C:
sta
R:
co
A:
pe
pu
w

Please return/renew this item by the last date shown

worcestershire
county council

Heaven Can Wait

Cally Taylor

First published in Great Britain in 2009
by Orion, an imprint of the Orion Publishing Group Ltd.
An Hachette UK company

3 5 7 9 10 8 6 4

A CIP catalogue record for this book
is available from the British Library.

ISBN 978-1-4091-0323-3

Typeset by Deltatype Ltd, Birkenhead, Merseyside

Printed and bound in the UK by
CPI Mackays, Chatham ME5 8TD

The Orion Publishing Group's policy is to use papers that
are natural, renewable and recyclable products and made
from wood grown in sustainable forests. The logging and
manufacturing processes are expected to conform to the
environmental regulations
of the country of origin.

The Orion Publishing Group Ltd
Orion House
5 Upper Saint Martin's Lane
London, WC2H 9EA

www.orionbooks.co.uk

For my parents, Reg and Jenny Taylor

Chapter One

What would you do if you thought you were about to die?

a) Scream and alert everyone in the immediate vicinity?

b) Tell no one and freak out on your own?

c) Pretend it wasn't happening?

Me, I pulled up my knickers and burst into tears.

I'd been worried about my health for a week. I was exhausted, my ankles were puffy and my wee was as frothy as a yellow cappuccino. According to the print-out in my hand that meant only one thing; I had an incurable, possibly fatal, disease.

My wedding was in less than forty-eight hours and breaking bad news to my fiancé was about the only thing that wasn't on my enormous 'to do' list. But I had to tell Dan. According to the Internet there would be twice-weekly visits to the hospital, dialysis machines, maybe even a transplant. That was a lot to take on, for any man.

Be strong, Lucy, I told myself as I opened the door to the living room. You can do this. Just be strong.

*

Dan was slouched across the sofa watching a documentary about the mating habits of a spindly yellow spider. His arms were crossed behind his head, his dark hair ruffled, his jaw rough with stubble. He was wearing low-slung jeans and his favourite top – a faded black Jimi Hendrix T-shirt that showed off his broad shoulders and strong arms. That was the thing about Dan, he could throw on any old thing and still look effortlessly gorgeous. Not that he cared, he was one of the least conceited people I'd ever met – which made me love him even more.

As I walked into the room he shifted his long legs to make space for me on the sofa, but I perched on the armrest instead. When the female spider bit the head off the male and ate him, Dan grinned across at me, his brown eyes shining with amusement.

'Given the choice between that and three-hour chats after sex,' he said, 'I'd definitely go for death by head-chomping, every time.'

He looked puzzled when I didn't laugh and I looked away at my hands and twiddled with my engagement ring. Oh God, how was he going to react to my news? Would he cry? Shout? Faint? Worse?

'Dan,' I said, 'I've got something really important to tell you.'

'What's up?' he said, his eyes still fixed on the screen.

'It's bad news.'

'Is this about the wedding?' He turned the television down, twisted onto his side, and gazed up at me.

'What's happened now? Baker put a lily instead of a rose on the top of the cake?'

I took a deep breath. 'I think I've got late-stage kidney disease.'

The remote control clattered to the floor as Dan sat up and grabbed hold of my hands, crushing the Internet print-out I'd been holding.

'You what?' he said, his eyes searching my face. 'You didn't tell me you'd been to the doctor.'

'I haven't.'

'Then how do you know you've got kidney disease?'

I squeezed his hands and rubbed my thumb over his fingers. He was obviously in denial. The Internet had warned me he might react like that. 'Because I looked up my symptoms on the web.'

He frowned and rubbed a hand over his jaw. 'What kind of symptoms?'

I stared at the TV. It felt weird to be discussing the state of my urine with my boyfriend. It's not something you really talk about, even if you have been together for seven years.

'My wee's frothy,' I said. 'There are bubbles in it and the Internet says frothy urine is a symptom of kidney failure.'

Dan laughed so hard he slipped off the sofa and landed on the floor. I stared at him open-mouthed, then reached forward and thumped him on the arm – hard.

'Why are you laughing, Dan? Stop it, you're freaking me out.'

3

He propped himself up on his elbow and reached for my hand. 'Sorry, Lucy. I shouldn't have laughed, not when you're at death's door and all. How long have you had these so-called symptoms?'

I counted the days in my head. 'About a week. No, definitely a week. They started last Friday.'

'And what did we buy on Friday that you said we really needed?'

I wriggled my hand out of Dan's grip and glared at him. There was me, pouring out my heart, and he was talking to me about food shopping. What the hell was wrong with him?

'I don't know, Dan. What *did* we buy?'

'A new toilet freshener that's supposed to get rid of limescale in a flash.'

'So what?'

He raised his eyebrows. 'You're not the only one who's seen bubbling urine in the pan for the last week.'

'What?'

'Lucy, you absolute doofus,' Dan said, poking me in the side, 'you've been weeing on the toilet freshener. You put it at the front of the toilet and it sticks out. That's what's been making our wee frothy.'

I stared at him in astonishment. 'So I don't have kidney disease?'

'No, Lucy,' Dan said, rolling his eyes. 'You don't.'

I burst out laughing. 'Oh my God,' I gasped. 'I'm such an idiot!'

Dan leaped back onto the sofa and pulled at me until I toppled off the armrest and landed on top of him.

He smiled up at me and pushed my hair back from my face.

'What would I do without you, Lucy Brown?' he said and kissed me softly.

I held his face in my hands and kissed him back. I felt like life just couldn't get any more perfect. And I was right, it wouldn't.

By the end of the next day I would be dead, but not from kidney disease.

Chapter Two

I was still smiling when I woke up the next morning. Dan was nestled beside me, the duvet soft against my skin. He was still asleep, his long, dark eyelashes fluttering as he dreamed. I traced my thumb along his cheekbone, then kissed him softly on the lips.

'Dan,' I whispered, 'we're getting married tomorrow.'

He shifted position, threw a heavy arm over my chest and pulled me closer.

'I love you,' he mumbled.

'I love you too,' I said and gently pushed his arm down to my waist and rolled over. It was ten o'clock. Ten o'clock! I grabbed my evilly long 'things to do' list from the bedside table and groaned. I'd hardly crossed anything off and I still had to:

a) Write out all the place settings. I'd decided on metallic silver pen on pebbles 'borrowed' from Brighton beach.

b) Finish making the table arrangements (long-stemmed lilies in clear glass vases).

c) Call the photographer to discuss the shots he was going to take. I still wasn't sure if the one of Dan admiring my wedding ring was too cheesy.

The list was far too long to do on my own. Dan would have to help me out. I looked back at him but he was snoring gently, his mouth slightly open, his face crumpled into the pillow. Even with sleep lines etched into his cheek, he still looked so damned handsome I couldn't help but stare at him.

I knew I was going to marry Dan as soon as I met him. Actually, that's not strictly true – it was about halfway through our first date. I'd suggested an art-house film at our local cinema, but it was so boring I almost fell asleep halfway through.

'Interesting film,' Dan said afterwards. 'Very, er, long.'

I didn't want him to think I was as dull as the film so I attempted to save the evening by suggesting we get some food. When Dan said we should go back to his place and share a takeaway, I jumped at the offer. So the date wasn't a complete write-off. There was still time to impress him with my sparkling wit and personality.

We made polite chit-chat as walked back to his place and then sat side-by-side on his threadbare sofa and tucked into a carton of chicken chow mein. The room was completely silent apart from the sound of chomping and swallowing and I was really quite enjoying myself – until my stomach gurgled ominously. Damn. In all the excitement I'd forgotten the effect Chinese food has on my digestive system. My belly had expanded to twice its size and the top button of my trousers was *this* close to popping off. *Not* an attractive look. I shifted in my seat to try and relieve the pressure.

'Do you fancy putting some music on?' Dan asked, twirling noodles on his fork, totally oblivious to my plight.

Good idea, yes, very good. Maybe a little walk across the room would help.

'I certainly do,' I said, standing up and surreptitiously sucking my stomach in. 'I'll have you know I've got fantastic taste in music, Mr Harding.'

Dan stopped eating and grinned up at me. 'Is that so? Go on then, impress me.'

'I will.'

I could feel his eyes checking out my arse as I sauntered across the room.

'Hmm, what have we here?' I said in my best 'I know my music' voice. The CDs at the top were a bit too heavy metal for my taste so I squatted down for a better look.

And farted.

It was like the mating trumpet of an elephant in the wild, only much, much worse.

I froze. If I didn't move it hadn't happened (oh please God let Dan somehow, miraculously, not have heard it). I clamped my hands to my burning cheeks and said the first thing that came into my head: 'Your floorboards really creak, don't they?'

Dan snorted with laughter. He laughed and he laughed and tears poured from his eyes until I thought he was never going to stop. Then I started laughing too. It was the goofy, unself-conscious grin on his face and the almost childlike gasp of his laughter that made me giggle. How could I not find it funny? If Dan could make me laugh at myself when all I really wanted to do was curl up and die of shame, I didn't want to spend the rest of my life with anyone else.

I tore my eyes away from his sleeping face, folded up the list and placed it on the bedside table. Things-to-do could wait, for a few minutes anyway, there was something I wanted to do first. I inched my way out of bed and towards the wardrobe on the other side of the room. And there it was, zipped up in an enormous waterproof bag, my dream wedding dress. I'd tried on loads with Anna and Jess, my best friends, before deciding which one to buy. A white dress was ruled out straightaway – with my long, dark hair and pale skin it made me look too washed-out. Slinky-style dresses were discarded too – unless you're a stick insect they cling to every lump and bump. And then we found this dress – ivory and strapless, the bodice finely boned with a wide, hooped skirt, delicately beaded with tiny pearls. It wasn't too plain and it wasn't too foofy. It was perfect.

'Lucy,' Dan said. 'What are you doing?'

I slammed the door shut and span round. 'You didn't see it, did you? Tell me you didn't see my wedding dress?'

Dan tucked the duvet under his chin and peered at me through bleary eyes. 'I've already seen it.'

'You haven't?' I said, the words catching in my throat.

'Of course I haven't, you numpty,' he grinned. 'You banned me from opening that door – remember?'

Ah yes, there was my handmade 'Do Not Enter Under Pain of Death' sign, Sellotaped to the door. I looked back at Dan suspiciously. 'Then why tell me you had?'

'I just wanted to wind you up.'

I sprinted across the room, jumped onto the bed and pummelled him through the duvet.

'You're not allowed to wind me up today, Daniel Harding.'

'Why not?'

'Because it's the day before our wedding, that's why,' I said, thumping him on the shoulder.

'Would now be a bad time to tell you I also found the present you bought me?'

'What?'

He grabbed me and pulled me against him. 'Ha! Got you again!'

I was going to call him a shit, or worse, but he kissed me before the words could leave my mouth.

At eight o'clock, after ten hours of frantic phone calls, lily disasters, silver pen explosions and several enormous strops, I kissed Dan goodbye at the front door. I was only going for a quick peck but he was rather more enthusiastic.

'Let's go upstairs,' he said, pausing mid-snog to grab my bum.

I slid his hands away firmly. He was supposed to be spending the night at his brother's flat and was already three hours late – not that he'd helped me do anything on my list. Oh no, he had to go out for five hours to do his own pre-wedding preparation which, I strongly suspected from the shower gel scent of his skin and his beery breath, involved going to the gym for a work-out, followed by several hours down the pub. Anyone would think he didn't care that tomorrow was the most important of both our lives. I looked at my watch. I had just under an hour to have a bath, prepare some food and tidy up the house before Anna and Jess came round for a pre-wedding girls' night in.

'Please?' Dan said again.

'No,' I snapped. 'You really need to get going. I've still got loads to do.'

He hung his head and gave me the big-brown-eyed sorrowful look that normally made me melt. 'I'll give you a back massage.'

I shook my head. 'No. Just go, Dan. Please.'

'OK, OK, I'm going, I'm going,' he said as I dodged his clumsy attempt to give me a hug and pushed him away.

I watched as he ambled down the path, his suit bag slung casually over his shoulder, his top hat cocked at a strange angle on his head. He paused when he reached the gate and turned round.

'Is something happening tomorrow?' he asked. 'I've

got this weird feeling I'm supposed to be somewhere.'

I raised my eyebrows and gave him 'the look', the same one that can stop small children screaming in a second. Dan just grinned.

'What?' he said. 'It's not too late to cancel, you know.'

My stomach flipped over and I felt sick. 'What do you mean, *cancel*?'

'The wedding,' he said. 'It's not too late to back out.'

I stared at him, a tight knot forming in my stomach. Did he have any idea how hard I'd worked so we'd have a wedding to remember? Did he realise how much of my social life I'd had to give up to get everything done while he went out drinking with his mates or watched films with his feet up? And had he ever thanked me? Had he ever said he appreciated all my hard work?

'That's not funny, Dan,' I said. 'It's *really* not funny.'

His grin slipped and he shrugged. 'You need to chill out, Luce.'

Chill out? Why do men always tell women to chill out when we're being perfectly rational? Besides, I had every right to be pissed off. At breakfast he'd tried to convince me he was going to say 'my awful wedded wife' during our vows and, during lunch, he'd lobbed a bread roll at me, claiming he was going to start a food fight at the reception. Now he was joking about cancelling the wedding. Was there no end to the hilarity? I tried to bite my tongue but the words tumbled out anyway.

'In case you haven't noticed, Dan, I've spent the last

year of my life organising this wedding and I haven't slept properly in days.'

'I've done stuff too,' he said, looking longingly in the direction of his red Mini. 'I booked the DJ for the reception.'

'Wow. You rang up one of your mates and asked him to bring his decks along. Well done you.'

Dan looked shocked. 'Do you know how long I spent going through all our records looking for the songs for the playlist? I wanted each song to be perfect, to represent special moments in our relationship to—'

I threw my hands in the air. 'So you listened to a few records, did you? God, how taxing for you, Dan. Because you hate listening to music, don't you? It's *such* a chore. I'd have liked to have sat on the floor drinking beer and playing tunes too, but instead I had to drive all over town picking up cravats and buttonholes and wedding favours and—'

'Can we just stop arguing now?' Dan interrupted, looking at me as though *I* was the one being exasperating. 'I thought I was supposed to leave. I thought that was what you wanted.'

'What I wanted, what I want, is for you to take our marriage seriously. You've been a real a pain in the arse today, Dan.'

He shrugged, opened the gate and nearly tripped over his own feet as he stepped off the pavement. 'I love you, Lucy Brown,' he shouted as he rummaged for his keys and let himself into his car.

I closed the front door, rested my forehead against the hallway wall and took a few deep breaths. Oh God. What was wrong with me? It wasn't like me to over-react to a bit of gentle teasing, but it was as though all the stress of the previous few months had just built up and up until I couldn't keep it in any more. Even so, I shouldn't have had a go at Dan. He'd just done what he always did when I was tired or stressed – tried to make me laugh. True, he could be an idiot sometimes, and more than a bit lazy, but he was still perfect for me in every other way. He was tall (I was five foot seven), dark-haired (me too, well, mousy but dyed) and quirk-ily handsome. I loved everything about him; from his firm bum and his warm brown eyes to the little kink in his nose from an over-enthusiastic rugby match when he was a teenager. And he loved me, even if I did suffer from an extreme sense of humour failure in times of huge stress. Not to mention being gullible, ridiculously over-emotional, and prone to hypochondria!

I'd call him before I went to bed, I decided as I sprinted up the stairs, to say sorry for being such a horrible bridezilla. I hadn't even said, 'I love you too,' when he'd left and I'd never done that before. I always said it back.

I paused at the top of the stairs and rummaged in my jeans pocket for my 'things to do' list. Next to item number ten – wedding present for Dan – was a ques-tion mark scribbled in biro. I'd bought him some silver cufflinks, but they weren't special enough. Cufflinks don't exactly say, 'This is the happiest day of my life,' do they? More like 'I'm a very unimaginative girlfriend. Next year I'll buy you a drill for Christmas.'

I shoved the piece of paper back into my pocket and wandered into the bathroom. There was less than an hour before Anna and Jess came round for a pre-wedding night of champagne and music and I needed to calm down and think. I threw off my clothes, turned on the radio, eased myself into the warm bubbles and thought happy thoughts. In less than twenty-four hours I'd be Lucy Harding, Mrs Daniel Harding. Goodbye, Lucy Brown!

When my fingers and toes were as wrinkled as raisins I stepped out of the tub and reached for a towel. That's when it hit me – the perfect present for Dan was in the attic. I'd gone on a decluttering spree two weeks before and he'd moved my wooden box of keepsakes into the attic for me. It was stuffed full with memories of our life together: flyers for gigs, photos, trinkets, letters, shells, postcards, and a cinema ticket from our first date. If I put the cinema ticket into the cufflinks box and gave it to Dan after the ceremony, it would be perfect – something new to celebrate our marriage and something old to commemorate our first date.

I just had to find it first.

I unclipped the hatch to the attic with the pole and stamped wet footprints into the carpet as I dragged the stepladder across the landing. I stepped up to the top rung of the ladder and reached up. The box was a few millimetres away from my outstretched hand.

'Shit.'

It was tantalisingly close. If I could just stretch a little bit further, I'd have it. I stood on tiptoes and lunged towards the edge of the box. The ladder squeaked and jolted, then tipped to one side. I screamed and grabbed at nothing as my towel slipped from my body and I fell through the air.

My first thought as I tumbled towards the carpet was – shit, I forgot the safety-catch. The second was – this is really, really going to hurt.

And it did, but only for a split second.

My head collided with the banister, my neck twisted, snapped, and I hit the carpet with a thump.

And that was that. I was dead.

Chapter Three

When I opened my eyes all I could see were grey, blurry legs stepping over me. Not one person stopped to ask if I was OK. Oh great, I thought as I rubbed my head, I've obviously collapsed in the middle of Oxford Street. How the hell did that happen?

I propped myself up on one elbow and looked down at my body to check for clues.

And realised I was stark bollock-naked.

'Nooooo,' I whimpered as I curled into the foetal position. 'No, not the naked shopping dream again.' If I didn't get up quickly, I'd progress to part two of the dream, where all my ex-boyfriends show up to point and laugh.

I waited for a lull in the legs and stood up slowly, one hand covering my pubes, the other clutching my boobs. I was surrounded by people of every age, race and religion on earth. They were wearing business suits, yashmaks, evening dresses, hospital gowns, wetsuits, overalls and nightclothes. And everyone was a pale, almost translucent, grey. It was as though I'd been invited to the most bizarre fancy dress party in the world.

Not that there was any music.

The whole place was silent apart from the shuffling of feet, the occasional moan or groan, and a distant whirring sound. Everyone stared straight ahead and when I did make eye contact with them, they looked at me blankly. It was like being a fresher at university again. But there wasn't any beer. Or DJs. Or disco balls. There weren't even any walls, just a great, dark cloud hovering ominously above us.

It was, I decided, the crappiest party ever. And it was time to leave.

'Excuse me,' I said, nudging the arm of a young woman wearing a Victorian costume.

She stared through me and carried on walking. I hurried after her, then stopped suddenly. My hands and legs were as grey as school rice-pudding.

'What's happened to me?' I said, grabbing the arm of a very old man with wild, wiry hair. 'Why have I gone grey?'

He shook me off and hobbled away.

'OK, enough now, I want to wake up,' I shouted. 'I've got a wedding to sort out.'

When nothing happened I felt light-headed and tingled all over. I hadn't suffered a full-blown panic attack since my parents had died, but I still remembered the warning signs.

'Lucy,' a male voice shouted over the hum. 'Lucy Brown, stay where you are.'

I froze. Someone knew who I was.

'Over here,' I shouted, releasing a boob and waving a hand in the air. 'I'm over here.'

The crowd parted and I spotted the top of a golden bald head moving towards me. I immediately squatted on the ground and tried to cover myself up with my hands. 'Oh God, please don't let it be an ex-boyfriend. Pleeeeeease.'

A couple of seconds later, a short, squat man burst through the crowd and held out his hand.

'You must be Lucy,' he said breathlessly. 'So sorry I'm late. I should have been here to greet you when you arrived.'

'What the hell's going on?' I said. 'I'm naked!'

'Ah, so you are,' he replied, as though it was the most normal thing in the world. 'Do you want a sheet?'

I watched as he rummaged in the inside pocket of his jacket and extracted a white sheet like a magician pulling scarves from a hat. He handed it to me with an apologetic look on his face and I wrapped it around me and stood up. My new friend was very short and very golden. He literally glimmered from the top of his shiny head to the tips of the rather hairy toes peeping out from beneath his tailored tweed suit. Thick bushy eyebrows framed his eyes and a wide nose sat in the centre of two very fleshy cheeks and above his smiling mouth. He was the spitting image of Bob Hoskins.

'Is this a dream?' I asked.

'I'm Bob,' said glowing man, holding out his hand. 'Pleased to meet you.'

I knew it. I just knew it. Stress always made me

dream about famous people, which sounds cool but isn't – especially when you end up dreaming you're having sex with Noel Edmonds. I couldn't watch *Deal or No Deal* without cringing for months after that one.

'Hoskins, right?' I smirked, shaking his hand.

'No,' he said, looking confused. 'Saint Bob, cousin to Peter. Come with me.' Before I had chance to respond, he grabbed my hand and launched himself back into the crowd. I stumbled and tripped as he dragged me behind him.

'Not far now,' he gasped. 'Nearly there.'

Just as I was about to beg for a breather, we squeezed through the last few people and approached a wide, wooden door. Bob let go of my hand and rooted through his pockets.

'Aha!' he said as he pulled a key from the inside pocket of his suit jacket, then opened the door. 'Do go in and sit down.'

I squinted around the room and tried to locate a chair. Everything glowed with light and I couldn't see a thing.

'Sorry,' said Bob, reaching into his jacket again. 'These might help.'

He handed me some sunglasses. They looked like something Elton John might have worn in the seventies, but I suppressed the urge to call the fashion police and slipped them on. Everything immediately dimmed and I blinked like a demented camel in a sandstorm.

The room was bigger than I'd first thought. It had a huge arched ceiling inset with carvings of plants, people and animals and a dark polished wood floor. Bang in the centre was a wide mahogany desk with two leather Queen Anne chairs at either side. Bob was sitting in the chair facing me.

He smiled. 'Take a seat, Lucy, let's have a chat.'

I gingerly lowered myself into the empty chair, fully expecting it to turn into a celebrity and shout, 'Get off me, fat arse.'

'Is this a dream, Bob?' I asked, tucking my feet under me when the chair failed to react.

He shook his head. 'What's the last thing you remember?'

'I got on a ladder to try and get Dan's present out of the attic,' I said, the words rushing out, 'and then I fell off and I hit my head.' I took a breath. 'I'm unconscious, aren't I?'

Bob shook his head again.

'I am,' I said. ' I'm in a coma in hospital and Dan's standing by my bedside playing me 'My Heart Will Go On,' by Celine Dion to try and get me to open my eyes, only he calls it 'My Fart Will Go On,' after our first date when I—'

'Lucy?'

'Yes, Bob.'

'You're not going to wake up.'

'I am.'

'No you're not.'

'I am.'

'Lucy,' Bob whispered, leaning forward, 'you're dead.'

'I'm going now, Bob,' I said as I stood up and moved towards the door. 'I'm going to tell Dan that I love him, that I'm sorry about the argument, and I can't wait to get married to him tomorrow and that …'

I tugged the door open. The mass of grey people swirled around outside.

'Wake up, Lucy,' I said, pinching myself hard on the arm.

The pinch didn't hurt so I slapped myself around the face. What was happening to me? Why couldn't I feel anything?

'Lucy,' Bob called, 'please come back in.'

I traipsed back into the office and gripped onto the back of the chair. 'Help me wake up please, Bob. I can't do it by myself.'

He stood up, straightened his suit and walked towards me. His lips twitched into a half smile but his eyebrows were definitely frowning.

'You're never going to wake up, Lucy,' he said. 'This is limbo, halfway between earth and heaven. You really are dead, I'm afraid.'

'Limbo,' I joked, 'is that a new nightclub in town?'

Then everything went black.

Chapter Four

For a small man, Bob was remarkably strong. He caught me as I crumpled towards the floor and held me tightly. He was as warm as a freshly filled hot water bottle and the longer he held me, the more peaceful I felt. When he slowly lowered me into my chair I felt as relaxed as if I'd drunk a bottle of wine all to myself (and I didn't feel sick).

'You OK, Lucy?' Bob asked.

I nodded. I was dead and should have been freaking out. Instead I felt as though I was floating on a cloud in the sunshine while fat cherubs fanned me with their wings.

I watched as Bob walked back to his chair and opened the large book on the desk. He flicked through the pages, pausing after each one to lick the tip of his stubby index finger.

'Am I going to hell?' I asked. My words slurred and my tongue felt loose in my mouth. 'I didn't mean to steal those earrings from H&M. They fell in my bag by accident.'

He laughed. 'No, Lucy, you're not going to hell. You're in limbo because you weren't ready to die.'

No shit, I thought, but was too zonked out to say.

'So,' he continued, running his finger down the page, 'you're Lucy Brown, aged twenty-eight, only child of Judith and Malcolm Brown, deceased.'

A jolt ran through me as he said my parents' names. Oh my God. Mum … Dad …

I hadn't seen them since I was twenty-two. I'd returned home from university for the Easter holidays and was annoyed because they were going on holiday to Rhodes without me. Bloody finals; two weeks all on my own with just a cat and an experimental psychology textbook for company. I didn't even have Dan to distract me from myself. He'd stayed up in Manchester to carry on working part-time as a waiter while he studied.

I'd only been at home for two days when my parents packed up and left. When they pulled out of the drive Mum wound down the car window and stuck her head out.

'See you soon, Looby-Lou,' she'd shouted. 'We love you.'

Two police officers visited the cottage to tell me the news. The policewoman sat me down in a chair and said, 'I'm so sorry,' while her colleague clanked cups in the kitchen as he made tea. It was a car crash on a windy mountain road, she said, just four days into their holiday.

The next two weeks were a blur. Dan came down to Brighton to be with me and all I was aware of was his arms around me and his soft voice in my ear. My parents' death devastated me. I thought I was permanently broken and I'd never be fixed, but Dan held me every night and told me he'd never leave me. I really thought we'd be together for ever. I didn't think either of us would die until we were old and grey.

'Lucy,' said Bob, his gentle voice interrupting my thoughts. 'Lucy, are you OK? Want to take a break?'

I put my hands to my face. My cheeks were wet with tears.

'Where are they?' I asked, my throat tight. 'Where are my mum and dad?'

'They're in heaven,' Bob said softly.

I sat up with a jolt and reached across the table. 'Can I see them? Can I talk to them?'

'You could,' Bob said. 'But you have a decision to make first.'

'What kind of decision?'

He looked away and rubbed his hands over his smooth head. 'You need to make a choice – between your parents and Dan.'

'What do you mean choose?' I asked, jumping out of my seat, no longer feeling the slightest bit calm. Bob grimaced and straightened his tie. 'I think you'd better come with me.'

I hurried after him as he strode towards a door on the other side of the hall. There was a way of seeing Dan again. But how? Maybe I wasn't totally dead and Bob could wave his heavenly wand to bring me back to life. That's why I wasn't in heaven with my parents. Or perhaps Bob would be able to magic Dan to the flat just in time to give me CPR. I'd open my eyes and he'd say, 'Thank God. Oh, Lucy, I thought I'd lost you,' and we'd kiss and get married and live happily ever after. Everything was going to be OK.

I held my breath as Bob fumbled the key into the lock. What was behind the doors? London? My street? My flat? A hospital ceiling? The doors opened with a creak. 'Here,' said Bob, bowing slightly and opening his hands, 'are your options.'

I felt my heart sink. Before me were two grey escalators. One had a glowing sign above it that said 'Up', the other 'Down'. The one going up disappeared into the grey cloud above our heads and the down escalator descended into a green mist.

Bob pointed at the up escalator. 'That one,' he said, 'will take you up to heaven, where your parents are waiting for you.'

I gasped. I couldn't help it. I couldn't quite believe that, right at the top of the escalator, my parents were waiting to see me again. I tried to swallow back the lump in my throat, desperate not to cry again.

'And that one?' I said, pointing to the down escalator. 'What happens with that one?'

'That one returns you to earth.'

I was right. I wasn't really dead. I was just in some weird halfway house. I stared at the up escalator and my heart twisted in my chest as I imagined my parents waiting in heaven for me, their beautiful, loving faces smiling, their arms outstretched. What I wouldn't give for a big bear hug from my tall, strong dad and a tight squeeze from my mum, the scent of L'Oréal hairspray and Christian Dior J'adore perfume filling my nose as she held me tightly. There were only three people in the world who'd ever made me feel safe and loved, and I was being asked to choose between them. How the hell was I supposed to do that?

I looked from the down escalator to the up escalator, and back again, feeling like my head was about to explode. Should I choose my parents or Dan? My parents, who had loved me and cherished me throughout my childhood and teenage years, and who I hadn't seen for six long, long years, or Dan who loved me more than anyone else in the world and wanted to spend the rest of his life with me?

I thought about my parents, their arms wrapped around each other and hopeful, welcoming looks on their faces, and then I thought about Dan – Dan who'd find my dead, naked body on the upstairs carpet, Dan who'd gather me into his arms and say my name over and over again as he cried and rocked me back and forth.

'I'm sorry,' I whispered to the up escalator. 'I love you so, so much, Mum and Dad, and all I've dreamed about for years is one more chance to see you both, to hold you, to tell you I love you, but …' – I wiped a tear from my cheek but another quickly took its place – '…but I'm not really dead. Not yet. Bob's giving me a chance to have my life back and Dan's all alone and he needs me. You understand that, don't you? We've got another chance to be happy and I think you'd want that for me. But I'll be back. One day I'll come back and we'll all be together and—'

'Lucy?' Bob said. 'Everything OK?'

I shoved him out of the way and sprinted towards the down escalator before I could change my mind. 'Thanks for everything but I'm going back to my flat now.'

Bob was quicker than Linford Christie after a bad burger. He darted in front of me and stood in front of the down escalator, arms spread wide.

'Wait,' he said. 'You can't take this escalator until I've explained everything to you.'

'What's to explain?' I said, trying and failing to squeeze past him. 'If I go down that escalator I'll be reunited with Dan. You said I could see him again, you said—'

'No I didn't,' Bob said like a petulant child. 'I said you'd better come with me. I didn't give you your options.'

'Which are?'

'You can go up to heaven, be with your parents and wait for Dan to die, or return to earth as a member of the living dead.'

'A WHAT?'

'A member of the living dead.'

I opened my mouth to speak, then closed it again as I took in what Bob had just said.

'I can only go back if I become a … a … zombie?' I said finally.

Bob held up a hand. 'We prefer the term living dead, Lucy. Anyway, you'd go back to earth as an undead and complete a task that would allow you to become a ghost. Only then would you be reunited with Dan.'

The only way I could be with Dan again was as a *ghost*?

'Lucy,' Bob said, 'are you OK?'

I shook my head, totally unable to speak. If I went up to heaven I'd have to wait for Dan to die which, if he lived to a ripe old age, meant I wouldn't see him for ... I counted on my fingers ... *fifty-one years!* I really was dead. I was a dormouse, a stiff, a corpse, a dodo, a doornail, a ... hang on, something didn't quite make sense ...

'Why can't I just become a ghost?' I asked. 'Why do I have to be a zombie first?'

'Living dead,' Bob snapped.

'Whatever.'

'In order for someone to become a ghost, as stated in clause 550.3,' Bob said, clasping his hands behind his back and looking very officious all of a sudden, 'the deceased must perform a suitable task for the good of humanity.'

'Such as?'

'Hmm,' he said, reaching into his jacket pocket and pulling out what looked like a black, plastic calculator. He pressed a few buttons, sighed and pressed a few more.

'You,' he said, looking up at me, 'would have to find love for a stranger who had never been in love before.'

29

That was it? All I had to do to become a ghost was find someone a boyfriend?

I'd match-made some of my friends when I was alive. OK, so none of the relationships had ever worked out, in fact one of my friends had said I'd mentally scarred her for life after her date with a taxidermist I'd met on the train, but that didn't mean I couldn't do it. I'd just been unlucky.

'How long would I have?' I asked.

'Twenty-one days.'

'Are you kidding me? Three weeks to find someone the love of their lives? It took me twenty-two years to find Dan.'

Bob shrugged. 'Twenty-one days is the standard term, Lucy. Any longer than that and wannabe ghosts get too settled on earth. It can be very traumatic if people refuse to go to heaven when they fail to complete their task.' He glanced in the direction of the grey-faced people behind us. 'Traumatic and busy.'

I felt bad for getting pissed off with the people who'd bumbled around me outside Bob's office. They were obviously shell-shocked by what had happened to them. Not that I could blame them. I'd just been told I could have a go at being some kind of celestial Cilla Black and it still didn't feel real.

'I've got another question,' I said.

Bob nodded.

'If I go back to earth as one of the living dead and pass my task I'll become a ghost which means I can be with Dan again ...'

'Yes,' Bob said. I had the distinct impression he was getting a tiny bit sick of me.

'Can I go to heaven afterwards?'

He shook his head. 'If you decide to become a ghost, that's it. If you choose to haunt a building you have to remain on earth for as long as that building exists. If you haunt a person you'll be a ghost for as long as the person is alive. You can only go to heaven when they die.'

'Oh God!'

'Ssh, he might be listening.'

'Sorry.'

'Do you need to think about what you want to do?' Bob asked.

I nodded vigorously. 'Can I have five minutes?'

'You've got all of eternity,' Bob said, 'but I'd rather you were a bit speedier than that. You can use my office if you'd like.'

I sat down heavily in the chair opposite Bob's and put my head in my hands. It just wasn't fair. My life had been going so well. OK, so my graphic design job was a bit tedious. I'd left art school dreaming of designing funky magazine covers and cutting-edge packing and I'd ended up designing boxes for supermarket own-brand washing power and leaflets for conservatories. Then there was the fact that our living situation wasn't ideal. The house was tiny and had a dodgy boiler that kept cutting out in the most freezing part of winter, leaving us cold and smelly for days on end. And I didn't have any living relatives, but I had friends, and I had Dan. Dan who'd promised to love me for ever. All I did was try and find a present for him that would put a big goofy smile on his face on the most special day of our lives, and God decided that was the perfect time to kill me off. How fair was that? It's not like I wanted too much from life. I just wanted to get married to the man I loved, have a half-decent career, and maybe have kids one day. Was that too much to ask?

A pang of guilt shot through me as I remembered the last time Dan had seen me alive. I'd pushed him away when he'd tried for one last hug and then I'd ranted at him about not helping out with the wedding. And then ... oh God ... I hadn't even bothered to say 'I love you,' as he left, and he'd driven away thinking I was angry with him. That was his last memory of me.

'Lucy?'

I looked up. Bob had poked his shiny bald head round the door. He looked vaguely apologetic.

'Sorry to hurry you, but there's a bit of a backlog of new arrivals waiting in limbo. Have you made a decision?'

I sat back in the chair and looked Bob straight in the eye.

'Yes,' I said. 'I have.'

'OK,' said Bob, ushering me out through the door. 'What's it to be?'

'I really, really want to see my parents but I can't go up to heaven without seeing Dan again,' I said. 'I can't spend the next fifty years wondering if he's OK. I *need* to be with him, Bob. I need to say sorry and let him know I love him.'

'Is that your final decision?' Bob asked, looking the tiniest bit disappointed. 'It would make the paperwork so much easier if you just went to heaven.'

'It's my final decision,' I said, sounding a lot more confident than I felt and a tiny bit like I was a contestant on a bizarre heavenly game show.

'OK, Lucy.' Bob thrust a large brown envelope into my hands. 'Everything you need is in here and if I've missed anything, I'm sure your new housemates will be able to fill you in.'

I stared at him. 'What housemates?'

'Lucy, you're about to join the House of Wannabe Ghosts. You'll meet your housemates soon enough.'

I clutched the envelope to my chest as Bob slid a key into a small slot in the front of the down escalator. When the red and white striped barrier slid back, he held out his hand. 'Good luck, Lucy. See you in twenty-one days.'

'Thanks, Bob,' I said, squeezing his hand tightly.

My heart, if I still had one, bounced in my chest as I stepped forward and grabbed hold of the handrail.

'Don't forget,' Bob shouted. 'You can come back whenever you want. You don't have to stick it out for three weeks. The instructions are in the manual.'

'Manual!' I shouted back. 'OK! Got it!'

The escalator juddered and I nearly ran back up the steps. What the hell was I doing? Who did I have to find love for? And would Dan really be pleased to see me if I became a ghost?

The escalator whirred and clunked and carried me down into the thick green mist. I was going back to earth and there was no turning back.

Chapter Five

Day One

'Ow,' I said, rubbing my nose and stepping back. 'What the hell?'

The escalator had stopped suddenly and I'd just charged head first into a white, painted door. With no handle. I stared at it for a couple of seconds and then tentatively tapped it with my toe. When nothing happened I knocked politely.

'Hello?' I said.

No answer.

'Hello?' I said, knocking harder. 'It's Lucy.'

When there was still no answer I started to feel a bit scared. I was far too unfit to run up a down escalator for a start. I *had* to get through the door. There was nowhere else to go.

I thumped the paint with both fists. 'Oi! Let me in!'

The door swung open revealing a tall, thin, middle-aged man with a mop of curly dark hair and a thick moustache below his large nose. He was wearing cords, an acrylic, lemon-coloured jumper and white socks with leather sandals.

'Can I help you?' he said.

'I'm Lucy,' I said, waving my envelope in front of his face. 'Bob sent me.'

The man rolled his eyes and sighed. Not exactly the warm welcome I'd been hoping for.

'Right,' he said, stepping back. 'You'd better come in.'

I took a step forward and immediately hit my head on a clothes rail. Coat-hangers, each one holding a pastel-coloured jumper or a pair of pale cords, jangled noisily as I stumbled forwards.

'Mind the shoes,' barked the man.

Beneath my feet were pairs and pairs of neatly arranged brown sandals, each set containing a pair of balled white socks. I was in a wardrobe and, from the look on the face of the man in front of me, it was his.

'All right,' I said, taking a step back. 'Keep your hair on. I didn't know it was your wardrobe.'

'Just hurry up and get out.'

I ducked my head, jumped forwards, tripped over my feet and sprawled head first onto a grubby sheepskin rug. It smelled like overboiled veg.

'Sorry,' I said, scrabbling back to my feet and staring around wildly. Where on earth was I?

A bedroom. Yes, definitely a bedroom. And a very nerdy one at that. In the corner of the room was a single bed with a Thomas the Tank Engine duvet cover. Beside it was a bedside table stacked high with books. Every wall was covered with posters of trains; there wasn't an inch of uncovered wallpaper.

I was just about to comment on the décor when the wardrobe door shut with a bang. Train Man was staring at me, his hands on his skinny hips. His skin wasn't peeling off and he didn't walk with a limp, but he was still the most singularly unattractive man I'd ever laid eyes on.

'Are you a zomb … living dead?' I asked.

'Yessssssssssssss,' he said slowly. 'I am.'

I looked him up and down and chewed on my fingernails. Just because he looked human, it didn't mean I did too. I looked down at my hands. They looked pink and soft, but that didn't guarantee my face wasn't hanging off. I patted my face to check for blood or drool.

'Something wrong?' asked Train Man.

'I'm not sure yet. Have you got a mirror?'

Train Man nodded and rummaged around in his chest of drawers until he found a shaving mirror.

I held my breath and peered into it.

OK, so I still had brown hair, blue eyes and angular eyebrows. I hadn't grown a preposterously large forehead and my mouth wasn't hanging down in a groaning zombie kind of way. The dark circles under my eyes freaked me out for a couple of seconds before I realised I'd removed my concealer before I had a bath. Phew. I was still me. A little bit peaky without make-up, but attractive in a forgiving light.

I handed the mirror back. 'Thanks … er …'

'Brian. I'll introduce you to Claire and then show you your room.'

There was another woman in the house. Thank God. Maybe she'd be someone I could talk to; a friend who'd understand how I felt and who'd tell me what the hell was going on!

Brian bumbled out of his bedroom and I followed him into a narrow corridor. The carpet in the hallway was as grubby as the one in the bedroom. Where it wasn't threadbare, it was decorated with huge, orange swirls. The woodchip walls were off-yellow and peeling and through an open door at the end of the corridor I could see a sink. It was grey with limescale and looked as though it hadn't been cleaned for years.

I was just about to ask if there was a second bathroom when Brian stopped at a closed door and knocked. 'Claire, we have a visitor.'

'Door's open,' shouted a female voice. 'I won't bite.'

Brian snorted and turned towards me. 'That depends on how close you get.'

I took a step back as he turned the door handle. Claire obviously wasn't the only one you shouldn't get too close to. Brian smelt worse than a pig in a sauna.

'Are you coming in or what?' shouted the voice.

I shuffled into the room after Brian and stood, slightly nervously, by the door. The room was filled with thick smoke, a stomach-churning mixture of cigarettes and incense sticks, and the walls were plastered with posters of a band I vaguely recognised. I say vaguely because black and red lipstick kisses were plastered over the lead singer's face; only his eyes and wiry, blonde hair were still visible. The floor was covered in clothes, most of them black, with the occasional dash of red or pink. In the corner of the room, sitting cross-legged on a single bed, was an overweight girl dressed in black leggings, an oversized crocheted jumper, army boots and a pink tutu. She looked at me through narrowed eyes. 'Who are you?'

'Lucy Brown.'

'Claire.'

'Pleased to meet you.'

'Whatever.'

Nice, another lukewarm welcome. Actually, it was worse than lukewarm, it was downright arctic.

It was hard to tell how old Claire was because she was plastered with make-up, but I guessed she was about eighteen. Her foundation was so pale she looked ghoulish and her eyes were piggy small beneath thick, black eyeliner and super-thin pencilled-on eyebrows. A black crocheted top revealed her bra strap and thick crêpe bandages around each of her wrists. She caught me looking and sighed. 'Oh goody, we get to play the death game again.'

'Sorry,' I said, trying and failing to avert my eyes from her wrists. 'What game?'

She rolled her eyes. 'We swap stories about how we died and the person who died in the most tragic way is brought back to life.'

I caught my breath. I'd died the night before my wedding. How much more tragic could you get? Maybe I'd win and—

'Jesus, you're gullible,' Claire cackled. 'Look at your

face. Aw, so sweet and hopeful.'

I looked desperately towards Brian but he shook his head. 'There's no death game, Lucy. Claire thinks she's being funny.'

'Well I laughed,' she said, sneering at Brian. 'Anyway, I committed suicide and he had a heart attack.' She tossed back her pink dreads. 'Your turn.'

'I broke my neck,' I said, 'falling off a stepladder.'

'Oops.'

I glared at her. 'On the night before my wedding.'

'Really?' she said, looking me up and down. 'And I thought you were on your way to a toga party.'

Bugger, I'd totally forgotten I was still wearing the bloody sheet. I folded my arms across my chest and tried my best to look nonchalant but Claire kept sniggering.

'OK,' said Brian, raising his arm to guide me out of the room and subjecting me to a whiff of his evil armpits, 'I think the introductions are over for now. Cup of tea, Lucy?'

I nodded. Even stinky, sandalled Brian's company was more appealing than Psycho-Goth-Cow's.

'See ya, Bride,' she shouted as I hurried out of the room.

'See ya, Goth,' I muttered as I shut the door behind me. Not my wittiest comeback ever.

I followed Brian across the hallway and down the rickety, uncarpeted stairs to what passed for the kitchen. A rusty stand-alone oven coated with grime leaned against one wall and a sink full of dishes cluttered the other. Every single work surface, apart from one, was covered with crumbs, dishes and empty food packets. What should have been a bowl of apples in the middle of the kitchen table had wrinkled into a bowl of what looked like old men's testicles.

'Sorry,' Brian said, sweeping a pile of newspapers and magazines off one of the plastic-backed chairs and onto the floor. 'It was reasonably clean when I got here. Then Claire moved in.'

I shrugged in sympathy and glanced at the tea-stained cups on the table in front of me. There was something thick and mouldy growing in one of them. It vaguely reminded me of the first meal I cooked for Dan (a particularly unsuccessful Thai green chicken curry).

'I've seen worse,' I lied, and sat down.

'This,' Brian said, pointing at the only clean work surface in the kitchen, 'is mine and so is this cupboard. I'll ask Claire to clear out one of her cupboards for you.'

'Thanks,' I said, though I secretly suspected the chances of her doing that were even smaller than me borrowing a pair of Brian's sandals for a girls' night out.

'How long have you been here?' I asked him as he retrieved two clean-looking mugs from the cupboard and filled the kettle.

'Five days.'

'And how are you getting on with your task?'

He shrugged. 'I don't really want to talk about it.'

He was obviously going to be a fat lot of good when it came to doing my own task, which reminded me – I still hadn't opened my envelope.

'Is it OK to open this now?' I asked, waving it at Brian.

'You haven't opened it yet? Other wannabe ghosts tend to open theirs on the escalator.'

I didn't feel like a wannabe ghost. In fact, I didn't even feel like I was properly dead. I felt like I was at university and I'd just moved into the worst houseshare in the world. I slipped my hand into the envelope and slowly pulled out the contents, careful not to let anything drop onto the filthy floor.

On the top of the pile of papers was a sheet headed 'Details of Task: Lucy Brown'. I skimmed the details:

Name of wannabe ghost: Lucy Brown

Age: 28

Cause of death: broken neck (that made me wince)

Reason for seeking ghost status: to haunt fiancé Dan (it sounded a bit creepy, written like that)

Task: to find a total stranger the love of their life

Name of stranger: Archibald Humphreys-Smythe

Age: 30

Occupation: Computer Programmer

Place of work: Computer Bitz Ltd, 113, Tottenham Court Road, London

'Oh God,' I said. 'He's a geek and he sounds posh.'

Brian placed a cup of tea on an empty cereal box. 'Who's a geek?'

'My task. He's called Archibald, for God's sake. What kind of family calls a little kid Archibald?'

'My dad was called Archibald,' Brian said.

I cringed. 'Shit, sorry.'

'Don't be.' He shrugged. 'He's dead too.'

I felt my cheeks grow hot and quickly looked at the next sheet of paper. It was a bound document, about three inches thick, and was titled 'Rules and Regulations for Wannabe Ghosts'.

'You might want to read that,' Brian commented. 'There are lots of things you can't do.'

'Like what?' I asked.

Brian looked strange when he smiled. His eyes disappeared behind his crinkled lids and his lips disappeared beneath his moustache. You could see his nose hair more clearly too and … ewwww … everything attached to it. How strange that someone so uptight about kitchen cleanliness could totally ignore his own personal hygiene.

'I'll let you discover that for yourself,' he said.

I reached for my cup of tea and peered into it. 'Can I drink this or is it going to go straight through me?'

Brian reached for his own cup of tea and took a sip. 'You're not a ghost yet, Lucy. You're temporarily human, sort of. You can eat, drink, sleep and defecate.'

'Nice.'

'You did ask.'

'Not about pooing, I didn't.'

'What did you ask about?' Claire was lounging in the doorway, observing us with a bored expression.

'None of your business,' I said.

'Is that so?'

Before I knew what was happening she'd leaped

forward and grabbed the first sheet of my instructions. When I tried to grab it back she skipped to the doorway and peered at it from her safe distance.

'Reason for seeking ghost status,' she read, 'to haunt fiancé Dan. Fiancé? Someone actually wanted to marry you?'

I glanced at the butter dish nestled next to the cereal box. Could Claire die twice if I stabbed her with the butter knife?

'Yes, as it happens,' I said.

'And you want to haunt him?'

'Not haunt, no. I just need to be with him. There are things I need to say.'

She laughed. It was a surprisingly high-pitched titter for such a generously proportioned girl. 'Liar! You want to check he hasn't moved on yet.'

'No I don't,' I said, jumping out of my seat and snatching the piece of paper out of her hand. 'I've been dead for less than twenty-four hours, for God's sake.'

'So when did you die, Little Miss Never Gonna Be a Bride?'

'Yesterday. Friday 23rd March at about 7.30 p.m.'

'What would you say,' Claire said, raising her pencil-thin eyebrows, 'if I told you today was Saturday 27th April?'

'I'd say you were a liar.'

'Yeah?'

I moved out of the way as she bent down and rummaged through the pile of newspapers and magazines

44

Brian had swept onto the floor.

'Aha!' she said, waving a copy of the *Daily Herald* in front of me. 'Proof.'

I grabbed at it. 'Let me see that.'

And there it was, in the top right-hand corner of the newspaper – Saturday 27th April. I swallowed hard and sat down. She was right.

'Brian,' I whispered, 'how can that happen? How can a month just disappear?'

'It's eternity up there,' he said, placing his mug back on the table and gesturing upwards with his thumb. 'There's no such thing as time.'

'So I really have been dead for a month?'

'I'm afraid so.'

'Poor little Lucy,' said Claire from the doorway. 'Worried Dan's moved on, are you?'

'Brian,' I said, ignoring her. 'I'd like to see my room now, please.'

'Of course.'

I thought Claire was going to swipe at me with her black talons as I swerved round her and followed Brian out of the kitchen. She didn't, but she did mumble 'Never the bride' as I approached the stairs.

I turned back. 'Rearrange these words, Claire: don't fuck why off.'

She raised an eyebrow and stared at me. I stared back, determined not to look away first. I was good at the no-blink game. I always beat our cat.

'You missed out the word *you*, Lucy.'

Oh.

Crap.

'Your room,' Brian announced, after I'd sprinted up the stairs at lightning speed, 'is next to mine.'

'Excellent,' I panted. 'I'm glad.'

And I was, even if there was a strange smell like an eggy mist creeping out from under his door. The further I was from Claire, the better. I wasn't about to admit it to Brian, but her comment about me wanting to check if Dan had moved on had really hurt. She was talking total bullshit, of course. Dan loved me, he wanted to marry me, and I'd only been dead for a month. Of course he wouldn't have moved on.

'Wow,' Brian said as he strolled across my room and sat down on my bed, 'you certainly like to be surrounded by stuff, don't you?'

What stuff? What was he on about? Oh my God. Were those Dan's shoes strewn around the base of the laundry basket? And was that the enormous pink elephant he'd won for me at Brighton Pier on the bed? There was more. Dan's contact lens solution, a pile of CDs and his PSP cluttered his bedside table, and the book I'd been reading, a box of tissues and half a glass of water were neatly arranged on mine. I clutched at the doorframe, suddenly feeling faint.

'It's my room,' I said. 'It's my room, mine and Dan's.'

Brian shot me a look. 'Well, yes. I told you it was.'

'But it's exactly like the room I had when I was alive.'

'Good, isn't it?' said Brian, bouncing so hard on the

bed the springs creaked. 'I don't know how they do it, but everyone who comes here gets a complete replica of the room they lived in before they died.'

'Why?'

'I've got no idea. Maybe they think it'll help us settle in.'

I thought it was horrible; like taking part in a twisted episode of *Big Brother* where, instead of making you do stupid tasks and then evicting you, they kill you off and then torture you by making you live a replica of your old life.

'I think it's sick,' I said.

Brian moved from the bed and walked towards me. For a horrible second I thought he was going to hug me. Instead he sidled past and opened the door to his room.

'I thought it was a nice touch, actually,' he said as he disappeared. 'I missed my train posters.'

I was just about to go after him when a creak on the stairs startled me and I jumped, hitting my hip on the dressing table. I gasped in pain and grabbed hold of it, nearly sending my jewellery box flying as I stumbled about. The box was exactly where I'd left it, the lid permanently open because I'd once dropped it on the floor and broken the hinge. It was piled high with tangled necklaces, clusters of single earrings (their pairs permanently lost) and the silver and jade bracelet Dan had bought me for my birthday balancing precariously on the top. I looked down at the third finger of my left hand. Oh no! My engagement ring had disappeared.

I rummaged through the box, spilling earrings and necklaces onto the floor. Where was my ring? Where was it? I threw open the drawers and tipped them onto the floor too. I'd definitely been wearing my ring when I said goodbye to Dan at the front door and then ... then ... I'd taken off my clothes in the bedroom and wandered into the bathroom. Please, I thought as I flew across the room towards my bedside table, please let it be here.

And there it was; a small platinum band with a single princess-cut diamond solitaire. Dan had chosen it himself from a shop in Bond Street and hidden it in his pocket when we went camping in the New Forest last year.

I'd been tired after the journey and just wanted to crawl into the tent and go to sleep, but Dan had insisted we build a fire first.

'It'll be fun,' he'd said, reaching into his rucksack and pulling out a firelighter, a small bundle of kindling, two metal skewers and a packet of marshmallows. ' Look, the stars have come out too. It's a perfect night for marshmallows.'

His smile was so wide and his eyes were so excited, I couldn't say no, and I soon set to work lighting the world's smallest bonfire as Dan threaded marshmallows onto the skewer.

'Lucy,' he'd said from behind me as I prodded the fire.

'Uh huh.'

'Lucy, do you want a marshmallow?'

'In a minute. I'm just trying to—'

'Lucy Brown …'

There was something in the tender way he said my name that made my heart flip. When I turned around he was on one knee, a diamond ring balanced on the top of a fat, pink marshmallow.

'Lucy Brown, will you marry me?'

I can't remember what happened then – it's all a blur of tears and kisses and yes, yes, yes, and more tears and more kisses – until Dan slowly slid the ring onto the third finger of my left hand.

'If that's a yes,' he'd grinned, 'you've just made me the happiest man alive.'

I slid the ring off the bedside table and pressed it against my lips as tears filled my eyes and dribbled down my cheeks. If I had any chance of surviving the House of Wannabe Ghosts and completing my task, there was one thing I had to do first. I had to see Dan.

Chapter Six

I thundered down the stairs, wrenched open the front door and peered down the street. The sky was streaked orange, red and gold, and all around me street lamps were buzzing as they flickered to life. Plan. I needed a plan. How about … hang on … why were my teeth chattering? And why was an old man across the street gawping at me as though all his Christmases had come at once?

Dammit! I was still wearing the bloody toga.

I hitched it up, slammed the door, and ran back to my bedroom. Clothes, I needed nice clothes, suitable clothes. But what kind of clothes did you wear when you were planning on visiting your grieving boyfriend to say, 'Hiya, bet you thought you'd never see me again?'

I wrenched open a drawer and pulled out a pair of black knickers, a matching bra, my Gap jeans, some stripy socks and a soft, grey jumper. I dressed quickly, wriggling into my jeans and sucking in my stomach like it was a perfectly normal evening. When I caught sight of my reflection in the full-length mirror by the door I smiled. I looked like me again. Me – Lucy Brown, five foot seven and a bit, size twelve (nudging fourteen if I had PMT), with green eyes and shoulder-length brown hair. I looked just as Dan would remember me.

It was only when the front door banged behind me that I realised I had no idea where I was. The street looked and sounded like a normal London street – terraced houses, small front gardens (some littered with rubbish, others gravel-covered and neat), pigeons pecking at splodges of chewing gum ground into the pavement and the wail of police cars and fire engines in the distance – but where exactly? Across the road a man was striding down the street, his expression steely. A woman tottered behind him on high heels, shouting, 'Mike! Wait for me!' whenever he got too far ahead. I thought about chasing after them, but they disappeared into one of the houses before I could get up the nerve.

Clues, I needed clues, or someone who had one. There were three teenagers further down the road. They were sitting on a low brick wall in front of a house, chatting and flicking their fingers in the air, laughing hysterically. I wandered towards them and tried not to feel nervous. Look street, I told myself. Think rap, think bling, think swagger. I glanced at my reflection in a car window. I looked like Eminem after a stroke.

'Excuse me,' I said as I drew closer to the teenagers, ' whereabouts in London am I?'

One of the boys, the one in the Burberry baseball cap, winked at me. 'Get lucky last night, did you?'

'No, I ...'

'Bit of a slapper, are you?' said the girl, hooking her

thumbs into her low-rise jeans and exposing a perma-
tan midriff, complete with belly ring.

'You can talk,' piped up one of the boys.

'Fuck off, Jase,' she said, turning to glare at him.
'You're the slapper.'

'Please,' I said. 'Could you just tell me where I am? I
need to get home.'

'Give me a tenner and I'll tell you,' said the girl,
holding out her manicured hand.

'Forget it,' I sighed. 'I'll work it out for myself.'

They laughed as I walked away. I could still hear
them cat-calling and screeching as I reached the end of
street, turned the corner and almost walked headlong
into a bus stop. I stared up at the numbers on the sign.
Oh my God, we were in Kilburn. I was only about
ten minutes from West Hampstead, where Dan and
I lived.

I rummaged in my bag for some money as a bus
pulled round the corner and peered into the notes section. There was two hundred quid in my purse! Where
had that come from? And where were my bank and
credit cards, my driving licence and my library card?
Everything that had my name on it had gone.

Arse, I thought, as I paid for a ticket and stepped
onto the bus, I should have read the bloody manual.
I stared out of the window as the bus carried me
closer to Dan. Everywhere I looked people were
walking, talking, arguing and laughing; they gathered
in small groups outside betting shops, queued for
computers in Internet cafés and shuffled in and out of

mini-supermarkets, plastic bags containing milk, bread and beer swinging from their wrists. I watched as the lights went on in the flats above the shops as people returned home from work and settled in front of the TV, carried plates of food into their living rooms or closed the curtains, shutting me out. They were all going about their normal lives as though nothing had happened. And nothing had happened really. It wasn't as though I was Princess Diana, Anna Nicole Smith or Heath Ledger. I wasn't famous or important and the public weren't in love with me. I was just Lucy Brown, aged twenty-eight, from London. Only a handful of people in the world knew I'd died and no one, apart from my new housemates, was aware I was back.

The elderly woman in the seat next to me started rummaging around in her bag and I turned to look at her. She was small and bony with a clear rain hat jammed over her blue-rinsed curls and pulled low over her deeply lined forehead. Poor woman, I thought, as she retrieved a mangled toffee from the bottom of her bag and popped it in her mouth, she's probably terrified of dying. Lonely, too. The least I could do was talk to her and help ease her fears. I was somewhat of an expert on death after all.

I cleared my throat. 'Excuse me.'

She glanced up at me and smiled. 'Are you after a toffee?' she asked, dipping back into her bag. 'I've probably got another one in here.'

'No, thank you,' I said. 'I just wanted to talk to you.'

'Lonely, are you?' she asked, tapping the back of my hand with her spindly fingers. 'That's OK, love, we all get lonely at times.'

'No, no,' I said, 'I just wanted to talk to you about death.'

'Death?' she repeated, frowning up at me.

'Yes,' I said, my eyes filling with sympathetic tears as I gently squeezed her delicate hand. 'I just wanted you to know that you have no reason to fear death. Everyone you have ever loved and lost is waiting for you in heaven. All you have to do is—'

'Help!' the old woman shouted, inching away from me and staring madly round the bus. 'Somebody help me. I'm being recruited for a cult. Help! Help!'

'No,' I said, my heart thumping wildly as everyone turned to stare at me, 'you've got me all wrong. I just wanted to—'

Before I knew what was happening, a middle-aged man had swaggered down the aisle and was pointing an accusatory finger in my face.

'You people!' he bellowed, his face puce. 'If you're not knocking on our doors at all times of the day and night, you're pestering pensioners on the bus. You should be ashamed of yourself.'

'I ... I ...' I stuttered, staring out of the window as I frantically searched for an explanation that wouldn't make me sound like a complete nutter. 'I ... oh, this is my stop!'

Seconds later the bus ground to a juddering halt and I sprang out of my seat, hot-footed it down the aisle and jumped off the step and onto the street. The sun had slipped over the horizon and a dusky haze had descended, broken only by the street lights that flickered and hummed, brightening patches of pavement with a warm orange glow. And there it was, the white sign with black writing that made my stomach flip over, White Street, NW6. My home.

I waited until a crowd of people strolled past the bus stop and tagged along behind them until I reached the street light nearest to our house, then stopped and hovered in the shadows.

The light was on, the curtains were pulled back, and the television was flickering in the corner of the living room. At the back of the room were two bookshelves, one filled with my books, the other filled with Dan's DVDs and computer games. On top of the bookcases was a carved wooden elephant I'd bartered for during a holiday to Thailand, two church candles on black metal stands, a silver statue Dan's team had won in the London Advertising Awards and a wilted-looking spider plant. In front of the bookshelves was a sofa. Someone was curled up on one side, hugging a cushion with one arm, his legs curled up underneath him.

It was Dan.

On the bus I'd imagined running up to our front door, pressing the bell and launching myself at him. Instead my armpits were damp and my mouth was dry. What would I say? What would Dan say? It's not every day your girlfriend comes back from the dead and knocks on your door.

I was still trying to get up the courage to do something when the TV flickered and illuminated Dan's face. He was looking at what looked like a photo. His shoulders were shaking and tears were pouring down his cheeks. My heart convulsed and I thought I might pass out from the pain. I'd never seen him cry like that. Ever.

I took a step closer to the window and knocked.

'Dan,' I mouthed. 'I've come back.'

He glanced up, a look of astonishment and delight on his swollen, red face.

'It's me!' I shouted, jumping up and down and waving frantically. 'I'm back! I'm so sorry about the argument, Dan. I was just being an idiot. I didn't mean what I said, honestly.'

Dan's expression changed in front of my eyes. Excitement faded to disappointment and he frowned. I froze, my hands still in the air, mid-wave. What had just happened? Why wasn't he smiling any more? Was he angry with me? I ran down the pathway and pummelled on the door.

Come on, I thought as the light in the hallway was switched on and the floorboards squeaked with the sound of heavy footsteps. Come on, Dan, just let me in.

The door opened slowly.

'Yes,' he said, peering through the gap. 'Can I help you?'

'Oh very funny,' I said, feeling as though I was about to explode with happiness. 'Just let me in and give me a hug.'

'Sorry?' Dan frowned. 'I can't hear you. Could you say that again?'

'I know I died,' I said, still grinning like a lunatic, 'and I'm still dead, sort of, but I've come back to be with you. I've just got to complete a task first. I've got to—'

'Who are you,' he said, looking me up and down, 'and what do you want?'

I felt sick. There was something about the expression in Dan's eyes that wasn't right. He seemed cold and distant and not the slightest bit excited to see me.

'Dan, it's me,' I said, reaching through the gap in the door and stroking his cheek. 'It's Lucy. Are you OK? Are you in shock?'

Dan jumped as though he'd been burned and swatted my hand away. 'What the hell do you think you're doing?'

'Let me in,' I begged as he started to close the door. 'Stop messing around. You're scaring me.'

'If you've lost your voice,' Dan said, 'there's a chemist down the street.'

Then he slammed the door in my face.

'Dan,' I screamed, pummelling the painted wood with both fists. 'Dan, it's Lucy. It's Lucy. Let me in.'

The door swung open again.

'Look.' There was a look of disgust on his face. 'I don't know who you are or what you want, but I really don't need this shit. Just go away.'

He shut the door again and I stared at the glossy blue paint and the shiny, silver thirty-three and swallowed

57

back tears. What had just happened? Why hadn't he recognised me and let me in?

I banged forlornly on the door a couple more times, still calling his name, but he ignored me. In desperation I moved to the window and tapped the glass. Dan was sitting on the sofa again, his head in his hands.

'I came back, Dan,' I sobbed. 'I came back to be with you.'

He got up and crossed the living room, his eyes on mine. For a heart-stopping moment I thought he'd recognised me again. Then he yanked the curtains closed and disappeared.

I didn't immediately go back to the House of Wannabe Ghosts. Instead I walked to Primrose Hill, sat on a bench in the dark and stared at the lights flickering and twinkling over London. They would have looked beautiful if I hadn't felt so utterly miserable and alone.

I couldn't block the image of Dan's crying face from my mind. I had never, ever seen him look so utterly bereft. In fact, in seven years I'd only seen him cry four times. They were:

1) When he came to see me after my parents died.

2) When his mum told him she had breast cancer. He didn't cry then, in front of her, but he did bury himself in my arms later, hiding his tears in the crease of my neck.

3) One year later, when his mum told him she was officially in remission.

4) When we watched *Schindler's List* on DVD. At

the end, when Schindler grasps a ring made for him by the Jews and cries, 'I could have saved more, one more Jew, two more Jews,' Dan made a loud gulping sound. When I turned the lights back on, his eyes were red raw.

That's probably a lot of crying for most blokes, and I'd never seen a man cry before. Watching Dan crumple because I was dead was the most horrible thing I'd ever seen and I knew, in the split-second when he'd looked up at me through the window and almost recognised me, that I'd made the right decision in coming back to earth. Nothing, I realised as the London Eye twinkled on the horizon, was more important than us being together again. He'd been there for me so many times when I was alive and now he needed me. Even if I was only a ghost, at least he'd know I was watching over him.

I stood up, feeling determined. If I was going to pass my task I had to get back to the House of Wannabe Ghosts and find out why Dan hadn't recognised me. There was no time to lose.

Chapter Seven

All the lights were burning inside the House of Wannabe Ghosts so I turned the handle and pushed. It was locked.

'Brian,' I screamed through the letterbox, terrified I'd be left standing on another doorstep. 'It's Lucy. Could you let me in?'

There was a loud boom from upstairs, the sound of heavy footsteps along the landing and then the door swung open.

Brian was dressed head to toe in combat clothes: a khaki shirt, camouflage jacket and trousers, and a pair of army boots slung over his shoulder. Three thick black lines were painted on each of his cheeks.

'Ah, Lucy,' he said, 'thank God, you've come back.'

'I'm glad you missed me,' I said, relieved he knew who I was. 'And I've got so much to ask you. First of all I need to know why—'

'We can chat later,' he said, holding up a hand. 'First we need to save Claire.'

'What from?'

'Her exact words were,' he said, wriggling his feet

into his heavy black boots, "'I'm going to kick the bitch's head in. Come and help me.'"

'What!' I said. 'You're not going to help her beat someone up, are you?'

'Of course not,' he said as he shooed me out of the doorway and slammed the door shut. 'I'm going to stop her. And you're going to help me.'

'No I'm not,' I protested. 'Claire was a complete bitch to me earlier and—' but Brian was already out of the gate and jogging down the street like a demented Action Man.

I turned back to the front door and gave it a shove, then a harder one, but it didn't budge. Bugger! I looked from the door to Brian. I'd have to go after him or spend the rest of the night sitting on the step waiting for my housemates to come back.

I sprinted after Brian, my thighs wobbling as I pounded the pavement and clutched the stitch in my side. Dead and still flabby and unfit. How unfair was that?

'Brian,' I panted as we approached the bus stop, 'were you ever in the Territorial Army by any chance?'

He nodded and passed a hand over his sweat-free forehead. 'I was, yes. How did you—' He pointed down the street. 'Bus!'

Sure enough, a red double-decker was pulling round the corner. It drew up beside us, Brian paid for our tickets and then charged up to the top deck. I followed behind, grabbing the handrail and dragging myself up the steps. He paused at the top of the stairs and stared around, his eyes darting left and right like a judge at a table tennis competition.

'I'm just looking for a seat where we won't be overheard,' he whispered as though we were on some kind of covert military mission.

I pushed past him, desperate to sit down, and slumped into a seat at the front.

'If we sit here,' I said, tugging at his wrist, 'we can look out of the window and check there aren't any submissives following us.'

'I think you mean subversives, Lucy,' Brian said, carefully positioning himself on the edge of the seat so our bodies didn't touch.

I felt myself blush. 'Yeah.'

'We're not looking for subversives,' he said, frowning at me. 'We're looking for Claire. She told me she was in the Dublin Castle pub in Camden.'

I stared at him in astonishment, temporarily stunned by what he'd just implied. It didn't matter that Claire was a bitch or Brian was smelly because we could communicate with each other via ESP. How cool was that?

'Can you read my mind too, Brian?' I asked hopefully. 'Can you tell what I'm thinking now?'

'Of course not.' He shifted away from me, looking at me like I was mad. 'I spoke to Claire on the telephone, Lucy. There's one in the hall cupboard, next to the kitchen.'

'Oh.'

There was a pause and I stared out of the window,

clicking my purse open and closed. On the streets below us north London was still bustling with life; angry drivers honked their horns, young men leaned up against kebab shops smoking cigarettes as they eyed up the girls that walked past. Men in suits, desperate to get home, negotiated their way through crowds of laughing teenagers, and couples, arm in arm, paused outside restaurants and peered at the menus.

'Brian,' I said finally, 'how come I've got two hundred pounds in my purse but all my cards and stuff have gone?'

He tutted. 'You haven't read your manual yet, have you?'

'I haven't had time,' I said, staring back out the window at a couple snogging passionately against a pub window. 'I went to look for my fiancé instead.'

'And?'

'It was really horrible.' My bottom lip wobbled dangerously and I willed myself not to cry again. 'He didn't recognise me, Brian.'

'Oh, Lucy,' he sighed. 'If you'd just read your manual you'd have realised that would happen.'

'But I still look like me,' I said, turning to look at him. 'I checked in the mirror.'

'I know you do,' Brian said, his eyes soft with sympathy, 'and I can see the same person you see. So can Claire. But other people, living people, they view us slightly differently, Lucy. It's what's called a temporal twist in perception.'

'What's that?' I asked. It sounded scary.

'Imagine I was a holding a clay model of a human being.' Brian held his hands in front of him. 'And then I squashed it slightly.' He pressed his hands together. 'It's still a clay model of a human being but it just looks slightly different. That's what happens with us.'

'But Dan recognised me,' I said. 'For a split second when he first saw me.'

Brian nodded. 'The temporal twist doesn't happen instantaneously. There's always a slight delay.'

'Does that affect our voices?' I asked. 'Is that why Dan couldn't hear me either?'

'No. It's familiar mutism,' Brian said. 'Rule 512.6: if you try to communicate with anyone who knew you before you died, your attempts will be thwarted. Speaking renders you mute and writing turns into gobbledegook. You might have discovered that, Lucy, if you'd bothered to read the—'

'Manual. Yes, Brian, you said.'

I was still trying to figure out the temporal twist thing when the bus swung round the corner of Camden High Street and turned onto Parkway. Friday-night revellers crowded outside Camden tube. Music poured out of clubs, pubs and restaurants and goths, emos, punks, metallers, hip-hop kids and homeless people spilled onto the pavement and into the night. We were surrounded by life and energy. No wonder Claire couldn't keep away.

'I saw my mum in Covent Garden once,' I said, swallowing hard, 'or I thought I did. It was about a month after she'd died.' I turned to look at Brian. 'Do you think that means she came back to earth to do a task?'

'Quite possible,' he said sagely.

'But she never showed herself to me as a ghost. Do you think she failed?'

He shook his head. 'Sometimes people pass their tasks and choose not to become ghosts.'

'But why, it doesn't make sense? Why go through all that trouble and then not show yourself to the person you lov—'

Brian held up a hand and stood up. 'This is our stop.'

It was absolutely heaving inside the Dublin Castle. I followed Brian's dark, fuzzy head as he squeezed between the crowds of drinkers and made his way towards the door at the back of the venue where a black and red sign said LU$T BOYS in the ugliest font I'd ever seen. As we got closer a skinny bloke in a tight black T-shirt and even skinnier jeans, held up a hand.

'How many?' he asked, peering out from beneath the lank fringe that curved over the end of his nose.

Brian dug around in his wallet and pulled out a twenty-pound note. 'Two.'

Skinny Boy grabbed Brian's note and stamped both our hands with a dark squiggle.

'You're in,' he said.

The door slammed shut behind us and a thumping, screeching, drum-battering wall of noise bombarded my ears. It was dark, stank of beer and sweat and there wasn't space to breathe, never mind move (it was even worse than limbo). Brian raised himself onto his tiptoes and peered through the gloom.

'Lucy,' he bellowed in my ear. 'I've spotted Claire and I can see blood.'

'Blood,' I repeated. 'Shit.'

I followed the line of Brian's finger and squeezed my way through the crowd, ignoring the elbows and boots that jabbed me as I pushed through. At one point something hit my back and warm liquid seeped through my jumper, dripped down my spine, and curled towards my bum crack.

Please let that be lager, I prayed, pushing on towards the stage.

It wasn't hard to spot the band. A short, peroxide-haired singer was screaming into his mike while the rotund drummer thrashed about with his sticks like he was having some kind of psychotic fit. Only the bassist stood completely still, his eyes closed, the plucking movement of his fingers the only sign he wasn't fast asleep on his feet.

'Look,' Brian said, grabbing my shoulder. 'There she is.'

Claire was flat on her back on the floor, her black boots cycling the air, her skirt up round her waist, exposing her fishnet-covered bum. One of her nostrils was smeared with blood and several of her dreads had come loose. A blonde woman in a red bra was sitting astride her, smacking Claire's head against the floor as Claire pulled at her clothes and threw badly aimed punches. They were both red in the face and breathless.

It was like watching two gothic beetroots take part in WWF.

Brian was rooted to the spot, his mouth wide open. 'Hey,' I said, thumping him on the arm. 'Do something! Stop them.'

He took a step forward, paused, and then stepped back again. 'I'm not sure basic military training has equipped me for this, Lucy.'

I rolled my eyes. 'Oh for God's sake. Just pull them apart. I'll help you.'

Adrenaline and stupidity propelled me out of the crowd and towards the scrap.

'Grab her,' I said, pointing Brian in the direction of the scrawny blonde. 'I'll get Claire.'

Brian pounced and wrapped his arms around Claire's attacker, lifting her clean into the air while I grabbed one of Claire's hands and attempted to pull her up. Before I had time to react, her free hand curved through the air and hit me square on the chin. I stumbled backwards, slightly dazed and then reached for her again.

'Piss off,' she screamed, her dreads flying round her head like a Gorgon's snakes. 'I can look after myself.'

'For God's sake, Claire,' I shouted, rubbing my jaw, 'I was trying to stop you being killed.'

'I can't die,' she hissed. 'Remember?'

'Yeah,' shouted some random bloke in the crowd. 'We're all gonna live for ever. Rock and roll!'

Across the dance floor the skinny blonde was

wriggling in Brian's arms and thumping him in the side of the head with both fists. His jaw was gritted but I could tell he was in pain.

'Claire,' I shouted. 'Do you want Brian to get hurt too?'

She looked across at Brian and her expression softened a little.

'Fine,' she said, levering herself up off the ground. 'I'll deal with *her* tomorrow.'

The crowd were still booing our retreat as we stumbled through the pub and out the front door, Claire laughing hysterically the whole way.

'Look,' I said as we stepped onto the street. 'There's our bus.'

'Fuck that,' Claire said. 'I'm too pumped. I'm gonna run all the way home.'

'Claire,' I shouted as she sprinted off. 'Stop!'

The bus whizzed past me and I stared after it.

Shit.

There wouldn't be another one for an hour, if that. Now what was I supposed to do? I watched Claire disappear into the distance and made a decision. I'd have to go after her. She was only a kid really. I cradled my boobs with one arm and started to jog. Hooray, I thought, more running.

'Leave me alone,' Claire hissed as I drew up beside her.

'Can't,' I panted, as Claire stopped running and began to walk instead. 'I missed the bus.'

'Fine.'

'Fine.'

We walked on in silence, words sizzling inside my head. I can't deal with long silences, they make me uncomfortable. The longer they go on, the more I worry I'm about to spit out what I'm thinking in a Tourettes-style word explosion. I glanced at Claire. Selfish-Bitch-Cow-Fat-Bastard-Goth-Twat.

'So,' I said, forcing a smile, 'are you going to tell me what happened tonight?'

'Why should I?' Claire said, speeding up her pace again.

I jogged along beside her, determined not to give up. 'Because I tried to help you and you thumped me, that's why.'

'Nosy, aren't you,' she said, raising an eyebrow. 'If you must know, that blonde bitch slept with Keith. I couldn't say anything because of the mutism thing so I slapped her instead.'

'Who's Keith?'

'Jesus, Toga Girl.' Claire glanced at me. 'Are you retarded as well as deeply uncool? Keith Krank is the lead singer of the Lu$t Boys. He was on stage tonight, you moron.'

'Why do you care if she slept with Keith?' I said, letting the moron comment slip.

'Because she slept with him half an hour after I did.'

'Tonight?'

'No, three hours before I died.'

'But you—'

'Killed myself. Yeah.'

How was I supposed to answer that? I'd never had a conversation with someone who'd committed suicide before. Or anyone else who'd died, for that matter.

'Was Keith your boyfriend?' I ventured.

Claire shrugged. 'Dunno. Does having sex with someone five times count?'

'I'm not sure.'

'He's a poet, you know,' Claire continued, eyeing me suspiciously. 'He's really sweet and sensitive and he works in a dogs' home when he's not playing with the band.'

'Dogs' home,' I repeated. 'Right. So how did you meet him? Are you a groupie?'

'No!' She glared at me as though I'd just accused her of being a Westlife fan. 'I auditioned to be in the band. And don't look so surprised, Lucy. I'm actually shit-hot at the guitar.'

'So why didn't they take you on?'

'How many fat girls have you seen in bands?' she said, rounding the corner.

I had a think. I needed to say something to make her feel better. I had to come up with someone who'd be an inspirational role model.

'How about Mass Cass from the Mamas and Papas?' I said. 'She was fat and talented, but she didn't commit suicide. She died while she was eating a sandw—'

'Fuck off, Lucy,' Claire snapped. 'You're such a bitch.'

She didn't say another word to me all the way home.

Chapter Eight

'Morning, Lucy,' the note on the fridge read. 'Gone round the corner to the café for a late breakfast. Do join us. Brian. PS It's <u>Monday</u>.'

I rubbed my eyes and read the note again.

What?! Monday. How was that possible?

I'd passed out on my bed on Saturday night after I'd returned to the House of Wannabe Ghosts with Claire and she'd stomped up to her room and played LU$T BOYS at full volume. I couldn't have slept all the way through Sunday. Could I?

I switched on the kettle and grabbed a grubby ceramic jar from the window sill. Coffee. Coffee would help me make sense of what was going on.

I twisted the lid and peered inside. Empty. Damn. If I wanted some caffeine I was going to have to join Brian and Claire in the café. Great, more Claire, just what I needed on a Monday morning. Still, I reasoned as I grabbed my task envelope and let myself out of the house, at least the note proved that Brian had made it home alive (well, technically dead, but you know what I mean).

As it turned out, Claire was surprisingly subdued over breakfast. She glanced up as I walked into the bright if slightly tired-looking café, but looked down again as I approached the table, her scraggy dreads falling over her face as she bit into a sausage.

'Hello, Lucy,' Brian said brightly as I pulled out a chair and sat down.

He looked awful. His left eye was purple and as bloated as an egg, and there were several scratches on his cheek.

'My God,' I said. 'You look terrible.'

Claire didn't have the grace to blush or look the tiniest bit guilty, she just kept forking her breakfast into her mouth.

Brian shrugged. 'It looks worse than it is.'

I ordered a full veggie breakfast and wolfed it down. Thirty-six hours of sleep had given me a huge appetite. Between mouthfuls, I questioned Brian about what had happened when I'd left the club. He was annoyingly non-specific, but it seemed the blonde hadn't taken well to being manhandled and she'd taken her frustration out on his face before they were unceremoniously thrown out by the bouncers.

'And then I came home,' Brian said, 'and went straight to bed.'

I sipped my coffee, relishing the taste of the warm,

bitter liquid. 'Why did I sleep for so long? I've never slept that long before.'

'Wow, call the *Guinness Book of Records*,' Claire mumbled.

I looked across at her. 'Sorry?'

'Fuck off, Lucy.'

I opened my mouth to reply but Brian held up a hand. 'I think your overly long lie-in was a result of the transition from limbo to earth. I slept for almost twice that long when I got here. You'd think the saints might factor that into the twenty-one days and give us a bit longer.'

'Yeah,' I said. 'I'm a bit worried about how much time we've got. This is day three and I haven't done anything about finding Archie whatshisname yet.'

'Don't be too hard on yourself,' Brian said, smearing his toast with a thick layer of butter. 'You had a bit of a tough first day and an even tougher evening.'

'Yeah,' I said, 'last night was a bit mental.'

Claire suddenly dropped her knife and fork onto her plate and pushed her chair back so suddenly it squealed on the tiles.

'Why don't I just go,' she said, 'and leave you two alone to bitch about me behind my back. Would that make you happy? Would it, Lucy?'

'I—' I began, but she was already halfway across the room.

'Looks like I'll be paying for her breakfast, again,' Brian said, as the door to the café slammed shut.

74

I stared at him. 'Why does she have such a problem with me?'

He wiped his thumb across his upper lip and flicked a bit of egg out of his moustache. It curved through the air and landed on a teapot at the table beside us. The old lady who was holding it squealed and dropped it.

'She has a problem with everyone,' Brian said, completely obvious to the fact that two pensioners were now trying to rescue their scones from a river of hot tea. 'It's not just you.'

I wiped my mouth with a napkin and picked up my envelope.

'I need to read the manual,' I said, 'and see if there's any way I can make Dan recognise me—'

'There isn't,' Brian interrupted.

'And then,' I continued, ignoring Mr Know-It-All-Egg-Tache, 'I need to find out some more about this Archie guy. Is there a computer and Internet connection in the house?'

Brian shook his head. 'No, not that I'd know how to use it, if there was. I'm more of a pencil and notebook kind of man. Maybe you could try the library?'

'The library? Right.'

'I'll leave you to it, Lucy,' he said as he stood up. 'I should really get on with my own task.'

'Great,' I smiled, opening the manual. 'Have fun.'

The manual was made up of seven different sections:

1) What you can do
2) What you can't do

3) On arrival – an orientation guide

4) House of Wannabe Ghosts housekeeping rules

5) What to do if you complete your task

6) What to do if you don't complete your task

7) What to do if you change your mind about completing your task

The second section – 'What you can't do' – was the thickest and my eyes immediately flicked to the line saying you cannot contact people who knew you when you were alive. It said: 'It is forbidden to try and contact anyone who knew you when you were alive. This includes, but is not restricted to: parents, siblings, partners, lovers, cousins, aunts, uncles, employers, employees, friends, acquaintances, business associates, club members, gym members, hobbyists, newsagents, shop owners, postal workers, doctors, police officers …'

The list was enormous so I skipped on a bit.

'Should you try and make contact with anyone who knew you while you were alive:

1) They will not recognise you

2) They will not understand you (see mutism on page 566)

3) Any signal or contact you initiate will be misinterpreted and misunderstood

4) Any attempt you make to try and communicate through writing, symbols, letters or technology will be rendered illegible and will not be understood

5) Any attempt you make to try and communicate a personal message through any other person will be

rendered incomprehensible (see also mediums and psychics on page 673)

So that was why Dan had been so weird with me. He wasn't being cruel or brainwashed, he just had no idea who I was.

Brian was right.

There was no way I could make Dan recognise me – or understand a word I said. Damn it. If the only way I could be with him was as a ghost, I'd have to complete my task. There was no other way round it.

I flicked through the manual and sighed. There was no *way* I could read it all, not unless I spent the next eighteen days studying it. I was just going to have to wing it and see what happened. But first, Mission Find Out More About Archibald Humphreys-Smythe.

Who knew libraries had Internet connections? And nice men in Simpson's ties who show you to a free computer and tell you how to log in? Not me but, so far, so easy. Now all I had to do was type Archibald's full name into Google and press enter and I'd get an email address for him or, if I was really lucky, a phone number and then I'd just ...

Your search – Archibald Humphreys-Smythe – did not match any documents.

What? Nothing? How could there be nothing at all? Google could find Osama bin Laden if you looked hard enough.

I tried again, this time typing 'Computer Bitz' into

the search engine. Please, I begged silently as I hit enter, it's where he works. It has to have a ...

Computer Bitz (London) – Specialists in Software Design and Development

Yes!

Oh, very good, an 'About us' link that should tell me who worked ...

No. Nothing about Archie, no mention of any staff at all, just some computer software mumbo-jumbo that went straight over my head. I clicked frantically on all the other links.

Nothing. Nothing. Nothing.

How the hell was I going to meet Archie if:

a) I didn't know what he looked like

b) I didn't have a phone number for him

c) I didn't have an email address for him?

My only option was to ring the number for Computer Bitz and ask to speak to him, but what would I say – 'Hi, want to meet girls and find love?' He'd think I was a cheesy late-night TV ad.

Oh, wait, there was a link I'd missed. It was in a tiny font, buried in the bottom right-hand corner of the page.

Careers

Please let there be a graphic design job, please let there be ... oh ...

Web designer wanted. Must be proficient in

Photoshop, HTML, Javascript and CSS. Eye for detail essential. Previous experience essential.
For more details call Graham Wellington on 0207 437 9854.

The only web experience I had was buying designer cast-offs on eBay, but my graphic design past meant I had excellent Photoshop skills and an eye for detail. I could get myself some books on web design and blag the other three requirements. I was a fast learner, after all. How hard could it be?

I borrowed a pen from Simpson's-Tie-Man and scribbled the number on the back of my manual. Now all I needed to do was fake and print off a CV, buy a couple of CDs and find some websites I could pass off as my work. Then all I had to do was go back to the house and make a phone call to Graham Wellington, whoever he was.

My stomach gave a little lurch. It was just a phone call. Easy-peasy. Right?

Chapter Nine

'Brian?' I shouted as I let myself back into the House of Wannabe Ghosts. Then, more tentatively, 'Claire?'

No answer.

'Brian? Claire?'

No one was home. Thank God. I really didn't want to make such an important phone call with Claire muttering snide comments in the background and I had the distinct impression Brian wouldn't approve of the outrageous lies I was about to tell. I didn't need an audience, I just needed to hurry up and make the call before I lost my bottle.

The phone was in the cupboard under the stairs, exactly where Brian had said. The lead was too short to drag it into the hallway so I had to squeeze inside. The cupboard smelt of mothballs and socks and my back ached as I hunched over the phone, but there was a dial tone. Good start.

'Hello,' said the voice on the other end of the phone. 'Computer Bitz. Graham Wellington at your service.'

At my service? What was he – a butler?

'Hello, Mr Wellington,' I said. 'My name's Lucy Brown. I'm phoning about the web design job.'

There was a pause. A long pause. I could hear Graham Wellington breathing down the phone.

'So,' I bumbled on, 'I've got a lot of experience and obviously I have all the skills you listed on your website and I was wondering if you need me to send in my CV or if—'

'Are you a nice girl, Lucy Brown?'

I raised my eyebrows at the inside of the cupboard. 'Sorry?'

'Are you a nice girl or a nasty girl? We only employ nice people at Computer Bitz.'

Oh my God. Who was this guy?

'I'm a ...' Oh God, I was going to have to say it, wasn't I? '... I'm a very nice girl.'

'Good, good.' Mr Wellington purred. 'Can you come in at 3 p.m. this afternoon? We'll have a little tête-à-tête, a little chat-ette, to get to know each other better.'

'Right, a chat-ette,' I said, double-checking the number I'd just called. No, it definitely didn't start 0898. I hadn't accidentally called a sex chatline. 'So you'd like to interview me this afternoon for the web designer job?'

Graham sighed. 'Oh, Lucy, Lucy, Lucy, interview is such an formal word. Do you need directions?'

'No, it's fine, thanks. I've printed out a map, just in case.'

He made a noise like a steam train hissing. 'Organised too. Very nice.'

I didn't know what to say to that. Luckily Graham

didn't seem to care. 'See you at three o'clock, Miss Brown,' he said. 'I'll look forward to getting to know you.'

'Yes, um, me too.'

The phone line went dead and I stared at the phone. What the hell was that all about? Still, I was one step closer to meeting Archibald Humphreys-Smythe so it had to be good.

I spent most of the afternoon trying to decide what to wear. You know where you are with a normal interview: smart suit, heels and tidy hair, but how on earth do you dress for a 'nice chat-ette'?

Were jeans casual enough or too sloppy? How about jeans with a jacket? Or a skirt and a jumper? A bikini and a sarong?

I emptied my wardrobe and most of my drawers onto my bed and tried on dozens of combinations before I finally decided on an outfit; a black polo-neck jumper, a knee-length red skirt and black opaque tights with black boots. Casual but not scruffy. I wrinkled my nose at my reflection. It would have to do.

But what about jewellery? Should I wear my engagement ring or take it off? I pressed it against my lips and deliberated. On the one hand it made me feel close to Dan but, on the other, I didn't want to risk Graham Wellington asking any weird questions like, 'So, Miss Brown, are you going to wear nice lace lingerie for your wedding night or nasty nylon knickers? We only like nice pants here at Computer Bitz.' I needed the interview to be as straightforward as possible. Particularly as I was about to lie my arse off about my qualifications and experience.

I twisted the ring from my finger and carefully placed it on my bedside table.

'I'm sorry, Dan,' I whispered. 'I'll put it back on when I've passed my task, I promise.'

OK, time to leave before I changed my mind. I grabbed my coat and hurried down the stairs and out of the front door.

And smashed straight into Brian.

'Oh my God, I'm so sorry,' I said, patting his arm. 'Are you OK?'

He grunted and shuffled past me.

'Brian?' I raised my voice. 'Is everything OK?'

'Huh?' he said, glancing back at me. 'Did you say something, Lucy?'

'Are you all right?'

'Yeah.'

He didn't look all right. Even his moustache was droopy. I glanced at my watch. Only twenty minutes left.

'I've got a job interview,' I said, 'but I'll be back later. We can talk then.'

'If you want,' he said.

Sweat dribbled down my back as I charged up Tottenham Court Road and counted shop numbers under my breath. 59 ... 61 ... 67 ... 91 ...

It was shocking, really. I'd lived in London for six

years and I still couldn't read a bloody map. How many times did I get lost on my way to Computer Bitz? Too bloody many, in fact, I was fairly certain I was still lost … Oh! … 113. At last!

I wrenched the door open and my jubilant grin immediately slipped. In front of me was the steepest staircase I'd ever seen. I swiped my brow with my jumper sleeve and groaned. If I got any hotter I'd drown in my own sweat. I looked back at the stairs. No, it was fine, I could do it.

I stomped up, step after step after step, until there it was, finally, the door to Computer Bitz. I glanced at my watch: 2.59 p.m. Right on time. If I was lucky the receptionist might take pity on me and let me have a sit down and a glass of water before my interview. I might even have time to pull a comb through my hair and transform myself from bedraggled stink-pot to efficient web designer.

I took a deep breath, pulled open the door, and fixed my mouth into the 'nicest' smile I could manage.

'Hello,' I announced. 'I'm Lucy Brown.'

A roomful of blokes stared back at me. I'd never seen so many men with long hair, beards, glasses, or a combination of all three and they were all gawping at me like I'd just beamed down from Planet Woman. The only clean-shaven bloke with short hair and no specs was wearing a *Red Dwarf* T-shirt.

Get Smegged indeed.

'Excuse me,' I said to the nearest beardy bloke.

'I'm Lucy Brown. I've got an interview with Graham Wellington at 3 p.m.'

Beardy peered at me through his curtain of thick hair.

'Just around the corner there,' he nodded. 'I think Graham's on the phone.'

I drifted around the corner, horribly aware I was being watched by dozens of pairs of eyes. Oh my God. Archie was somewhere in the room. If I just shouted out his name he'd react and I'd know who he was.

But I couldn't do that. Silly idea.

If I started screaming 'Archie, Archie' at the top of my voice he'd probably flee through the nearest exit and I'd never get to play Cupid. I had to play it cool.

'No,' bellowed a loud northern voice that made me jump, 'you're wrong. I'm the expert on voice-activated software, not you.'

In front of me, leaning casually on a wide desk, was a middle-aged, ginger-haired man with a generous pot-belly hanging above black trousers that were a size too small. His face was so red he looked as though he was about to burst something, and not just his trousers.

I cleared my throat politely.

Belly Man looked me up and down. 'Yes,' he said into the phone, 'that would be acceptable. Now, if you'd just suggested I take charge of the marketing at the beginning of the conversation we would have saved each other a lot of valuable time.'

'Lucy Brown,' I mouthed. 'I'm here about the—'

'Sit.' Belly Man gestured for me to sit down in one

of the chairs lined up against the wall in front of the desk.

I sat, feeling like I was about to be told off by the headmaster at school. Belly Man snapped his mobile phone shut and lowered himself into his chair.

'Graham Wellington,' he said, beaming at me across the desk. He had the whitest teeth I'd ever seen.

I squirmed in my seat and tried not to look unsettled. 'I'm Lucy. I spoke to you earlier.'

Graham leaned back in his chair and folded his hands behind his head. I almost expected him to put his feet up on the desk and let out a massive yawn. He didn't. Instead he said, 'Ah yes, the nice Miss Brown.'

'That's me.'

'Sooooo, Lucy ...'

Here it came – the first interview question and probably one I didn't know the answer to. Blag-head on, Lucy, I thought. Put your blag-head on.

'Do you like wine, Lucy, or beer?'

'Wine,' I shot back without a moment's hesitation. A strange question, admittedly, but at least it was one I knew the answer to.

Graham shook his head. 'Wrong! Here at Computer Bitz we like a nice pint of beer after work. But the question is, should we make an exception for you, nice Lucy Brown?'

Hmmm. Obviously a trick question, but what was the right answer? I'd just have to chance it.

'I think you should make an exception for me, yes,' I said. 'Equal opportunities and all that.'

Graham smirked. 'Ooooh' he said. 'Equal opportunities. Very feminist. Are you a lesbian, Lucy Brown?'

If I was a cartoon character my eyebrows would have flown off my face and danced above my head. Somewhere in the office someone snorted with laughter.

'Just joshing, Miss Brown.' Graham leaned forward and peered at me from across the desk. 'A sense of humour is important in this job. You do have a sense of humour, don't you?'

'Well yes,' I said. 'Of course. Ah ha ha.'

I continued to titter, unsure when to stop until Graham interrupted me.

'We do have another member of staff of the female variety, but she works from home. Accountants, eh? Number-munchers, the lot of them.'

'Number-munchers,' I tittered. 'Oh yes, very funny. Very good.'

Graham nodded and looked pleased. Thank God.

'So,' he said, 'tell me a little about yourself, Lucy.'

Finally, a proper interview question. I'd even rehearsed this one on the tube, lies and all. I reached across the desk and handed Graham a plastic sheet containing my fake CV and a CD and print-outs of various websites I'd found on the net. None of them had a 'designed by' tag at the bottom so I was pretty certain I could get away with claiming they were mine. Finders-keepers and all that.

'Well,' I began as Graham flicked through them, 'I've designed websites for everyone from bands to estate agents to photographers to crane firms to actors to—'

Graham held up his hand. 'Not the boring stuff, Lucy. We all know you can do the web stuff.'

Do we, I thought. I don't.

'Tell me about you,' Graham continued. 'Tell me the juicy stuff.'

'I'm … ' What the hell could I say? I couldn't tell him I was a dead almost-bride, my fiancé thought I was mute and I lived with a train-spotter and a goth and …

'I'm single,' I lied.

Graham nodded encouragingly. 'Go on.'

'And I like reading, dancing and singing karaoke, although I'm not very good at singing, and I like going to the cinema and the pub. I love going on holiday, particularly beach holidays.'

I glanced across at Graham. Was I saying the right thing? He cracked his knuckles, stood up and walked round the desk. He was, I realised with a sudden lurch of horror, heading for one of the seats next to me.

'So,' he said as he sat down, his generous thigh pressed against mine, 'tell me about these beach holidays.'

His aftershave was overwhelming. It smelt like a mixture of musk, pepper and oranges. I cleared my throat. 'What would you like to know?'

Graham scratched his head, revealing the cufflinks on his shirt sleeves. Silver handcuffs. Uh-oh. I stared at the carpet and tried hard not to look too alarmed.

'What do you like to do on beach holidays?' Graham asked.

Oh God. If I'd been at any other interview I would have made my excuses and left. In fact, I probably would have left the minute Graham had made the lesbian comment, but I desperately needed the job. I had to get it so I could get to know Archie. It was the only lead I had.

'I like the beaches,' I said, 'and I like swimming and sunbathing.'

Graham leaned towards me. He was so close I could count the sweaty pores on his nose.

'Do you skinny-dip, Lucy?' he asked, almost blinding me with his glow-in-the-dark teeth.

OK, now was the time to tell him to sod off and run away. Fast.

'No,' I said instead. 'I don't.'

'Shame,' he said, looking down at my chest, 'you've got a fine pair.'

Thwakkk!

My open palm made contact with his cheek before I knew what I was doing. Graham jumped back, clutched at his jaw, and stared at me, his eyes wide.

'Um,' I said, standing up. 'Um.'

And then I ran round the corner, out of the door and down the stairs. I didn't stop running until I was halfway down the street.

Then I shouted, 'Fuckkkkkkkkkkkkkkkk!' at the top of my lungs.

Chapter Ten

Drink, I thought as I pushed open the door to the White Horse, my favourite pub in the whole of West Hampstead and just a stone's throw from my old house … and my new one. Drink lots. ASAP.

'Glass of dry white wine please,' I said to the first barman that caught my eye. 'Large one.'

He raised his eyebrows. 'Hard day?'

'You could say that,' I sighed.

I carried my drink to the darkest corner of the pub and sat down heavily in a chair. What was I going to do? Who slaps their potential boss during the most important interview of their life? Me, that's who. I'd totally screwed up my task and it was only day three.

I could ring up and apologise, but there was no way a grovelling 'sorry!' would change anything. The chances of Graham replying, 'Oh, how lovely, an apology. I don't think you're a psycho-bitch from hell any more. Want a job?' were less than nil.

Oh shit, oh shit, shit, shit. What had I done? How the hell was I going to get to know Archie now? I didn't know anything about him apart from where he worked.

I rested my head in my hands and stared around the pub. It hadn't changed at all since I'd last been in with Dan. The walls were still panelled with dark wood, the oak floor sticky with spilt beer and the beams so low Dan had to duck his head when he walked in. Unlike the harsh, bright glare of a wine bar, the White Horse was dimly illuminated by wall lights topped with dusty crimson shades and wine bottles stoppered with candles on the tables and window sills. There was something very calming and warm about the pub's dark nooks and crannies, where you could hole yourself up with a drink and remain undisturbed for hours. That was probably why Dan and I had spotted so many famous people in the pub. It was somewhere to hide. Not that there was any sign of Pete Doherty or Sadie Frost at the moment, but the regulars were in, as usual. Sleeping Man was in his favourite corner, his mouth open, half a pint of bitter on the table in front of him. Shopping Woman was sitting at one of the round tables in the middle of the room, two bags of food at her slippered feet. Bob the Talker was, as always, propped up next to the bar, being ignored by the bar staff. Despite the horror of my predicament it was good to be back in my local. It made me feel safe. I'll just drink and people watch, I decided as I took another sip of wine, until I'm drunk. There was nothing I could do about the Archie situation anyway. It would have to wait until day four.

The bell above the door chimed loudly and I looked up. Wine slopped in my glass and I nearly dropped it. Anna and Jess had just walked in.

My Anna and Jess. My best friends in the whole world.

I watched, open-mouthed, as they made their way to the bar. They both looked great. Jess, who was my best friend at uni, worked as a make-up artist in the theatre. She was exactly as I remembered her – short, cute and messy – her black hair pulled into an untidy ponytail, fixed in place with a silver clip, a black pinafore dress over a white T-shirt and a pair of ridiculously clumpy boots on her feet. And she looked happy. Things must be going well with Stuart, I thought. Excellent.

Jess looked great, but it was Anna who really made me gawp. Her hair was shorter and sleeker than normal. Her blonde curls had been replaced with a straight, smooth bob that curved under her jawbone. She'd also swapped her boho flowing skirts and loose, off-the-shoulder tops for smart jeans, heels and a fitted blue top with a low neckline that showed off her impressive cleavage. She looked magnificent, there was no other word for it. All the men in the bar dribbled into their pints as she angled herself through the crowd and pressed her bosom against the bar. Wow, I thought, I wonder if she's got a new man?

I'd met Anna at one of Dan's friend's parties three years before and we'd clicked immediately. She made me laugh my arse off and she was the most singularly fascinating person I'd ever met. She'd worked as a lap-dancer for a year after university to fund a trip around the world where she'd swum with dolphins, lived with a Nepalese family, worked in a Romanian orphanage, trekked the Inca Trail, and learned four languages. Then she'd returned to London and wangled herself an amazing, high-paid job in the city.

Right before I died, she'd been on a hunt for a sperm donor. She was obsessed with getting pregnant before she hit thirty-five and the old biological clock had started to tick, loudly. But Anna wasn't looking for a husband. In fact, she wasn't even looking for a boyfriend.

'I'm done with men,' she'd said when her eighteen-month relationship with Julian ended when she found out he was cheating on her. 'More trouble than they're worth. I don't need one to have a baby. I just need the sperm.'

She'd even created a list of 'must-haves' in her potential sperm donor which included:

1) Nice face
2) Height (no shorter than six foot, no taller than six foot five)
3) Intelligence (degree absolutely necessary, IQ over 135 preferred)
4) Sense of humour
5) Warm and passionate personality
6) Close group of friends
7) Good health (very, very important)
8) No sexually transmitted diseases (obviously)

Anna's plan was to find the right man, date him for long enough to find out if he met her criteria, get him to agree to go to a STD clinic to be tested before they had sex for the first time, and then claim she was going on the pill. She would then have sex with him until she got pregnant and break up with him (without telling him about the pregnancy). Then she'd stop answering her phone, 'disappear' from his life and go through the pregnancy alone.

Jess and I had tried to talk her out of it, but when Anna set her heart on something, that was it – there was no stopping her. She'd get it – no matter what it took. She'd given everything a go in her quest to meet the perfect man. She'd tried speed-dating, Internet-dating, dark dinner dates ('too freaky'), singles zoo dates, singles balls ('too many balding Hooray Henrys') and danger dates ('the roller coasters mess up your hair'), but no one matched up to her ideal.

I stared at her as she and Jess wound their way through the crowd, drinks in hand. Had she found someone since I died? Was that why she'd changed her image?

Oh my God. They were walking towards me. Maybe they'd actually recognised me—

No. The two men at the table nearest to me were draining their pints and Anna and Jess hovered beside them. One of the men clocked Anna as he stood up.

'Hello, sexy,' he said, adjusting his tie.

Anna sneered down at him. 'Dream on, loser.'

'Your loss,' the man shrugged.

'Only if I lost my sight,' Anna fired back. 'Have you looked in the mirror recently?'

Jess giggled as the men walked away. She sat down with her back to me, but she was so close I could smell her perfume. She'd worn the same sweet, flowery scent for years, and it had become synonymous with her in my mind.

I shivered. I was sitting *this* close to my best friends and I couldn't say a thing to them. The bloody mutism rule meant I couldn't even tell them how much I missed them.

'So,' Anna said, leaning towards Jess, 'how are you?'

Jess fiddled with her hair clip. 'Not bad. I've been working on a new production of *As You Like It*. It's been mental and some of the actresses have seriously pissed me off, but there are more important things in life than work. I've been thinking about that a lot since …'

She looked at Anna who finished her sentence. 'Lucy died.'

'Yeah. Things have changed since she died. I've changed. Me and Stuart have changed. We're so much closer now.'

Anna's expression softened. 'I know what you mean about changing.' She touched her hair. 'When my hairdresser asked me if I wanted to try something different I said yes. I felt like I'd changed after Lucy died, and my style didn't match who I'd become. Does that sound weird?'

'Yes and no,' Jess said. 'I wasn't really talking about changing superficially, Anna, I—'

Anna laughed. 'Are you saying I'm superficial?'

'Not at all,' Jess said hurriedly.

'I miss Lucy,' Anna said, stroking the rim of her wine glass with a manicured finger. 'Did you know she always used to ring me every Sunday morning at ten o'clock? I told her not to ring me until the afternoon because I like a lie-in, but she kept on doing it. It used to annoy the hell out of me, but I miss it now. I keep waking up at ten o'clock on Sunday, but the phone never rings.'

Oh. Oh, Anna. My wine caught in my throat and I swallowed it quickly before I choked and drew attention to myself.

'Have you seen Dan?' Jess asked. 'I keep meaning to give him a ring, but I don't know if I should.'

'Actually, I rang him a couple of days ago,' Anna said, putting her drink back on the table. 'He said something really freaky had happened and he needed to talk to me about it. We're having a drink in here on Thursday night.'

Me, I thought, almost jumping out of my chair. I was the freaky thing. He thought he saw me outside the house. That's why he wants to talk to you, Anna. Thursday, I mentally repeated. Come back to pub on Thursday. Oh. My. God. I'd get to see Dan again.

'I'm so glad you're meeting up with him,' Jess said. 'When I spoke to him at the funeral I got the impression he didn't really want to talk to anyone.'

Anna sighed. 'Yeah, well, you can't really blame him, can you?'

'I suppose not.'

They fell silent again and Anna fiddled with the stem of her glass. It was strange seeing the two of them alone. It had always been the three of us on a night out, or me and Anna or me and Jess. They got on brilliantly when we were all together, but they never met up without me. It was like their friendship didn't really exist if I wasn't there. It was good to see they were getting to know each other at last.

Anna propped her chin on her hands and stared at the wall above my head. Talk about me, I silently urged her. Talk about what happened when you found me. I know it sounds morbid to obsess about what had happened after I'd died, but I had so many unanswered questions. Who had found me on the hallway floor? Did many people go to my funeral? Was I buried next to my mum and dad?

'So,' Jess said finally. 'How's the sperm donor hunt going? Still looking?'

Anna raised her eyebrows and shrugged. 'Kind of, half-heartedly. Part of me thinks I'd better get it sorted quickly, just in case I die first—'

I laughed, I couldn't help it. It didn't come out as a proper laugh of course, more of a wheezing snort. Anna glanced at me, frowned, and looked at Jess.

'What?' Jess asked.

Anna looked at me again. 'Nothing. What was I saying?'

'Part of you thinks you should get it sorted in case you die …'

'Oh yeah, and the other part thinks, I just can't be arsed. Knowing my luck, I'd give birth to a boy and he'd grow up to be a complete bastard.'

Jess laughed and clinked her glass against Anna's. 'I've missed you, Anna. We should do this every week.'

Anna smiled. 'I'd love to, Jess. By the way, I love your pinafore. Where did you get it?'

They continued to talk about clothes, shoes and shopping for the next hour and I zoned out. When you're dead, no one really cares what you're wearing (apart from Claire, obviously). I bought myself several more glasses of wine and dipped in and out of the girls' conversation, waiting for them to change the subject back to me or Dan. At one point they both started reminiscing about one particularly disastrous camping trip we'd all gone on where I'd headed to the toilets in the middle of the night without a torch, tripped over the guy rope of another tent, and landed on a couple who were having sex. It took all my self-restraint not to try and join in.

By ten o'clock I was very, very drunk and laid my head down on the table. I just wanted to close my eyes for a couple of …

The barman shook me awake. 'Hey,' he said. 'It's eleven-thirty. Time to go home, Bad Day Girl.'

I stared up at him through bleary eyes. 'Huh?'

'Forgotten your bad day already, have you? That's good.'

It was true, I had. I'd totally forgotten about slapping

Graham Washington and totally screwing up my chance to meet Archie.

I glanced at Anna and Jess's table. They'd gone.

Chapter Eleven

Tuesday 30th April
Day Four

'Lucy,' Brian bellowed from the door. 'Lucy, phone!'

'What day is it?' I mumbled, peering at him through bleary eyes.

'Tuesday,' he said. 'And there's someone on the phone for you.'

I slumped back onto the sheet and closed my eyes. 'Tell them I'm dead.'

Brian snorted. 'It sounds important.'

'Who is it?'

'Some guy called Graham something. Wellington, I think he said.'

'Shit,' I said, sitting bolt upright.

What did Wellington want? Could a dead girl go to prison for attempted assault? Oh God. How would I complete my task if that happened?

I slid off the bed and stumbled out of the room and down the stairs. The door to the cupboard was open and the phone was off the hook. I grabbed at it.

'Hello.'

'Lucy Brown?' said a familiar voice.

I swallowed hard. 'Speaking.'

'Lucy Brown, this is Graham Wellington.'

'Oh my God, Graham, Mr Wellington, about what happened, I—'

'Lucy,' he said sternly, then, 'is it OK if I call you Lucy?'

'Yes.'

'Lucy, it has been brought to my attention that my conversation with you yesterday was a little unprofessional.'

'Well, yes. It was, but—'

'And I have been advised that certain employment tribunals do not take kindly to a few old-fashioned compliments.'

What? Since when was 'you've got a nice pair' an old-fashioned compliment?

'And, in the light of that,' he continued, 'and obviously as a result of your very fine web design skills, I'd like to …'

He paused.

'You'd what?' I said, my heart jumping around in my chest like a toddler on a trampoline.

'Offer you the job. When can you start?'

I burst out laughing. I couldn't help it. It was utterly ridiculous. I'd lied about my qualifications, the man had insulted me and I'd slapped him. And I'd got the job!

'Is that a "no"?' There was fear in Graham Wellington's voice.

'No,' I said, 'that's a "yes". I can start tomorrow.'

'You can?' he squeaked. 'That's fantastic. You are obviously a very nice girl indeed, Lucy Brown. I'll see you tomorrow.'

'OK. Bye then.'

'Goodbye.'

I was still sniggering to myself as I wandered into the kitchen and poured water into the kettle. Brian appeared at the doorway and raised an eyebrow.

'Everything OK, Lucy?'

'Yes, Brian,' I said, swirling water and washing-up liquid into a dirty mug. 'It's brilliant. I've got a job.'

'You have? Well done.' He frowned. 'Why is that good?'

'Because,' I said, 'tomorrow I get to meet Archibald Humphreys-Smythe. I'm one step closer to completing my task.'

'Oh, good for you,' he said, his smile not quite reaching his eyes. 'Good for you.'

The rest of the day dragged by. There was no TV in the house and the small, cranky radio in the kitchen buzzed intermittently which made it impossible to listen to anything for more than a few minutes without screaming. Claire was out (where, I had no idea) and Brian only popped out of his room every couple of hours to make a cup of tea or use the bathroom.

I was officially bored.

At six o'clock, unable to bear my own company for one second more, I tapped on Brian's door.

'Come in,' he said.

He was lying on his bed in his underpants, holding a book called *The Encyclopaedia of Electric Trains 1879 – Present Day*.

'Hello, Lucy,' he said, looking up. 'Take a seat.'

I walked towards the chair, pausing as I passed the wardrobe. It was the one I'd stumbled out of when I'd arrived from limbo.

'Brian,' I said. 'Do you mind if I have a look in the wardrobe?'

He nodded. 'Mmm hmm. Go ahead.'

I pulled open the door and peered inside. The cords and pastel jumpers were still there, so were the neat rows of sandals and socks. What about the escalator? Was that still there?

I parted the hangers and reached for the door handle at the back of the wardrobe.

'Don't!' shouted Brian. 'You'll die!'

I jumped back as though I'd been electrocuted. 'What!' I said, staring at my hand.

'Just my little joke,' he grinned.

'Very amusing.' I looked back at the handle. 'What happens if I turn this?'

'Nothing.'

'Really?'

'Seriously, nothing. You can only open it if there's someone on the other side.'

I wiggled the handle and pushed. Nothing happened.

'But what if I want to go back?' I asked, shoving the door.

'Then you use the other door,' Brian said, flicking over a page of his book.

'What door?'

'The one in *your* wardrobe.'

Hmmm. Interesting, and also horribly tempting. If I ever felt like giving up my task I could just jump into my wardrobe and scramble my way back up to limbo. Not that I'd ever do that, of course.

'Sit down and relax,' Brian said as I banged the wardrobe door shut. 'You're making me feel stressed.'

I plonked myself into the wicker chair by the window, pulled my knees to my chest and stared round Brian's room, desperate for something to entertain me. Could his posters be any more dull? How could anyone feel moved by the sight of a train?

'Brian,' I said. 'Have you come back to haunt a train?'

He peered at me over the top of his book. 'No, Paddington Station.'

'A station?'

'Yes, you have a better vantage point for train-watching from Paddington.'

Was he winding me up? I raised my eyebrows at him but he didn't smirk or giggle. He seriously wanted to haunt *a train station*.

'Um, right,' I said. 'So you've been here for what … nine days now?'

'I have.'

'And how's the task going?'

'I don't want to talk about my task, Lucy,' Brian mumbled, raising his book so it covered his face.

'Why not? Maybe I could hel—'

The bedroom door slammed open and I jumped. Oh. Great. Claire was back. And she didn't look happy.

'Could you go?' she said, leaning against the doorframe. 'I need to have a word with Brian. Alone.'

I looked at my flatmate but he was still hiding behind his book. Coward.

'Ask me nicely,' I said, grinning at Claire.

She feigned a smile. 'Piss off.'

'See,' I said, as I squeezed past her. 'It doesn't hurt to be nice, does it?'

'Bye, Bride,' she said, and slammed the door shut after me.

I hung around on the landing for a couple of seconds and then pressed my ear against Brian's door. What was so private Claire couldn't say it in front of me? Hmmnnnggg, came Brian's low voice. Hmmnnnggg. Hmmnnnggg. Hmmnnnggg. I couldn't make out a single word he or Claire were saying. Now what was I supposed to do to entertain myself?

I wandered into my bedroom, opened my wardrobe door and peered inside. Brian was right. Behind my hangers and clothes was another white door, identical to the one in his room. I stroked the handle.

Open it? Don't open it? What's the worst that could happen?

I could be whisked off to limbo, never see Dan again

and he'd spend the rest of his life wondering if I'd died thinking he was a waste of space.

Oh. OK. That was pretty bad.

I threw myself onto my bed and grabbed the photo from my bedside table. It was of me and Dan on our first holiday together in Menorca. Dan was grinning like a loon and I was laughing my head off. It was a perfect holiday. The sand was white, the sea was cold and clear, and the sun was glorious. One afternoon, when Dan was feeling unusually energetic, he challenged me to a swim-off.

'See that buoy over there?' he'd asked, pointing into the distance.

'Yeah,' I'd nodded.

'I'll race you to it.'

I squinted at the buoy. It was a long way away and I wasn't a particularly fast swimmer.

'Only if we both swim breaststroke,' I bartered.

'OK,' Dan had said, holding out his hand. 'You're on.'

We pelted down the beach, threw ourselves into the cool water and started to swim. We were pretty well matched at first, but then Dan put his head down and started to pull away from me. Before I knew it, he was about ten metres ahead. There was no way I was going to win.

I stopped swimming, flipped onto my back and sculled with my hands. It was so quiet I could almost hear myself breathing. On the beach, ant-sized people scuttled around, shook their towels free of sand and settled themselves on sun-loungers. I'd felt like some kind of mermaid or oceanic god, surveying my world. It was bliss.

'Hey,' said a disgruntled voice beside me. It was Dan, red-faced and puffing. 'You gave up.'

'I didn't give up,' I said, covering my eyes as he splashed me. 'I just stopped to admire the view.'

'Wow,' he said, staring back at the beach. 'That's pretty bloody fantastic.'

'I know.'

Overhead, a seagull squawked as it surfed in the wind.

'How do you imagine heaven?' Dan asked, sculling beside me, his hairy toes peeping above the water.

'I dunno. Fields of poppies, sunshine, fluffy clouds, relatives running to meet me?'

'I think it looks like this,' he said.

I smiled. 'Really?'

'Yeah.'

'So what happens when we both die?' I asked. 'Do I live in poppy-field heaven and you live in sea heaven?'

Dan reached for me then and pulled me towards him. I wrapped my legs around his hips and we bobbed up and down in the water, the waves lapping around us.

'I hope heaven is a bit of both,' he'd said. 'Then we'll be together.'

'I like the sound of that,' I said, kissing him full on the lips.

*

The sound of raised voices and a door slamming snapped me out of my daydream.

'Brian!' Claire was screaming. 'Brian, come back.'

I jumped off my bed and sprinted across the room. My gothic flatmate was standing at the top of the stairs, bellowing after Brian, who was speeding towards the front door shouting, 'Leave me alone!' at the top of his voice.

'Hey,' I said. 'What the hell's going on, Claire? What did you do to him?'

She glared at me. 'I didn't do anything to him. I just asked if he'd help me with my task and he went off on one and stormed out.'

I wasn't sure I believed her.

'I'm going after him,' I said. 'You stay here.'

'Do what you want,' she snarled. 'I don't give a shit.'

By the time I'd pulled on my coat and escaped out of the front door, Brian was already halfway down the street.

'Brian!' I shouted after him. 'Brian, wait.'

Instead of replying or slowing down, he speeded up, striding down the street like a man on a mission.

Dammit. What the hell was wrong with him?

I followed him for a good ten minutes, ducking into people's gardens and behind bushes whenever he crossed the road and looked both ways. When we reached the tube station a light bulb went on in my head. Brian was heading for Paddington Station. I'd put money on it.

I waited until he boarded the train and then darted out from the stairs and jumped into the adjacent carriage. And trapped the hem of my coat in the door as it closed.

Shit.

The rest of the carriage grinned at me as the train chugged forward and I yanked at my coat.

'Come on,' I said, 'come on, you bugger'.

I put my heel on the door for leverage and pulled. Come on! Come on! My coat slipped free and I stumbled backwards, tripped over someone's suitcase, and landed in the lap of a sleeping businessman.

'Sorry,' I gasped as he woke with a snort. 'Sorry, sorry.'

I struggled up and grabbed hold of the overhead rail. Anna Friel, in an advert for a West End play, grinned down at me.

'Sod off, you smug cow,' I muttered under my breath, 'you had it easy in *Pushing Daisies*.'

'This is Paddington,' the guard announced as the train slowed to a halt. 'All change for Paddington train station, the District and Circle lines and the Hammersmith and City line.'

The doors opened and I peered through them. Brian was striding towards the exit. Quick, after him. I jumped off the tube and hurried down the platform.

The up escalator popped me out in the middle of Paddington Station and I stared around wildly. Now where had Brian gone? I panicked silently and scanned the concourse. He'd said something in his bedroom about Paddington having the best vantage point. I stared up at the roof. But where? I'd have to ask one of the guards.

'Excuse me,' I said, approaching the first one I spotted. 'Could you please tell me the best vantage point for watching the trains?'

He looked me up and down and grinned. 'You forgot your anorak.'

'Actually,' I said, the blood rushing to my cheeks. 'I'm not a trainspotter. I'm looking for someone.'

'Uh-huh,' he said, pointing into the distance, not sounding entirely convinced. 'Most of them hang out over there.'

'Right, thanks,' I said and set off towards the back of the station. Ah, there he was. Brian's fuzzy, dark hair was bobbing around in the middle of the crowd crossing the bridge.

I climbed the stairs and sidled up to him. He was leaning on a low metal wall, staring at the trains chugging slowly into and out of the station. He looked like he'd been crying.

'Brian,' I said, putting my hand on his shoulder. 'It's Lucy. Are you OK?'

He jumped and swiped at his eyes with his sleeve. 'What are you doing here?'

'I was worried about you.'

'You shouldn't bother,' he said, turning back to the trains. 'You've got enough on your plate as it is.'

'But I do worry,' I said, moved by the sight of his sad, blotchy face. 'The only people I've got in this strange living dead world are you and Claire. We need to look out for each other.'

Brian snorted. 'You think Claire's going to look out for us?'

'OK, well not Claire, but I still worry about her. She's like the bitchy little sister I never had.'

It was true. I had started to think of Brian and Claire as my pseudo-family. Claire was my annoying little sister and Brian was my strange, smelly uncle. There might have been other living dead people on earth, but we didn't know who they were or where they lived. The only people we could talk to about what we were going through were each other.

'What's up, Brian?' I said. 'Come on, let's go somewhere and have a chat.'

For a second I thought he was going to tell me to sod off and leave him alone. Instead, he shrugged his shoulders.

'OK,' he said. 'The café on platform one does a nice cup of tea.'

We sat at a table in the window, Brian with his pot of tea and me with a cup of coffee and a flapjack (I'm great in a crisis, I just need something sweet to get me through it).

'So,' I said. 'What's the problem? Is it your task?'

Brian nodded miserably and stared out of the window. 'I'm never going to complete it.'

'Why? Can't you find the person on your Task Objectives sheet?'

'Oh, I found him all right.'

'That sounds hopeful,' I said brightly.

Brian dropped two sugar cubes into his cup and stabbed them with his spoon. 'It's not.'

God, sometimes having a conversation with Brian was like drawing teeth.

'Why don't you tell me what happened?' I said.

'OK, not that it'll help.' He sighed and stirred his tea. 'I have to get a fifteen-year-old boy called Troy Anderson to admit he's a railway enthusiast. He secretly loves trains, but his friends think it's a deeply uncool hobby.'

Not just them, I thought, but didn't say.

'Have you talked to him about it?' I asked.

Brian raised his teacup to his mouth and took a sip. I waited as he slowly lowered it again, clattering it onto the saucer as he did so, and blotted his moustache with a napkin.

'I did speak to him briefly,' he said. 'Well, I introduced myself.'

'And? What did he say?'

'Fuck off, you paedophile.'

'Oh.'

I took a sip of coffee and tried to work out what to say next. When I looked back up, fat tears were rolling down Brian's cheeks.

'Oh God,' I said, grabbing his big hand. It felt cold and clammy and his fingers were shaking. 'It can't be that bad. Maybe you could try talking to him again?'

Brian shook his head and a tear dripped off his jaw

and landed on his pastel-yellow jumper. 'Why would he talk to me again? He thinks I'm a complete freak. I'm never going to complete this task, Lucy. And I'm running out of time.'

'Is it the end of the world if you don't pass your task?' I asked. 'Maybe you'd like it in heaven?'

'No,' Brian sobbed. 'No, I wouldn't. I want to be here. I need to be here.'

'But they're just trains,' I said softly.

'That's like me telling you Dan is just a man,' Brian said, his eyes wide.

'But he's the love of my life.'

'And trains are mine.'

There was something very tragic about a middle-aged man feeling that way about lumps of metal but, in a way, I understood him. Trains made him happy. They gave him a reason to get up in the morning. They probably made his heart beat faster too.

'Brian,' I said, not really thinking through the implications, 'why don't I help you with your task?'

He stared at me for a long time and then placed one of his big paws on mine.

'Would you?' he said. 'I'd be eternally grateful.'

'It'll be fine,' I said. 'Don't worry. We'll both pass our tasks. You'll see.'

He beamed at me across the table and I cringed inwardly. I wasn't exactly making great waves with my own task so how the hell was I going to complete two?

Chapter Twelve

Wednesday 1st May
Day Five

Typical. Just bloody typical.

My first day at Computer Bitz and it was raining. I'd spent *hours* straightening my hair and now it was plastered to my head like a stringy helmet. And my best suede boots were soaked. So much for making a good impression on Archie. He'd just have to take me as he found me.

I took a deep breath, turned the door handle, and strode into the office.

'Morning!' I said with exaggerated cheeriness.

Beardy Number One stopped typing, glanced up at me, and swiftly looked away again. He looked worse than I remembered. His long, greasy hair was scraped back into an elastic band and he was wearing a black T-shirt with 'Gamer' on the front in big white lettering. There was a blob of jam on the G.

'Good God,' Beardy said, staring intently at my boots. 'We didn't think we'd see you again.'

'What can I say?' I shrugged. 'I was desperate for the job.'

Beardy raised his eyebrows. Now he was looking somewhere over my left shoulder.

'Is Mr Wellington in?' I asked, leaning slightly to the left.

'No. He'll be in later today.' OK, now he was looking at my boots again. 'But we've set up a desk for you if you want to get yourself settled in.'

He unfolded himself from his chair and stood up. Gosh, he was *tiny*. He was about five foot five and so skinny I could see his shoulder blades through his T-shirt.

'You'll be glad to hear we got you a top-spec PC,' he said, weaving through the crowded desks. 'Follow me.'

Shit, I thought as he stopped in front of an empty desk in the centre of the room. Everyone will be able to see my screen.

'OK,' Beardy said to the middle of my forehead. 'A few introductions, if I may.'

Oh my God. I was going to get to meet Archie. I glanced around the room. Which one was he? Please, I prayed, please let him be the clean-shaved, short-haired one with 20-20 vision (I could always get him to ditch the *Red Dwarf* T-shirt and replace it with something more fashionable).

'This,' Beardy said, pointing to a spotty-faced guy with long, red hair who had the desk to the right of mine, 'is Geoff.'

I held out my hand. 'Hi, Geoff. I'm Lucy.'

'All right,' he mumbled, his eyes glued to the glowing screen in front of him.

Beardy seemed to think the introduction had gone well and pointed at the guy with bottle-top specs and long, greasy, black hair to my left.

'This is Nigel,' he said.

Nigel looked up and gave me a yellow-toothed smile.

'Pleased to meet you,' he said, shaking my hand weakly.

'One more for now,' Beardy said, pointing behind me.

Oh. It was Get Smegged Guy. Archie. It had to be. He had warm brown eyes and high cheekbones. Beyond the T-shirt and oily side-parting, he was actually a very nice-looking guy.

I smiled down at him and held out my hand. 'Hi, I'm Lucy.'

'Joe.'

DAMN!

'I could introduce you to this lot,' Beardy said, waving at the rest of the room while I deflated like a leaky balloon, 'but Graham wants us all to go out for a drink at midday so you'll meet everyone then.'

'OK,' I said, plonking myself into my chair. 'Sounds great.'

'I've got your log-in details here.' Beardy handed me a piece of paper. 'And Nasty installed all of the software you need.'

I looked up at him. 'Did you just say Nasty?'

'He's our network guy. Nice bloke. If anything goes wrong with your computer give him a shout.'

'Why's he called Nasty?'

'Because that's his favourite word to diagnose a problem. It's like his catchphrase. Most people don't know his real name. Anything else you need to know, Lucy?'

'Your name,' I said. 'You never told me your name.'

Beardy flushed with embarrassment and held out his hand. 'Oh, yes, right. How very rude of me. I'm Archibald Humphreys-Smythe.'

Chapter Thirteen

I wasn't sure whether to throw up my hands in despair or jump out of my chair and smother him with a bear hug. Instead I nodded and said, 'Nice to meet you, Archibald.'

I continued to stare at him, my heart thumping madly, as he wandered back to his desk by the door. I'd found Archie. I'd actually found him! But how was I supposed to find love for a short, skinny guy with long, greasy hair who couldn't make eye contact for more than a few seconds? Had anyone invented a dating site called www.loveageek.com?

'Everything OK?' Nigel asked, raising an eyebrow at me. 'You're not planning on doing a runner, are you?'

'No, nope. Just, er, getting my bearings.'

Right. Yes. I was at work. I had to at least *pretend* to do my job while I worked out what my next move was with Archie. I swivelled to face my monitor. Oh no, I'd been given a PC. I hadn't used one since IT classes at school. *Everyone* used a Mac in my old job.

OK. First things first, turn it on. Shouldn't be too hard.

I pressed a large oval button with some blue squiggly

writing on it and the monitor flickered to life. Phew. It was booting up. I glanced to either side to see if anyone was watching me but Geoff and Nigel, fat headphones jammed over their ears, were too busy typing to pay me any attention.

Excellent. Now all I had to do was Google the web design programme to work out how to use it before anyone noticed I had no idea what I was doing.

A shadow fell over my monitor as I tabbed between the program and the Internet instructions. I turned and stifled a scream. The man staring down at me was at least six foot eight, and had the biggest forehead and the thickest, blackest eyebrows I'd ever seen. He looked like Lurch from the Addams Family.

'Hi,' he said, holding out a spade of a hand. 'I'm Nasty.'

'Lucy.'

'Everything OK?' he said, crushing my hand.

'Yeah, yeah fine. Just, you know, getting on with my work.'

Nasty smiled. There was an enormous space between each of his tiny, peg-like teeth. He looked like a giant who'd been given a child's incisors by mistake.

'I just need to turn off your PC for a sec,' he said.

'OK, no problem.'

I closed down all the programs on screen and then panicked. How did you shut down a PC? I couldn't remember.

'Um,' I said, hovering my mouse over various buttons

and icons. I could feel myself starting to sweat. 'Do you want to do it?'

'No,' Nasty snapped. 'Just shut it down. You know, Start, Turn off computer.'

The typing on either side of me stopped. Geoff and Nigel were watching me and smirking.

'OK,' I said as the machine made a funny noise and started to shut down. 'Done.'

'Now turn it off,' Nasty said.

What was he on about? The screen was black. It was off, wasn't it? I stared blankly at him and shrugged helplessly.

'Turn it off at ... the ... main ... switch,' he said slowly.

I was just about to poke the oval button with the blue writing when Nigel giggled. I glared at him.

'The main switch is at the back,' Nasty said.

'Right, yes. I knew that.'

I stood up, walked around Geoff and approached my PC from the back. A million wires and cables poked out at various angles but where was the main Off button? I glanced hopefully at Nigel and Geoff. They grinned inanely back. The room suddenly seemed very still. Even Archie was standing up at his desk by the door, looking bemused.

'The Off switch,' Nasty snapped, 'when you're ready. I don't have all day.'

I lunged forward and flicked the first switch I could see. There was a loud bang and then poof! a cloud of smoke billowed out the back of the PC.

Oh. Crap.

The entire office was silent for at least thirty excruciating seconds and then someone started to clap. Another pair of hands joined the clapping and then another and another. Before I knew it, every single person in the room was clapping and cheering. I stared at Nigel in desperation, but he was snorting with laughter and high-fiving Geoff. I seriously considered crawling under the desk and staying there.

'Nice one, Lucy,' someone yelled.

'Umm,' I said, looking at the network manager from under my eyebrows, 'I think I killed my computer.'

He raised a dark eyebrow. 'Nasty.'

During lunch, a sandwich and a pint of beer at the local pub, Nigel explained I'd accidentally flicked the voltage switch instead of the Off switch. I hadn't killed my computer, but Nasty had taken it away to give it some nerdy TLC and make it work again.

'I wouldn't worry, Lucy,' Geoff said. 'On Nigel's first day he mistook a variable for a string.'

Everyone burst out laughing and I tittered, even though I had no idea what they were on about. Note to self: Google some geek jokes.

'I should have mentioned in my interview that I'm a Mac girl,' I said when the laughter finally died down, 'but I didn't want to make a fuss.'

'Good on you,' muttered Archie from the other end of the table.

'Yeah,' said someone else. 'Open source software all the way.'

Suddenly everyone became animated again, babbling away about Linux and Redhat and loads of other terms I didn't understand. I glanced across the table to see what Archie was up to, but he'd slipped away and was standing at the bar, twisting his watch nervously and making no effort to attract the barmaid's attention. I stood up, butterflies fluttering madly in my stomach, and sidled up beside him.

'Thanks, Archibald.'

He jumped, glanced at me and immediately looked away. 'What for?'

'For saying "good on you" when I said I was a Mac girl. I thought everyone would laugh at me.'

He didn't say anything, but I thought I spotted a small smirk cross his lips.

'Oh I get it,' I said. 'You're smiling because everyone's already laughed at me.'

'Sorry,' he said, pulling at his watch strap and blushing furiously. 'We shouldn't have done that. No one wants to be embarrassed on their first day.'

'It's a bit late for that.'

He was still making no effort to catch the barmaid's attention, so I frantically waved her over.

'I'll have a gin and tonic this time,' I said, 'and ...' I looked at Archie, who seemed to have shrunk to almost half his diminutive height. 'What would you like?'

'A half of bitter please.'

Bitter? No one under the age of forty drank bitter.

'A half of bitter,' I said.

We stood side-by-side in an awkward silence as the barmaid clanked ice cubes into a glass and pressed it against the gin optic.

'So,' I said, attempting conversation again, 'if you didn't have to go back to work after lunch what would you be doing instead?'

Archie shrugged his skinny shoulders. 'Some coding or play some games.'

'What kind of games?'

'Computer games, of course.'

Dark brown bitter spurted into a half-pint glass as the barmaid yanked the handle back and forth and I gazed at it, perplexed. There had to be more to Archie's life than coding and gaming or I was in deep trouble. How many women's ideal man is a short, long-haired geek? Not any I'd ever met. Still, maybe he had a nice car or a lovely house, *something* that might make him a bit more of a catch.

'So,' I said, taking a sip of my drink, 'where's home then, Archibald? Have you got your own place?'

'Not as such,' he said, shaking his head.

'What does that mean?'

'I live with my grandmother.'

'Grandmother,' I spluttered. 'How nice.'

Chapter Fourteen

Thursday 2nd May
Day Six

Bugger. Archie was nowhere to be found on Thursday morning. His purple anorak wasn't hanging over the back of his chair and his monitor was off. He'd steered clear of me on Wednesday afternoon and who could blame him? I'd practically spat gin at him when he told me who he lived with.

'Nige,' I said as I lowered myself into my seat. 'Is Archibald about?'

He peered at me over the top of his specs. 'Why, got a soft spot for him, have you?'

'No.' I blushed furiously. 'I just wanted to ask him a question about, er, the software I'm using.'

'Ask Nasty.' He tilted his head towards the network manager's desk. 'That's his job.'

Nasty caught my eye and flashed his beady teeth at me.

'Maybe later,' I muttered, cringing at the memory of my 'nasty' computer explosion. 'I've got to do a report for Graham on the website first.'

It was a shame Archie wasn't in, but I had bigger things to worry about. Anna was meeting my fiancé for a drink that evening. I was going to see Dan again!

My stomach flipped over as I walked into the White Horse just after six. I had no idea what time Dan and Anna were meeting up but I didn't want to risk missing them. I looked a state in my crumpled work clothes but I didn't care.

'Ah, it's you,' the barman said, taking in my creased black linen trousers and ink-stained white T-shirt as I propped myself up at the bar. 'Another bad day?'

I shook my head. 'Actually, it's been OK so far. I'll have a white wine please.'

I carried my drink to a table in the corner of the pub and sat down. Ten minutes passed but there was still no sign of my fiancé or my best friend. The pub had really filled up and I started to worry. There was a free table next to me and another one on the other side of the pub. How was I supposed to listen in to Dan and Anna's conversation if they sat there?

I was hit by a cold blast of air as the pub door opened and I looked up. A tall man with dark hair and a confused expression stepped into the pub. It was Dan! He was wearing jeans and the wonky green jumper I'd knitted him just after we first moved in together. He looked skinnier than the last time I'd seen him and his jaw was rough with stubble.

Our eyes met and I caught my breath.

Maybe the manual was wrong. Maybe, if you loved

someone enough, you *could* see through the temporal twist. Maybe he knew who I was.

Dan frowned and looked away. He had recognised me, but not as Lucy, as the weird, mute woman who had pounded on his door. My heart dropped to my stomach as he sat down at the free table on the other side of the bar and looked everywhere but at me.

Five minutes later, Anna walked in. She looked even more radiant than the last time I'd seen her. Her hair was smooth and glossy and her skin was flawless. She was wearing jeans, heels and a white, Bardot-style, off-the-shoulder jumper. If she wasn't my best friend I would have hated her.

She smiled when she spotted Dan and drifted towards him. He beamed up at her, kissed her on the cheek and said something I couldn't lip-read. Seconds later he was out of his seat and buying drinks at the bar.

Now what? I needed to get close enough to eavesdrop on their conversation but there were two big problems:

1) There were no free tables on that side of the bar

2) I didn't want to get too close and risk Dan thinking I was stalking him.

I sipped at my wine and frantically gazed around the room. There was a stool at the bar, about a metre away from Dan and Anna's table, next to a blonde man who had his back to me. There was only one thing for it. I had to pretend to chat him up whilst secretly listening in to Dan and Anna's conversation. I necked most of my wine, dipped my fingers into the little bit left in the bottom of the glass and rubbed at the stain on my T-shirt (the printer at work wasn't working so I'd tried shaking the cartridge to see if it was empty. It wasn't). Instead of making it look better, it made it look as though I'd spent the day working down the mines. Shit. I pulled on my jacket and buttoned it up to the neck. I looked like Miss Jean Brodie, but I had no choice. Dan and Anna already looked deep in conversation. I stood up and ever-so-casually sauntered over to the bar.

The barman tore himself away from the magazine he was reading just long enough to pour me another glass of white wine while I plotted my next move. The blonde guy who, on closer inspection, was actually peroxide blonde, still had his back towards me and was totally oblivious to my presence.

'Excuse me,' I said, tapping him on the shoulder. 'Do you mind if I sit on that stool?'

He span round and looked me up and down. There was something very familiar about his glazed pale-blue stare and the metal ring in his nose.

'Help yourself,' he said.

I manoeuvred my way around him, aware that if I reached out my left hand I could stroke the top of Dan's head, and stepped up onto the stool. Peroxide Guy downed a shot of what looked like tequila and followed it with a large gulp of his pint. I took a sip of my wine and glanced across at Dan just in time to hear him say, 'I miss her too, Anna, but sometimes I ...'

The rest of his words were lost in the hubbub of pub

chatter and I felt like screaming. Sometimes what? Sometimes he forgot about me? Sometimes he thought life wasn't worth living?

I felt a sudden pain in my forearm. Peroxide Guy was prodding me with the grubby finger of his right hand.

'Hey,' he slurred. 'Do you know who I am?'

I was going to ignore him, but Dan was staring right at me. He'd obviously noticed I'd moved table. Crap. I had to do something to stop him from freaking out and leaving the pub. I forced a smile in Peroxide Guy's direction.

'Why don't you tell me who you are?' I said, lightly stroking the top of his hand in what I hoped was a flirtatious manner.

'You heard of the Lust Boys?' he slurred, lurching so far back on his stool I was worried he was about to fall off. And the penny dropped.

'You're Keith Krank,' I said.

At the table to my right Dan's eyes were welling with tears.

'When I was a little boy,' he said, 'I said I'd marry the first woman who liked Indiana Jones. Do you have any idea how excited I was when I called Lucy to arrange a second date and she told me she was watching a repeat of *Raiders of the Lost Ark* on TV? It sounds silly, but I really thought we were going to spend the rest of our lives together and then she, she, left me ...'

My stomach twisted with pain. It wasn't fair. It really wasn't fair.

'Oi,' Keith said, jabbing my ankle with the tip of his pointed, patent boot. 'If you know my name, then you do know who I am, you big liar.'

I tore my eyes away from Dan and glared at Keith (totally forgetting I was supposed to be flirting with him).

'I wasn't lying. I just didn't recognise you straight-away.'

'Liar,' Keith said, grabbing his crotch. 'You want a bit of Keith meat.'

'Actually,' I said, 'I just ate my dinner.'

I could only see the back of Anna's head so I couldn't see her expression when she reached across the table and placed her elegantly manicured hand on top of Dan's. He pulled away and swiped his eyes with his sleeve.

'Hey.' Pale fingers waved in front of my face. 'Hey, did you hear what I said?'

'Sorry?'

'You want some Keith meat?' he said again, leering at me.

Why did drunks always forget what they'd said five seconds before?

'No thanks, Keith,' I repeated. 'I'm not hungry.'

'Horny? Yeah, that's more like it.'

Oh for God's sake. What was it Claire had said about Keith? That he was sensitive and a poet? He was about as sensitive as industrial sandpaper and his incessant drunken rambling was preventing me from listening in to Anna and Dan's conversation. I looked around the pub, desperate to find something to distract him.

'Keith,' I said, beckoning him with a finger.

He lurched forward. 'Yeah?'

'Why don't you wait for me in the ladies' loos and I'll join you in a second.'

His mouth fell open with delight. 'You're gonna do me in the bogs?'

'Yes.' I cringed. 'I'm going to do you in the bogs. Go and wait for me.'

'All right!'

He slipped off his stool, staggered to his feet, and took a few unsteady steps. He was halfway across the room when he stopped and lurched his way back to me. 'Where's the Ladies?'

'Follow the bar round until you get to the end,' I said, pointing in the general direction, 'and they're right in front of you.'

Grinning wildly, he wandered back across the bar, knocking into punters and spilling drinks as he moved. Below me, Dan and Anna were still deep in conversation. Anna's body jolted back and forth as though she was crying and Dan reached forward and wrapped her hands in his.

'I thought I'd feel her presence around me but I can't,' he said. 'She's definitely gone.'

Don't give up on me, Dan, I silently begged, please don't give up on me. I'm coming back.

'The last thing Lucy said to me,' Anna said, 'was, "see you later, gorgeous, we're going to have so much fun." That really sums Lucy up, I think.'

Dan nodded and said nothing. I could tell what he was thinking. He was thinking about how we'd argued about the wedding preparations and who'd done what before I'd died. Please, I silently begged Anna, please don't ask him—

'What,' she said, 'were Lucy's last words to you? If you don't mind me asking.'

Dan shook his head. 'I don't really want to talk about it.'

I didn't get to hear Anna's response because, right at that second, Keith Krank lurched back into view.

'Hey,' he bellowed. 'You didn't come. I waited for ages.'

I tried to speak but I was choking on my own misery. I could barely breathe.

'Hey,' Keith shouted. 'You were going to fuck me, you said.'

The noise and chatter immediately stopped. Everyone in the pub was staring at us. Keith put his face so close to mine I could smell the beer on his breath.

'You were going to eat the Keith meat!' he shouted. 'Why didn't you eat the Keith meat, you dick-teasing slag?'

I pushed him away and slipped off my seat.

'Hey.' He grabbed my shoulder as I tried to slip past him. 'Where do you think you're going?'

I pulled away from him, but he had a tight grip on my coat.

'Oi,' said another voice. It was Dan. He was standing up and glaring down at Keith. 'Let go of her.'

Keith looked up at him and narrowed his eyes. 'Piss off, Lanky Boy.'

'Leave her alone,' said Dan, grabbing hold of Keith's hand. 'She hasn't done anything to you.'

Before I knew what was happening, other people were scraping their chairs on the floor and standing up. Keith's bravado faded quickly and he let go of my coat.

'She's a slag,' he said as he pushed me roughly away. 'You can have her.'

His shove pushed me right into Dan's chest. I froze, my face pressed against the warm wool of his jumper.

'You OK?' Dan asked, wrapping an arm around me. 'The barman's having a word with that jerk. Why don't you sit down? Have a drink with my friend and me?'

The smell of his aftershave and his tender, reassuring hand on my shoulder was more than I could bear. I wriggled out of his arms, looked up into his gentle, puzzled face, and ran from the pub.

Later, in bed, I wrapped my arms around the enormous pink elephant Dan had won for me on Brighton Pier and buried my face in its soft fur. I could still remember the spicy musk of Dan's aftershave, the warmth of his body as he'd wrapped a protective arm around me after Keith's drunken shove. The last time he'd worn that green jumper was when he'd surprised me with a visit to Disneyland Paris in December the year before. I'd complained to Dan about how stressed I was about a late-running project I was working on, and he'd suggested a weekend away to cheer me up. I'd got really excited until he said that some home-cooked food at his parents' house in the Norfolk countryside was just what I needed! When he insisted I pack comfy shoes and thick jumpers I didn't suspect a thing (his parents' house was freezing!), but when he insisted we hop off the Metropolitan Line at St Pancras instead of Liverpool Street, I knew something was definitely up.

'What's going on?' I asked as he squeezed my hand tightly and led me to the Eurostar terminal. I stared up at the gleaming roof that curved above our heads like a metal cathedral ceiling and gawped at the champagne bar. 'Where are we going?'

'Didn't I tell you,' Dan said, his smile reaching all the way up to his eyes, 'my parents emigrated to France last week.'

'No way!' I said. 'Why didn't you tell me?'

'Because it's not true,' he said, letting go of my hand and darting across the concourse before I could thump him.

'But,' I said, hurrying towards him, my suitcase rolling along behind me, 'I haven't got my passport. We can't go anywhere.'

'I've got your passport,' Dan said, grabbing me around the waist and pulling me into him. 'And we're going to Disneyland, Luce.'

My squeals of delight could probably be heard across the channel.

Twenty-four hours later, my face was pressed into Dan's jumper again as he held me close on a cold winter's night and we watched a hundred colourful fireworks squeal and explode above the Magic Kingdom as Minnie, Mickey and Donald frolicked around on a float and a beatific Cinderella blew kisses into the crowd.

'I don't deserve you,' I said, looking up at Dan, my throat tight with emotion. 'I don't deserve to feel this happy.'

'Yes you do,' he said. He touched my chin, gently tipped back my face, then kissed me softly on the lips. 'Who else would I wind up, if I didn't have you?'

'So you only love me because I'm the most gullible girl in the world?' I asked, sticking out my bottom lip and faking a sulk.

'No,' Dan had said, looking deep into my eyes, 'because you're the most beautiful.'

I pulled the pink elephant closer to me, crushing it in my arms as tears rolled down my cheeks and soaked its soft fur.

'I'll find love for Archie, Dan,' I whispered. 'I will. Whatever it takes.'

Chapter Fifteen

Friday 3rd May
Day Seven

I sprinted into work on Friday morning and paused in the doorway, gasping for breath. Bloody Keith Krank. It was his fault I'd slept through my alarm. If it wasn't for him I'd have gone to bed at a normal time instead of sitting up for hours thinking about Dan and—

Hang on.

Archie was curled over his desk, his fingers on the keyboard, gaudy sweater hanging on the back of the chair. Wherever he'd been the day before, he was back! Project 'Find Archie Love' was back on.

'Hi, Archibald,' I said, mopping my sweaty forehead with my sleeve.

'Mmm,' he replied, peering intently at his monitor.

'Good to see you back,' I persevered. 'Hope you're feeling better now.'

'What?' he said, looking up.

'You were away yesterday. I assumed you were off ill.'

'Something like that,' he mumbled, blushing from the base of his neck to his eyelashes.

He looked so awkward I suspected he'd been suffering from an embarrassing illness like explosive diarrhoea or something. But there was no need to be ashamed. We all get ill.

'Imodium is very good,' I said. 'I took it once when I had a prawn curry that was so bad I was on the loo for—'

'I wasn't ill,' Archie mumbled, looking horrified. 'I was doing a few ... things ...'

Oh. OK ... Time to go and sit at my desk.

I'd only been logged on for ten minutes when an instant message popped up on my screen. It was from Graham:

Hello, Lucy. Please come to my desk for a quick chat.

Oh shit. 'Chats' at my old job normally meant a bollocking or the sack. I swallowed hard. What if Graham had rumbled my dodgy CV? I couldn't lose my job. I still didn't have Archie's home phone number.

Everything OK? I typed back, my heart beating wildly.

Yes, we need to talk about the website, remember?

I sighed so loudly Nigel stopped typing and peered at me over the top of his glasses.

On my way I replied, ignoring my colleague and grabbing the notes I'd scribbled down the previous day. I had some bullshitting to do.

*

Graham's sombre blue tie had been replaced with a red bow tie and his bushy hair was gelled into a shiny side-parting. It wasn't a good look.

'Hi, Graham,' I said, hovering in front of his desk.

'Don't stand on ceremony, Miss Brown.' He waved me towards a chair. 'Sit down, sit down.'

'I wrote a few notes about the website,' I said, perching on the edge of my seat. 'Should I just read them out, or would you like to take a look?'

Graham propped himself up on his elbows and put his chin in his hands. 'Read. You have my full and undivided attention, Miss Brown.'

'Right,' I said, my finger shaking as I pointed to the first item on my print-out. 'First off – the colour. It's too gaudy and it doesn't portray a strong corporate image.'

Graham frowned. 'Carry on.'

'The animated bits look cheap and tacky and distract the visitor,' I said, getting into my stride. I might not know anything about coding websites but I knew bad design when I saw it. 'The font is too big, the lay-out is skewed, the menu is in the wrong place, there are far too many random photos taking up all the white space and generally the whole website gives an impression of unprofessionalism. Whoever designed it is a colour-blind idiot.'

Graham nodded. 'Right, so if you could give any advice to the designer, what would you say?'

'I wouldn't give them advice,' I said, pleased with his studious reaction to my critique. 'I'd tell them they were sacked.'

'Would you?' He raised an eyebrow.

'Yes.'

'Well, I'm afraid you can't sack me because I'm the Managing Director.'

Oh shit.

I cleared my throat. 'I didn't, I mean, I didn't think—'

'I was a coder myself once, Lucy.' Graham sat up straight in his chair and folded his arms. 'Website design isn't rocket science, you know. Any of the boys here could do the website, but they're too busy. That's why we employed you.'

Ouch. Graham might not have wanted to fire me at the start of the conversation but he probably did now.

'Right, of course,' I said. 'Sorry, I didn't quite get round to listing the good points about the website.'

'Which are?'

I looked down at the non-existent positive notes I'd made. 'The words that describe the voice-recognition software are good.'

'And?'

'And, um, the photo of you using the software is very … informative.'

Graham ran his hands through his hair and adjusted his bow tie. 'It is, isn't it?'

'It's great,' I gushed. 'The lighting is wonderful, the angles are great and, er, your desk looks very tidy.'

'And the model?'

'Sorry?' I said blankly.

'I think the word you're looking for is handsome.'

I gritted my teeth. 'You look very handsome in the photo, Graham.'

'Right then,' he said, standing up, 'off you toddle and sort out the website. Let's see if you can do any better.'

'I'll do my best,' I said, a bead of sweat dribbling down my back as I turned to go. I was halfway back to my desk when Graham shouted my name.

'Yes?' I turned slowly.

'If I don't like it you're fired.'

I stared at him, my eyes wide.

'Just joking,' he said.

By the time one o'clock rolled around, my head was buzzing with HTML tags, Javascript coding and photo libraries and I was desperate for a break. Archie had mysteriously disappeared again so I turned to Nigel.

'Are you going to the pub again today?'

'Nah,' he said, shaking his head. 'I'm going to work through lunch. Me and Geoff are collaborating on a little side project.'

I turned to look at Geoff, who nodded vigorously in agreement.

'Some of the other lads are going though,' Nigel added. 'Apparently they're going to discuss the pros and cons of server-side Javascript versus client-side. Why don't you join in?'

'Maybe not,' I said, shrinking into my seat. 'I've got a few things I should get on with so I'll probably just grab a sandwich.'

Nigel glanced at his watch. 'Sally the Sandwich should be round in a sec. She does a mean egg mayo with cheese.'

Sure enough, ten minutes later, there was a booming thump at the office front door. Sally the Sandwich was obviously a mountain of a girl.

'Come in!' Nigel yelled.

I turned, fully expecting to see a Russian shot-putter walk through the door.

'Hello,' boomed a tiny Chinese girl, her bleach-blonde hair tied in bunches on either side of her head. She was wearing a red and white checked shirt and a tiny little denim skirt, covered with a white apron with 'Sally the Sandwich' embroidered on the front in bright pink. On her feet were the most ridiculously oversized pink trainers I'd ever seen. She could have given the Spice Girls a run for their money.

'Egg and cheese?' she said, approaching Nigel and extracting a doorstop of a sandwich from the bottom of the pile.

'You got it.'

'Hiya,' she said, glancing at me. 'You new?'

'Yes, I'm Lucy.'

When I stood up and held out my hand, I felt like a giant. Sally was even tinier than I'd first thought. She couldn't have been much more than four foot eleven.

'What can I do you for?' she grinned.

I bought a sausage and tomato baguette and sat back down. Sally glanced at Geoff but he was munching on a wilted ham and lettuce sandwich he'd brought in from home.

'See you tomorrow then,' she said, hoisting her basket into the air as she strode back out of the office. 'Nice to meet you, Lucy. Bye boys.'

The rest of the afternoon dragged by. When Nigel pushed his chair back from his station and stretched his arms in the air, I glanced at my watch in surprise.

Shit, it was 5.30 p.m.

Archie had reappeared at the end of lunch but I hadn't had time to speak to him. I had to grab him quickly before he escaped.

I got to his desk just in time. He'd put on his jacket, strapped his courier bag diagonally across his body, and was reaching over to turn off his monitor.

'Archie,' I said. 'What are you doing this weekend?'

'Going to a LAN party,' he mumbled as he inched towards the door.

I had no idea what a LAN party was, but anything with the word 'party' at the end of it couldn't be bad, could it?

'Can I come?' I said, feeling the blood rush to my cheeks.

Archie looked up at me with surprise and ran his fingers through his lank hair. 'You want to come to the LAN party?'

'Yes. I'd love to.'

'You do realise it's likely to be a forty-eight-hour thing,' he said seriously. 'You'll need some serious stamina.'

Wow, more of a rave than a party then. Oh. My. God. What if Archie was on drugs? Maybe that's why he'd missed work. A drug-taking geek. Who'd have thought it?

'I can do forty-eight hours, no problem,' I lied. 'Where's the party?'

'Can I ring you tomorrow morning with the details?' he said, glancing at his watch. 'I need to be somewhere, like, now.'

I had to bite my lip to stop myself from grinning as I scribbled down the house phone number on a post-it note and handed it to him. If Archie could ask a woman for her phone number, there might be hope for him yet. He glanced at the piece of paper and stuffed it into his back pocket.

'See you then, Archie,' I called merrily as he shot out of the office door.

'Archibald,' he mumbled and disappeared.

Chapter Sixteen

I was in an unusually good mood when I strolled back into the House of Wannabe Ghosts. In just one day I'd managed to:

1) Not get sacked from my job
2) Win an invite to an amazing-sounding party

That meant a whole forty-eight hours to work my magic on Archie and find out what his ideal woman was like. Then all I had to do was convince him to let me help him find her. Brilliant, I thought as I strolled into the kitchen and took a Diet Coke out of the fridge, it's all going so well.

'Lucy,' Claire said, appearing out of nowhere and blocking the doorway.

'Yes,' I squeaked, freezing in my tracks.

'Why did you tell me to fuck off when you got home last night?'

Oh shit. I'd completely forgotten I'd done that. It was her fault for calling me 'Bride' as I'd stumbled through the door in tears.

'Because I was, er, angry with you for something that happened to me,' I mumbled.

'Which was?' she said, scooping up her woolly

extensions and wrapping a thick elastic band around them.

Uh oh. Was she tying her hair back ready for a fight?

'I met Keith Krank,' I said, taking a step back and knocking into the kitchen table. A cereal bowl tumbled to the floor and shattered with a crash.

'Really?' Claire pushed her crocheted jumper back from her hands, rolled it up to her elbows, and took a step towards me. 'Where?'

'How about we go for a drink and talk about it?' I stuttered as shards of crockery crunched under my feet. 'Somewhere local.'

If she really was going to beat me up, I wanted witnesses and easy access to an ambulance to ferry my battered body off to casualty afterwards.

Claire looked me up and down through narrowed eyes and I swallowed hard.

'Fine,' she said, just as I was considering lobbing the Diet Coke at her head and making a run for it. 'But you're paying.'

It was bustling in the Queen's Head, a run-down, old man's pub round the corner from the House of Wannabe Ghosts. All the tables were taken so we propped ourselves up at the bar. I ordered the drinks.

'So,' Claire said, grabbing a pint of cider and blackcurrant from the hands of our geriatric barmaid, 'what happened with Keith then?'

'Well,' I said. 'I ... um ...'

How could I explain what had happened, without her assuming I'd tried to pull Keith? However I phrased it in my head, the consequence was always the same – Claire would go mental and beat my head in. Hang on. I didn't have to tell her it was *me* Keith had made a move on, did I?

'I was having a drink in the White Horse,' I said, gripping my glass of white wine, 'and Keith walked in. He was really, really pissed.'

'Good old Keith.' Claire grinned. 'That's his favourite pub. Who was he with?'

'He was on his own, but not for long.'

'What do you mean?'

'He approached a girl who was sitting on her own at the bar and tried to convince her to go into the toilets with him.'

Claire reached for her cider and eyed me warily. 'Did she?'

'No. Keith called her a slag and a bitch and God knows what else. It was awful. The girl was really upset.'

I waited for Claire to react. According to her, Keith was a lovely, sensitive animal-saving guy, so finding out what he was really like was probably going to come as a bit of a shock.

'That's it?' she said, twiddling with her nose ring.

I stared at her, open-mouthed. 'What do you mean, that's it? The guy was a total twat. He embarrassed himself in front of the whole pub and ruined the girl's evening.'

'Tell me something I don't know.'

I frowned. 'What do you mean?'

Claire rubbed a hand over her face and looked away. Suddenly she didn't look quite so scary any more. In fact, she looked impossibly young and vulnerable. 'He used to do stuff like that to me all the time but, unlike the girl you told me about, I would go into the loos with him. That didn't stop him slagging me off afterwards though.'

'You're kidding?'

She shook her head and drained the last of her pint. 'I wish I was. After we'd done it he'd always go back to the band's table and tell me to piss off and sit at the bar. Then he'd tell them what we'd got up to and they'd all laugh and make comments about me.'

I was horrified. Claire was a pain in the arse, but no one deserved to be treated so cruelly.

'What kinds of comments?' I asked.

'Stuff about how fat I was, or how ugly, or how I was such a desperate groupie I'd do anything.'

'Oh, Claire, that's horrible. Why the hell did you keep sleeping with him?'

She slammed her empty pint glass on the bar and gestured to the barmaid. 'When Keith was sober, he was OK,' she said, lowering her voice as her empty pint was refilled, 'nice, even. I guess I thought if I spent enough time with him the shit drunken stuff would stop. But it didn't.'

'You should have just left him, Claire. You could have found someone loads better.'

'Look at me,' she said, holding her hands wide. 'Who'd want this?'

There was nothing wrong with her. Beneath the trowelled-on make-up she was a very pretty girl. How she looked wasn't a problem, it was the enormous great chip on her shoulder.

'Lots of people would want you,' I said. 'If you didn't give yourself such a hard time and act like a bitch all the time.'

'It's a bit late now,' she said, nibbling on her bottom lip. 'I'm dead.'

She had a point. Or did she? Could the dead still find love? I made a mental note to find out when we got back to the house. Quite why I wanted to help her I wasn't entirely sure. Maybe because I could still remember what it felt like to be a teenager and feeling like you didn't fit in. I'd been a dorky-looking teenager, with braces on my teeth and terrible skin. I was so self-conscious about my metal mouth I didn't kiss anyone until they were finally removed when I was seventeen. I'd also met my fair share of creeps.

'So what are you going to do, Claire?' I asked, draining my drink and setting the glass back on the bar.

She grinned. 'Complete my task and get my revenge. I'm going to haunt Keith and the band for ever. Let's see how they like having a groupie they can't get rid of.'

'Is that a good idea?'

'It's a great idea,' she said, a wry smile on her face. 'Those guys are going to pay for what they did to me.'

'Claire,' I said, my stomach flipping over. 'Why have I got a bad feeling about this?'

She just grinned.

Chapter Seventeen

Saturday 4th May
Day Eight

Bubbles tickled my nose as I leaned forward and Dan ran his soapy fingers up and down my back. The bathroom was dark apart from the gentle glow of flickering candles, and the sweet smell of Molton Brown seamoss bubble bath filled the air.

'Would Madam like some chocolate?' Dan whispered, slipping a piece of Dairy Milk between my lips. 'And some Barry White on the stereo?'

I nodded, though personally I think Bazza White is a bit *too* cheesy for a seduction scenario.

'Your wish is my command,' Dan said, reaching for the remote control.

I leaned back, relaxing against his chest, his arms around me his lips ... his lips ... what the hell was that annoying noise? Was the CD stuck? It didn't sound like the walrus of love, it sounded like, like ...

A phone.

Shit!

Saturday. LAN party. Archie. Phone. Wake up, Lucy!

There was a terrible tearing sound as I sat bolt upright in bed and clutched at my face. A page from the manual was stuck to my left cheek. Hmm. I must have dribbled in my sleep. Classy.

I winced as I peeled it off and rubbed my stinging skin. I'd only managed to read a couple of sections before dozing off but I hadn't found anything that answered the question about whether or not Claire would be able to find love in heaven. Maybe Brian would know? But that could wait. The phone was still ringing.

I swung my legs over the edge of the bed, hurried out of my room and stumbled down the stairs.

'Hello?' I gasped into the receiver.

'Is that Lucy Brown?' said the polite, posh voice on the other end.

'It certainly is,' I said, picking bits of paper off my cheek and flicking them onto the floor. 'Is that Archibald Humphreys-Smythe?'

Archie laughed. He had a much deeper laugh than you'd expect for a man of his size.

'Are you still keen to go to the LAN party?' he asked.

'I most certainly am.'

'Excellent. Where do you live? I'll be round to collect you in half an hour.'

I stared at the phone. 'What?'

'Forty-five minutes suit you better?'

What kind of party started at 11 o'clock on a Saturday morning?

'Why so early?' I asked.

'Well, we need to get set up. It is going to be a marathon session.'

How big was this party going to be that we needed to spend most of the day setting it up? Despite my reservations I was starting to expect a fantastic night out.

'I live at 108, Buckley Road,' I said. 'See you in forty-five minutes then?'

'Righto.'

The phone went dead. I crouched in the cupboard for a couple of seconds, feeling excited and nervous. This was my big chance to get to know Archie and I mustn't blow it. But first things first – what to wear?

Exactly forty-five minutes later, the doorbell rang. My heart pounded and I took one last look at my reflection in the mirror. Hair washed and dried? Check. All slivers of manual permanently removed from cheek? Check. Sparkly silver halter-top and very short black skirt? Check. Ridiculously high heels? Check. OK, I was ready to go. I took a deep breath, tottered across the hall and down the stairs and wrenched open the front door.

Archie, dressed in beige slacks and a black T-shirt proclaiming 'I love Elves', gawped at me. His eyes flickered from the top of my head to the toes peeping through the ends of my shoes and back again.

'Ummmmm,' he said, his mouth gaping like a gold-fish. 'Ummmmmmmm.'

I put my hands on my hips and grinned at him. 'The correct response, I think you'll find, is wow!'

'Yes, of course,' he said, shuffling from one foot to the other and twisting his fingers. 'It's just …'

Had I got the wrong end of the stick? Was it more of a dinner party than a rave? Or maybe it was a ball, that would make sense, he was posh after all.

'It's just … will you be comfortable in that outfit?'

Comfortable? High heels were a constant agony, but that was the price you paid. It was something men, Archie included, would never understand.

'I'll be fine,' I said. 'Don't you worry.'

'OK, let's go. My car's over there.'

He stalked off down the path and I staggered after him until he reached the cutest, shiniest white VW Beetle I'd ever seen, and stopped.

'This is Herbie,' Archie said, opening the passenger door. 'After you.'

I clambered into the small car as elegantly as I could. My initial doubts about my outfit were fading and I was starting to enjoy myself. Archie was a total geek (who goes to a party in a T-shirt that says 'I love Elves'?), but he was a complete gent and we were about to set off on a little mini-adventure together.

'Seatbelt?' he said, as he slid into the driver's seat.

'All buckled up and ready to go, Bimbo Baggins.'

'Huh?' Archie looked puzzled.

'You know, from *Lord of the Rings*?'

'I think you mean *Bilbo* Baggins, Lucy.'

'Right, yes, of course,' I said, trying desperately not to laugh.

Archie turned the key in the ignition, revved the engine, slipped the gear lever into first and pulled out into the road.

'Ready to party?' he asked. Beneath the extreme bushiness of his beard I spotted the shyest of smiles.

'Hell, yeah. Let's go. Have you got any music?'

'In the glove compartment.'

I reached forward, flipped it open and rummaged through the enormous pile of CDs inside. I'm not sure what I was expecting a geek like Archie to listen to, but it sure as hell wasn't rap and hip-hop. Old school at that. Not entirely my cup of tea though. I was more of a rock and indie kind of girl. I flicked through the CDs: Beastie Boys, Doctor Dre, Run DMC, Public Enemy, NWA.

'Are these yours?' I asked.

'Who else's would they be?'

I raised an eyebrow, popped the Beastie Boys CD in and rolled down the window. 'Fight for Your Right To Party' (quite appropriate, I thought) blared out of the speakers above the back seats and hit me in the back of the head with the force of the bass. I looked round. There was something on the backseat.

'Archie, why did you bring a laptop?'

'What?' he said, glancing at me and turning the stereo down.

'Your laptop. It's on the backseat. How come?'

'Because I need it of course. Where's yours?'

'I didn't bring one.' I looked down at my empty lap and frowned. 'I was going to bring a bottle of wine but I forgot.'

The brakes squealed and I lurched forward as the car stopped. CDs jumped off my lap and spilled onto the floor. Oh shit, I'd obviously made a major faux pas. Posh people *always* take booze to parties.

'Want to go back?' Archie said, as the cars behind us started to honk their horns. 'There's still time to go and get your laptop.'

What? Oh my God. Maybe at *really* posh parties you have to take a laptop or something equally expensive instead of a bottle of wine as a present. You know, like visiting dignitaries bring the Queen tiaras and jewels and stuff.

'But I haven't got a laptop,' I said desperately.

Archie put the car back into gear and pulled away. 'No worries, Nigel will have one you can use.'

'Nigel's going to the party?' I asked, surprised.

'Of course,' Archie said, 'and Geoff. It wouldn't be much of a party if there weren't enough laptops to go round.'

What the hell was he on about? Were we going to some kind of laptop orgy? What if LAN stood for Loving a Nerd? Uh oh. What if all the laptops had webcams connected to the Internet and the boys were expecting me to dance or strip or—

'Not far now,' Archie said, interrupting my silent freak-out. 'Nearly there.'

We pulled into a quiet suburban road and parked. Two old ladies ambled down the street; one of them was dragging a shopping bag on wheels, the other was pushing herself along with a Zimmer frame. It wasn't exactly party central.

'Are we here?' I asked.

Archie turned off the engine and got out of the car. 'Number twenty-seven,' he said, pointing at a terraced house with a red door.

I stood back to let him go down the pathway first. The butterflies in my stomach freaked out as he rang the doorbell.

What the hell had I agreed to?

Chapter Eighteen

The door opened slowly.

'Archie!' Nigel said, then his eyes flicked towards me. 'Bloody hell.'

I smirked. There was something very wrong about a geek checking me out so blatantly. What was even worse was how good it made me feel. I did a nervous shimmy. 'Glad you like it.'

'It's not that … it's just,' Nigel laughed, 'aren't you a bit overdressed?'

I glanced at Archie, but he was gazing at his trainers.

'Never mind,' Nigel said, ushering us through the door. 'Come in, the fun's through there.'

I wandered down the hall, through the door he'd pointed to and found myself in a very dark, slightly musty-smelling room. The curtains were closed and most of the furniture had been pushed up against the French windows. Four desks had been grouped together in a square in the centre of the room. At one of them, sitting behind a laptop, was Geoff.

'Hi, Geoff,' I said, peering through the gloom, still totally confused. The room didn't look like it was set up for an orgy *or* a party. What on earth was going on?

'Y'all right?' Geoff muttered, his eyes fixed to the screen.

Nigel sidled past me and typed something into the other laptop.

'I've got Coke, Red Bull, Lucozade and bags of Kettle Chips in the kitchen if you fancy a snack,' he said, glancing back at me. 'I thought we could get pizza later when the munchies kick in, ordered online of course.'

'Excellent idea,' said Archie, sitting down on one of the spare seats. 'Do take a seat, Lucy.'

I perched on the edge of one of the chairs and watched as Archie plugged his laptop into a socket in the wall and started messing around with leads and some kind of black box that was flashing in the middle of the desks.

'Archie,' I said, staring suspiciously at the black box. 'Is there anything I can do to help?'

'Oh,' he said, looking uncomfortable. 'Sorry, have you got a spare laptop, Nige? Lucy forgot hers.'

'No probs,' said Nigel, standing up. 'It's an ancient beast I'm afraid, Lucy, and the graphics card is a bit crap, but it'll do.'

He sloped out of the room and I heard the sound of heavy footsteps clomping up the stairs.

'Archie,' I whispered as he suddenly disappeared under his desk. 'When does the party start?'

'As soon as we're set up, I should say,' his muffled voice replied.

'But where's everyone else? Where's the DJ? How can we dance with these desks taking up all the room? It's really dark in here too – don't you have any disco lights?'

A deep rumbling laugh drifted up from beneath the desks and there was a loud thump. Archie's grinning face popped out.

'Sorry,' he said, pushing his straggly hair off his face. 'I laughed and banged my head.'

'Why?' I asked, feeling more confused by the second.

'Lucy, do you even know what a LAN party is?' Geoff snorted.

'Well yes, of course,' I stuttered. 'It's a rave in a field. LAN is short for land. Isn't it?'

Archie and Geoff looked at each other and burst out laughing.

'What?' I said as they continued to roar. 'What did I say?'

'LAN,' Geoff said between bursts of hiccupping laughter, 'stands for Local Area Network.'

'What?'

Archie's mouth fell open and he stopped laughing. 'A LAN party,' he said slowly, 'is when people connect their computers so they can play multiplayer games together.'

'I knew that,' I squeaked. 'I was just messing with you.'

Archie and Geoff were still smirking when Nigel

strolled back into the room and placed a laptop in front of me. I stared at it, unsure what to say next.

'I could take you back home if you like,' Archie said gently. 'You don't have to stay if you don't want to.'

I looked from the laptop to my horribly short skirt and totally unsuitable shoes. No wonder the boys had all stared at me as though I'd just beamed down from another planet (which, in a way, I had). So much for being the Queen of Blag.

'Um,' I said. 'Um.'

If I stayed I'd have to spend the next forty-eight hours of my non-life playing computer games and the only one I'd know was one of Dan's football games. Even then I'd just peered over his shoulder, nagging him to turn it off so we weren't late for the cinema.

I looked back at Archie. He looked genuinely worried, as though he was the one responsible for my stupidity. Sod it. There wasn't really a choice to make, was there?

'I'd love to stay,' I said, smiling warmly at him. 'But you're going to have to teach me how to play the game.'

'Excellent,' he said, visibly relaxing. 'While I install the software and connect you to the hub' – he reached for my laptop – 'you need to decide what kind of character you want to be in the game we're going to play. Do you want to be a human, orc, elf or one of the Undead Scourge?'

'Hmmm,' I said, trying to keep a straight face, 'I get the feeling I'd be quite good at being undead.'

Chapter Nineteen

Sunday 5th May
Day Nine

We finally stopped for pizza just after midnight.

Well, I stopped, Nigel and Geoff kept playing and munched on pepperoni slices between fights. I'm pretty sure Archie wanted to carry on playing too but he took one look at me, surrounded by furniture and scrunched up on the sofa at the other end of the room, and wandered over with a slice of pizza in one hand and the box in the other. He hovered beside me, suddenly self-conscious after a night of open smiles and eye contact.

'Archie, Archibald,' I said, quickly correcting myself. 'Sit down, for God's sake. You're making the room look messy.'

I shuffled down the sofa to make space for him, but he still squashed himself up at the opposite end and pulled his knees to his chest. He nibbled at his pizza and stared longingly at Nigel and Geoff who were giving each other high-fives.

'Are you enjoying yourself?' he asked. 'I'd feel terrible if you were having a horrible time.'

I punched him lightly on the arm. 'I'm having a wonderful time, Archie. I'd tell you if I wasn't.'

He gave me a sly look. 'You called me Archie.'

'Yes ... and?'

'I've decided I quite like it when you call me that.'

I grinned and shifted position, tucking my feet under my bum. My heels were history and I'd swapped my outfit for a faded-blue sweatshirt and a pair of Nigel's black tracky bums earlier in the evening. I felt much, much more comfortable, if not a bit of a failure in the fashion stakes.

'Does everyone call you Archibald?' I asked.

'Well yes, everyone at work ... and my grandmother.'

'And your girlfriend?'

Archie choked on his pizza. 'I don't have a girlfriend,' he mumbled, staring at the floor. 'Unfortunately.'

Result! So he actually wanted a girlfriend. That was a very good start. You couldn't find a soulmate for someone who didn't actually want one.

'Do you know many girls?' I asked, reaching for another slice of pizza.

Archie shook his head. 'I don't really get chance to meet any. When I'm not at work I'm ... er ... busy doing things.'

'What kind of things?'

'Just things.'

'Oh for God's sake, Archie, just tell me. I can't help you find a girlfriend if you won't talk to me.'

Archie raised his eyebrows. 'You want to help me find a girlfriend?'

'Yeah, why not? I used to be a bit of a matchmaker when I was ...' I caught myself in time. '... younger,' I finished. 'I used to matchmake a lot of my friends when I was at uni.'

'Were you good at it?'

'Oh yes,' I lied. 'Two of the couples got married. They have kids now and everything. Anyway, what are these *things* that take up so much of your time?'

Archie licked his lips and his sharp Adam's apple bobbed up and down. I felt horrible for pushing him when he was so obviously uncomfortable but I had to know what I was up against. If he had some kind of action-packed schedule I'd have to work around it.

'I do jobs for my grandmother,' he said quietly. 'It pretty much takes up most of my free time.'

'Is your gran very old?' I asked sympathetically. The poor woman was obviously infirm.

'She's just turned seventy-two,' Archie said.

That didn't sound *too* old. There were plenty of famous people around who were even older than that and still working. Good old Brucie Forsyth was eighty and still pulling dance moves on TV and Honor Blackman was still a total glamour puss. But maybe there was something wrong with Archie's grandmother?

'Is she ill?' I asked.

Archie hugged his knees so tightly to his chest I thought he might snap. There was a sadness in his eyes that made me want to hug him. So he lived with his grandmother. It wasn't a huge deal, not really. If she was anything like her grandson she'd be short, shy and really quite sweet.

'My grandmother's actually very healthy,' Archie said, 'but she's only got me. My father was sent to Dubai by his firm four years ago and mother went with him. I was planning on joining them after a couple of weeks, but Grandfather died suddenly and everyone decided I should stay behind and move in with Grandmother.'

'Didn't you mind?'

Archie frowned. The look in his eyes had been replaced with an altogether more stoical expression. 'It was the right thing to do.'

'I'm sorry,' I said. 'It must have been awful. If it's any consolation, I know how you feel.'

'Do you?' he said, looking at me with surprise.

'Not about looking after your grandmother, no, but I lost both of my parents when I was in my early twenties. I know what it feels like to be alone.'

Now it was Archie's turn to look distressed. 'Oh God, Lucy,' he said. 'I had no idea.'

'It's OK,' I shrugged. 'Why would you?'

For a few seconds we said nothing. We just sat there on the sofa and looked at each other, a kind of unspoken mutual understanding filling the silence.

'Oi,' Nigel shouted, 'you two! Your characters are getting whipped. You might want to get over here some time today.'

And the moment popped like an over-inflated balloon.

*

The next thing I knew, something light yet scratchy was bouncing off my forehead. I opened an eye and peered across the room. Nigel was throwing Kettle Chips at me.

'Hello, sleepy,' he laughed.

'What?' I said, rubbing my eyes and yawning. 'I was just resting my eyes. I'm re-charged and ready to fight!'

I hadn't meant to fall asleep. After Nigel interrupted the chat I'd been having with Archie we returned to our laptops and launched ourselves back into the game. I kept going until 5 a.m. before I decided to return to the sofa and have a Red Bull to recharge my batteries. It obviously hadn't worked.

'You can go back to sleep if you want to,' Nigel said between mouthfuls of crisps. 'We've decided to end the marathon early because these two are a couple of lightweights.'

A heavy-lidded Archie and a yawning Geoff nodded in my direction.

'What time is it?' I asked.

'Four o'clock in the afternoon.'

'No way!' I rolled myself upright and stretched. 'Did my character die?'

'Nah,' said Nigel, 'we logged you out when we realised you'd passed out. You came last but you've still got ten credits. You can use them the next time you play.'

I picked up a Kettle Chip and lobbed it back at him. 'Who says I want to play with you lot again?'

Nigel stuck out his bottom lip and fake-sulked. 'You don't?'

'Well, maybe, if you're nice to me at work.'

'Never going to happen!' he laughed. 'In fact, now I've got to know you, I'm going to make your working life hell—'

'Lucy,' Archie interrupted, pushing back his chair and standing up. 'I'd like to go now, if you don't mind. I've got, um …'

'Things to do?' I smiled. 'Give me a sec while I go and get changed.'

It didn't take me long to get changed into my own clothes, fold up Nigel's offerings and place them neatly on top of his bed. After a quick hug goodbye with my surprised-looking hosts (it felt like the right thing to do – our characters had been through so much together, after all), I got into Archie's car.

The drive back to the house was quiet, but it was a tired, companionable silence and our little chat the night before had left me feeling I'd definitely made some progress with him. I didn't want to push for more.

'OK, Lucy,' Archie said as he pulled up outside my house. 'You're home.'

I stifled a yawn and flashed him a grateful smile. 'Thanks, Archie. I had a wonderful night.'

He nodded. 'Me too.'

I opened the car door and was just about to step out when I had an idea.

'Archie,' I said, ducking back into the car, 'how do you fancy coming speed-dating with me one night next week?'

'What!' he said, his eyes wide. 'Oh God, no. That sounds utterly terrifying.'

'It won't be.' I patted his arm. 'I promise.'

'You can't be serious,' he said, leaning away and looking at me as though I'd just suggested he join me for a spot of naked bungee jumping off the top of Big Ben. 'Me ... do speed-dating? Lucy, I really don't think—'

'It'll be fun,' I said desperately. 'You'll enjoy it. Honestly.'

'Hmm,' Archie said dubiously, twiddling with his beard and studiously avoiding my pleading gaze.

'Please, Archie,' I begged. 'Please say you'll come. It would mean the world to me.'

'But why?' he said, looking back at me.

'I need to find my soulmate,' I said truthfully, Dan's smiling face flitting through my mind, 'and going speed-dating with you might just help.'

'Hmm,' Archie said again. I could almost hear the synapses firing in his brain as he tried to decide what to do.

'Please.' I gave him my best plaintive look and crossed my fingers behind my back.

'OK,' he said finally, his frown dissolving into a smile. 'Seeing as it's for you.'

It wasn't quite the enthusiastic response I'd been hoping for, but just getting him to agree to come with me was a result.

'Are you sure?' I said. 'You're not going to chicken out at the last minute?'

Archie chuckled. 'I can't promise I won't be nervous

166

but my word is my word, Lucy, and I said I'd go.'

I held out my hand. 'Shake on it?'

Archie squeezed my hand and pumped it up and down.

'There,' he said. 'Happy now?'

'I will be. I intend to be very, very happy, Archibald Humphreys-Smythe.'

I was still smiling as I traipsed up the stairs, collapsed onto my bed and reached for my photo of Dan.

'Hi,' I said, stroking his cheek. 'Did you miss me?'

Yes, Lucy, I replied in my head. I really, really miss you.

'I miss you too,' I said. 'More than you can ever imagine.'

'Don't worry,' I said. 'Things are going really well. Archie's a lovely bloke and he's going to let me help him find a girlfriend. How good is that?'

Photo Dan just kept smiling.

'I'll find him someone in no time, Dan.' I kissed him softly on the mouth. 'And then we'll be together again. Just you wait.'

Chapter Twenty

Monday 6th May
Day Ten

I counted the days on my fingers. One ... two ... three
... I'd tumbled into the House of Wannabe Ghosts
on Saturday 27th April, which meant I'd been back on
earth for ... I smacked straight into a lamp post and
apologised profusely ... ten days. TEN DAYS?!

How had that happened? How could I be on day
ten already? I only had twenty-one days to complete
my task and I was nearly halfway through. OK, so I
knew a bit more about Archie and he'd agreed to go
to a speed-dating event with me, but still ... talk about
cutting it fine.

Monday, I thought, yanking open the door to
Computer Bitz; Jess and Anna said they'd meet up for
drinks every Monday night. My stomach lurched. If I
was going to see them again I'd have to return to the
White Horse. What if Keith Krank was there?

'Morning, Lucy.' Archie positively beamed at me as
I stepped into the office.

'Morning,' I said, returning his grin and weaving through the room to my desk.

'Miss Lucy Brown.' Nigel greeted me like a long-lost friend as I sat down. 'How the hell are you?'

'Very well thank you, Nigel.'

Geoff looked up. 'Nnngh.' Even his grunt was more cheerful than normal.

'Morning, Geoff.'

I grinned at my colleagues and felt my spirits rise. Maybe I could complete my task after all. There were at least three people in the world who didn't think I was a sad loser.

The day passed in a flash and by the time five-thirty rolled around I was fidgeting in my seat, desperate to get to the White Horse. My phone rang, just as I was packing up my stuff.

'Hello?' I said, thinking someone must have the wrong number. No one had rung me on my work phone before.

'Lucy?' said the voice on the other end of the line.

'Speaking.'

'It's Brian.'

'Brian!' I said, flustered. 'How did you get this number?'

'I rang directory enquiries and they put me through to a guy called Graham Wellington who put me through to you.'

Oh God, I hoped Brian hadn't said anything weird to him.

'What's wrong?' I asked. 'Has something happened?'

He laughed. 'No, no, I just wondered what you'd like for dinner.'

Dinner? Since when had we started cooking for each other? Since I'd arrived at the House of Wannabe Ghosts my nightly diet had become a never-ending cycle of pasta and pesto with grated cheese or baked beans on toast.

'You're cooking, Brian?'

'Well yes, after you kindly offered to help me with my task, I thought the least I could do was cook you dinner to say thank-you.'

Damn. I'd completely forgotten the conversation we'd had at Paddington Station. I'd been so involved in my own task, I hadn't given Brian's a passing thought.

'But I haven't done anything yet, Brian,' I said, feeling horribly guilty.

'It's a thank-you in advance then. What do you fancy?'

Oh, he was such a sweet man. Still smelly, but definitely sweet.

'I'm so sorry, Brian,' I said. 'But I've already got plans for tonight.'

There was a pause. He wasn't expecting me to invite him along, was he? I'd learned from my Keith Krank experience that talking and eavesdropping simultaneously was virtually impossible.

'Could we do dinner tomorrow night instead?' I suggested.

My housemate ummmed so loudly into the phone I had to hold it away from my ear.

'Brian? Does that sound OK?'

'Ah, yes, yes,' he finally said.

I looked at my watch. It was nearly six o'clock. I had to get moving. 'See you later then.'

'OK,' he sighed.

It was cold outside and I pulled my jacket tightly around me as I trudged up the hill to the White Horse. What if Anna and Jess didn't show up? What if they went to a different pub? If that happened I'd never discover what Dan's reaction to the Keith Krank incident was. I'd fallen into his arms, for God's sake. I *had* to know how he felt about that.

I felt sick with nerves as I pushed open the door to the pub and walked up to the bar.

'White wine, please,' I said, before the barman had chance to speak. I really didn't fancy a protracted discussion about what had happened the previous weekend.

When he turned his back and reached down to the fridge I glanced around the room. Anna and Jess were sitting at exactly the same table they'd sat at a week before. This time Anna had her back to me, but I could see Jess's small, smiley face. She was frowning and nibbling at her fingernails. What on earth was Anna telling her?

'Three pounds fifty please,' the barman said, sliding my drink towards me.

I practically threw the money at him. I had to find out what was going on.

'It was awful,' Anna said as I quietly pulled out a

seat at the table behind them and sat down. 'The poor woman was being totally abused by this drunken twat. Dan had to step in.'

Yes! She was talking about me. I shuffled my weight so I was on the edge of my seat and leaned towards them, trying my best to look casual.

'Really?' Jess said, her eyes wide. 'What happened then?'

'The girl fell against Dan and he put his arm around her and tried to comfort her, but she just pushed him away and ran off.'

'No!' Jess said, enthralled. 'Then what happened? Did the twat follow her?'

'Nah, he was too pissed to get back on his stool, never mind run anywhere. The barman went to look for the girl and, when he couldn't find her, he threw the twat out.'

Jess nodded. 'Glad to hear it. It sounds awful.'

There was pause. Anna was probably sipping her drink.

'You haven't heard the weirdest bit,' she finally said. 'Afterwards, Dan told me he thought the girl was the same one who'd knocked at his door earlier in the week.'

'What girl?'

Me, I felt like saying. It was me, Jess.

'That's just it,' Anna said. 'He'd never seen her before. She just turned up outside his house and was staring at him through the window. Then she banged and banged on the door until he opened it.'

That's a bit of an exaggeration, I thought. I only rang the doorbell once the first time. And I didn't stare. I gazed lovingly.

'And then what happened?' Anna had Jess on the end of a hook.

'Well,' Anna said, running a hand through her hair, 'the girl tried to speak to him but nothing came out. Apparently she was mute.'

'And Dan was sure it was the same girl who fell against him in the pub last weekend?' Jess asked.

'Pretty sure, yeah.'

'Did you hear her speak?'

'That's the weird thing.' Anna lowered her voice and I craned to hear. 'Neither of us did, but she must have spoken to the drunken twat.'

'So why pretend to Dan that she was mute?'

'No idea. He thinks she's weird.'

And so will you if you turn around and realise Weird, Mute Girl is sitting right behind you, I thought, suddenly feeling conspicuous. I rummaged around in my pockets until I found a hair band. It was twisted around a lump of tissue and a chewing gum wrapper. Lovely. I unpicked it hurriedly and tied back my hair. Now all I needed was a hat, a false nose and some sunglasses.

'So how is Dan?' Jess asked.

Anna sighed. 'Well, he wasn't too great, to be honest, not when we first got to the pub. But he perked up a bit after the twat was kicked out. I made him laugh so much at one point that he snorted beer out of his nose.'

Nice, I thought, if slightly revolting. Good old Anna. She'd probably told Dan all about her recent dating efforts. They were invariably awful and always raised a laugh (although, according to Anna, were never that funny at the time).

'So,' Jess said, 'when are you seeing him again?'

'Actually' – Anna giggled in a surprisingly school-girl-like way – 'I already did. I invited him round for dinner a couple of nights ago. Nothing fancy, just a bit of chicken tarragon and saffron potatoes with tiramisu for dessert. We had a much more chilled time than in the pub. It was nice, really, really nice.' She tittered again.

They'd had dinner and I'd missed it? Damn. Ask what they talked about, Jess, I thought. Ask her if Dan talked about me. I tried to beam my thoughts into my friend's head, but her psychic skills were obviously having an off day.

'That was nice of you,' she said instead. 'I don't imagine Dan's been eating well.'

'He hasn't,' Anna replied. 'That's why I suggested we go out for dinner on Thursday. I thought we'd try the new Thai place that's opened up in Swiss Cottage.'

Jess's face fell. 'Thursday? Oh, what a shame! Stuart and I have already made plans. We'd have loved to have joined you.'

'That is a shame.'

How weird. Anna was using her fake voice on Jess. Whenever she lied to someone her voice would become softer, lighter and tilt up at the end of a sentence: I'd

174

heard her use it a hundred times before, particularly with casual acquaintances: 'I love your new hairstyle. Asymmetrical cuts are all the rage.' 'What a beautiful tie-dye skirt.' 'Doesn't yellow suit you.' But why would she lie to Jess? Didn't she like her as much as I thought?

'I've been worried about Dan and how he bottles things up,' Jess said, totally oblivious to the fact she'd just been snubbed. 'He's not the sort of guy to open up to his male friends, but he'll talk to women. It's good he's talking to you.'

'I know,' Anna said. 'That's what's so nice about him. He's got this really sensitive, open side, but he's a man's man too. The best of both worlds really. I don't think Lucy would want him to mourn her for the rest of his life. She'd want him to move on.'

What? WHAT?! Why would she say that? The shock made me choke on my drink. I grabbed onto the table, unable to breathe or swallow, my mouth full of wine. The urge to cough scratched at the back of my throat and I pressed my lips tightly together. Don't cough, don't cough, don't …

White wine squirted out of the corners of my mouth and sprayed the back of Anna's perfectly coiffured head.

'Anna,' Jess said loudly. 'I think the woman behind you is choking on something. Smack her on the back, quick!'

Before Anna had chance to turn round I was sprinting across the pub, my jacket and bag in one hand, the other covering my mouth.

Chapter Twenty-one

Tuesday 7th May
Day Eleven

Even with a mug of coffee in my hands and my duvet around my shoulders, I couldn't stop shivering. Why on earth had Anna said I'd want Dan to move on and meet someone else? I'd never said that. Not once! And we'd had *loads* of drunken chats, about all kinds of things.

Once, in the early hours of the morning after a night out clubbing, Dan and I had a conversation about death. I don't know what it is about those few hours before the sun comes up that sparks weird conversations, but I suspect it's a result of the stillness you feel when most of the country is asleep. Anyway, I lit a couple of candles and we lay, fully clothed, on the bed. Dan lit up a cigarette, puffed heavily on it and exhaled with a sigh. I tucked my hands under my head and watched the smoke drift upwards and curl around the paper lightshade.

Five of us had started the night off in the pub. It was

only supposed to be a couple of drinks and then home when the pub shut, but one drink lead to another, and another, and before we knew it, we were discussing which club to go to. Anna had wanted to go on the pull in some cheesy happy house place, but I insisted we go to a place in Camden that played all the indie classics. After a bit of an argument, it went to a vote, and we trooped off to World Headquarters. It was a good night but ended abruptly in the middle of 'I Wanna Be Adored' when Jess and Stuart had a screaming row and stormed out of the club. After that, the atmosphere felt flatter than a hedgehog on the M25. Dan and I decided to call a cab, but when we looked for Anna we found her in the corner of the club, her tongue down the throat of some bloke who looked like he hadn't even left sixth form. She didn't even come up for air when we told her we were leaving; she just gave us the thumbs-up and waved us away.

When we reached the flat Dan poured us both a whisky and suggested we chill out on the bed for a bit before we went to sleep.

'Lucy,' he'd said, putting out his cigarette and lighting another one. 'Did you know that more people die at 3 a.m. than at any other time in the day?'

I glanced at the alarm clock. It glowed 02:56.

'Is that true?'

Dan nodded. 'Yeah, I read it somewhere. It's to do with the internal body clock and everything slowing down at that time.'

I pushed the alarm clock away and rolled over,

wrapping an arm around Dan. 'We'd better stay awake for a bit longer then.'

Dan rested his cheek against the top of my head. 'If I died, how long would you wait before you moved on and found someone else?'

I pulled away and looked up at him; even though he'd shaved before we left the house, there was stubble on his jawline. 'Where did that come from?'

Dan shrugged. 'I dunno. So, go on then, how long would you wait till you moved on?'

'Dan, that's morbid.'

'No it's not. It's just a question.'

'Hmm,' I said, searching his eyes to work out whether he was messing around or wanted a serious answer. 'I'd wait at least two years, I reckon.'

Dan raised his eyebrows. 'Two whole years? I was thinking more like two weeks.'

'Idiot,' I said, thumping him hard on the arm.

Dan rolled onto his side and propped himself up on his elbow. 'Lucy?'

'Yes, Weird Boy.'

'If anything happened to you …' He broke off and looked away, his jaw clenching and unclenching, his whole body tense.

'What?' I said, suddenly feeling nervous. It wasn't like him to be so intense.

Dan rolled onto his back and stared up at the ceiling.

'If anything happened to you, Lucy,' he said slowly, 'it would totally destroy me.'

I stared at him, my heart in my throat, as he raised his cigarette to his lips, inhaled deeply and blew out the smoke in a slow, steady stream. When he turned his head to look at me, I felt a rush of love so violent, so intense, I thought I might pass out. Instead I reached for his hand and squeezed it tightly.

'That's not going to happen, Dan.'

'What?'

'Me dying first,' I said, a small smile creeping onto my lips. 'You're the smoker, remember.'

'Ah yes,' Dan said, the corners of his eyes crinkling. 'You do realise I'm going to have to keep smoking for ever now, don't you?'

I grinned, grabbed the cigarette out of his fingers and stubbed in out in the ashtray.

'Hey,' Dan said. 'Why'd you do that?'

I rolled onto him and held his beautiful, bemused face in my hands.

'So I could do this,' I said, and kissed him.

I pulled the duvet more tightly around my shoulders and hugged my coffee to my chest. What Anna had said made no sense at all, unless – my stomach lurched horribly at the thought – unless Dan *had* said something to her. I'd heard him tell her he couldn't feel my presence in the house since I'd died. Maybe he thought that was my way of telling him to move on? Or maybe he believed that I wouldn't mind if he found someone else because I'd been so pissed off with him when I'd died? I sipped my coffee but the liquid did nothing to warm the chill I felt in my chest. There was no time to lose. I had to complete my task and become a ghost as soon as possible. And that meant finding Archie's soulmate as quickly as I could.

I launched my speed-dating plan as soon as I got into the office. I browsed through a couple of London-based websites and picked one running speed-dating events every evening. All I had to do was make sure Archie would show up.

'Archie,' I said, crouching by his desk.

He tapped away at his keyboard, seemingly deep in thought.

'Archie!'

He looked up and flashed me a smile. 'Yes, Lucy.'

'Are you free tonight?' I whispered.

'Let me just check.'

He consulted his electronic personal organiser and spent forever tapping buttons and scribbling on the screen with the stylus thing as I bobbed up and down, waiting for him to answer my question.

'Yes,' he said, just as I thought my knees were going to buckle under me, 'unless Grandmother needs me to do something. What have you got planned?'

Damn. I'd forgotten about his grandmother, but I wasn't going to let that faze me.

'A speed-dating event,' I said brightly.

'Tonight?' His grin faded.

'What's up? I thought you were up for it? You did say on Sunday afternoon that you'd come.'

'I was, I just, er,' he mumbled, twisting his beard and staring at his monitor. 'I just thought I'd have more time to psych myself up before we went speed-dating.'

'And how were you planning on doing that?'

'I'm not sure.'

'Well then,' I said, reaching across the desk and flicking off his monitor, 'just ring your grandmother and tell her you're going out tonight. We shouldn't be out for more than a couple of hours so it's not as though you're going to be home late.'

'I can't promise anything,' he said, switching his monitor back on and giving me a look. 'She might make a fuss.'

'Oh, please,' I begged. 'Please do this for me.'

'In that case, Lucy Brown,' he smiled, 'I'll see what I can do.'

By five o'clock I was jiggling up and down in my seat. Every time an instant message popped up on my screen my heart skipped a beat, but it was always Nigel sending me a link to a 'funny' website or Graham checking up on my progress. I hadn't heard a peep from Archie all afternoon and there was only half an hour of the day left.

I looked towards the door. Oh – good news, Archie was on the phone. Bad news – he was frowning. Oh please, Archie, I silently begged, please say you'll still come.

A sharp jab in my side made me look round. Nigel

was staring at me over his glasses, a bemused look on his face.

'Has someone developed a bit of a crush?' he sniggered.

'What?'

'Bit short for you, isn't he?' he said, gesturing over his shoulder with his thumb.

'You think I fancy Archie?' I asked, horrified.

'Well, you haven't stopped looking over there all afternoon.'

'That's because ... because ... I've been waiting for a courier to show up.'

'Really?' He raised a quizzical eyebrow.

'Yes, really. I'm waiting for a ... er ... component.'

'What kind of component?'

'It's for, for ...'

I stared at my screen in desperation. Component? Why the hell did I say that? Everyone knows you can't blag a geek when it comes to technical stuff. I should have just said I was waiting for an emergency pack of tampons to be delivered. That would have shut him up.

'It's for ...'

A message envelope popped up on my screen and I almost squealed with relief. It was from Archie.

'One second, Nige,' I said. 'I just have to deal with this urgent request from Graham.'

Hi, Lucy the message began. *Good news! I CAN go speed-dating with you tonight (though I still can't believe I agreed to go in the first place. I blame you for taking advantage of me when I was too tired to think straight!) Anyway, I have to go home first. Can I meet you there? Where/when? A.*

Brilliant! I'd really started to believe he wouldn't be able to make it.

That's excellent, I typed back, *we both need to be at the Amber Bar, Poland Street (Soho), at 7.30 p.m. The event starts at 8.00 p.m. Shall I wait for you outside?*

No, Archie typed back. *Would be safer for you to wait inside. I might be a bit late, but I'll definitely be there by 7.45 p.m. That OK?*

I deliberated whether or not I should give him some grooming tips while we were chatting (his beard was looking particularly unkempt today and he was wearing a horrible yellow gamers T-shirt with 'Ding! Welcome to Level 70' on the front in red), but I figured even a geek knew how to dress for a date. Besides, I didn't want to come across as patronising.

That's great, I typed back. *See you then.*

Around me, Nigel, Geoff and Joe were stretching and standing up. It was 5.30 p.m. Time to go home and get ready. I had a soulmate to find!

Chapter Twenty-two

What would Archie wear? What would he talk about? Could he even hold a conversation with a stranger for three minutes? I twisted my key in the lock and burst into the House of Wannabe Ghosts, my head buzzing with questions. A gorgeous aromatic smell drifted into the hallway from the kitchen and I inhaled deeply; garlic, onions, spices and … oh, God, I was supposed to be having dinner with Brian and I'd totally forgotten. Shit!

I hurried into the kitchen to find him standing at the cooker. He'd twisted a tea towel into a Karate Kid-style headband. It made his unruly frizz stand to attention like a bearskin helmet.

'Hi, Brian,' I said as he added pieces of chicken to the sizzling pan. I jumped away as they spat and popped in the hot oil, but Brian didn't flinch.

'Brian.' I tapped him on the shoulder. 'Are you OK?'

'Not really,' he mumbled.

I paused. 'Is this about your task?'

'Yeah.'

A pang of guilt shot through me. God, I was such a

shit friend. I was so involved in my own task I'd practically abandoned my housemates. I'd promised to help Brian but I hadn't done a thing. And now I was going to have to blow him out about dinner too. I looked at my watch. I only had just over an hour to get ready and get back into central London for the speed-dating event.

'Brian,' I said softly. 'I'm really, really sorry but I can't have dinner with you after all. I'm so close to completing my own task and if I go out tonight I might find Archie his soulmate. I know I promised I'd help you and I will. I promise.'

'Don't worry, Lucy,' Brian mumbled. 'You go and do what you have to do. Don't worry about me.'

'But I am worried.'

He shrugged and reached into the cupboard for a tin of tomatoes, leaving me feeling torn. I would help him, I would. But I had to find Archie a love match first.

By the time I got changed, travelled across London and fought my way through the crowds of people who'd descended on Soho en masse, it was 7.50 p.m.

I paused outside the bar to catch my breath and crouched down to check my reflection in the wing mirror of a parked car. My hair was behaving itself for once, but my eyeliner had already gathered into fat, gloopy balls near my tear ducts. I picked them out and stared at my reflection. The Lucy Brown that Archie, Nigel, Brian and Claire recognised stared back at me. That was me, the real Lucy, but who did Dan, Jess and

Anna see? What did Weirdo Mute Woman look like? Did she have blue eyes instead of brown? A smaller nose? Blonde hair?

A group of Polish students knocked into me as they pushed past and I jumped. What was I doing? I didn't have time to fanny around, wondering what I looked like. It was 7.55 p.m. Time to speed-date!

It was dark inside the bar, apart from a few low-hanging lamps beaming soft light over circular tables, arranged in rows to one side. A cheesy jazz soundtrack floated out from hidden speakers and groups of people huddled together near the bar. I peered at them and swallowed uncomfortably, my throat suddenly dry. What if Archie wasn't coming? What if he'd changed his mind?

My heart gave a little leap as I spotted his small, dark head towards the back of the room. He'd tied back his hair, which was a huge improvement, but his choice of outfit was, quite frankly, horrific. Beige chinos, trainers, a white shirt, a tweed jacket and a … a … cravat.

But he was talking to someone! Archie was talking to a real, live woman and he couldn't have been in the bar for more than a few minutes. It had to be a good sign.

I hurried towards them, my fingers crossed behind my back.

'Hi, Lucy,' he said as I drew close. 'I've got someone here I'd like you to meet.'

My God, talk about a fast worker. He hadn't even sat down at the tables yet.

'Lucy,' Archie said as the woman slowly turned to look at me, 'this is my grandmother.'

A short, stocky woman gazed up at me. She had a hard, lined face, thin, unsmiling lips (smothered in blood-red lipstick), and a generous nose. Her blonde hair was swept back off her face and fixed in a chignon so tight it looked as though it was cutting off the blood supply to her forehead. So much for the warm, friendly granny type I'd imagined. She looked like Cruella de Vil at a Sloane convention.

'Lucy Brown,' I said, holding out a hand and taking in her tweed skirt, sensible shoes, frilly white blouse and string of pearls.

'So you're the desperado?' she said, looking me up and down.

'Sorry?' I said.

'Archibald told me you were desperate for a boy-friend.' She squeezed my hand so tightly I winced.

Archie, the idiot, was looking everywhere but at the awkward scene playing out in front of him. Why the hell had he brought his gran along?

'I'm not desperate,' I said between gritted teeth. 'I just thought speed-dating might be fun. Are you here to watch?'

Mrs Humphreys-Smythe threw back her head and laughed uproariously. It sounded like the battle cry of a seagull attacking a bin bag.

'Oh no, darling,' she purred, slapping my arm slightly too hard. 'I'm here to join in.'

I glanced at Archie with alarm. He stared at his shoes.

'Grandmother thought tonight might be a laugh,' he mumbled.

'But you have to book,' I said desperately. 'There won't be space for anyone else.'

'All arranged,' said Mrs Humphreys-Smythe, smiling smugly. 'We were fortuitous. Someone dropped out at the last minute and the organiser said he'd be delighted for me to take the spare place.'

I doubted that very much. It was supposed to be a speed-date for people in their twenties to forties, but I had the distinct impression that Archie's grandmother wouldn't take no for an answer, whatever the organiser might have said.

'But aren't the men here a little, er, immature for you?' I ventured nervously.

'I'm widowed, darling,' Mrs Humphreys-Smythe squawked, 'not dead.'

'Obviously,' I said, my ears ringing. 'It's just that—'

My comeback was interrupted by the loud and very insistent clanging of a bell. Everyone instantly stopped talking and turned to see where the noise was coming from. The event organiser was standing on a stool, waving wildly with one hand and shaking the life out of a small brass handbell with the other.

'OK, everyone,' he bellowed. 'If you'd all like to form an orderly queue, I'll give you your name badges, a score sheet and a pencil—'

'I've already got a big pencil,' shouted some wag at the bar.

'Then I'd like you all to take your place at the tables,' the organiser continued, ignoring the tittering. 'If all the ladies could sit with their backs facing the bar and the men opposite them? When three minutes are up, I'll ring the bell again. The men should then move one place to their right. Ladies, stay seated please.'

We queued up like schoolchildren to receive our badges and then took our seats. I tried to slip away from Archie's gran, but she shoved the woman who was going for the table next to me out of the way and parked her generous behind on the chair.

I smiled tightly at her and stared desperately around the room. Where the hell was Archie? He'd better not have backed out. Oh. He was sitting at a chair on the far side of the room, staring at the ceiling and fiddling with his ugly cravat. So much for my plan to whisper helpful hints to him between dates. He was going to have to go it alone.

'Lucy, darling,' Mrs Humphreys-Smythe said in an overloud whisper as my date settled himself into the seat opposite me and looked at me with an expectant grin on his face, 'I don't know what your plan is, but if your intention is to take Archibald away from me, you've got a fight on your hands.'

She smiled tightly and turned away. I stared at my date, open-mouthed.

'Friend of yours?' he said.

*

For the next hour and a half I was an air hostess, a primary school teacher, a deep-sea diver, a trombone player, a stripper (that one went down particularly well), a street sweeper and a cardiologist, as a succession of men sat opposite me, chatted for three minutes, and then left. I couldn't tell you what they looked like or a single thing any of them said. I was too busy peering through the gloom at Archie, wondering if he'd hit the jackpot yet. Beside me, Mrs Humphreys-Smythe tittered and flirted her way through the evening, scaring date after date with her terrifying laugh and her overfriendly habit of grabbing their hand and not letting go until the bell went. By the time a rather nervous Archie shuffled his way to my table I was fuming.

'Archie,' I hissed as he sat down, his chair practically in the middle of the room in his effort not to get too close, 'why on earth did you bring your *gran* here?'

'I had no choice,' he stuttered, twisting his score sheet in his hands. 'She said there was no way I was going to leave her at home on her own and, if I was going out, she was going out too.'

'But she's a grown woman!'

He looked from his gran to me and back.

'I didn't want to let you down, Lucy,' he said miserably. 'I thought it was better to turn up with my grandmother than not come at all and leave you on your own.'

That made me feel crappy. Poor old Archie, he was just trying to do the right thing.

'But don't *you* want to meet someone?' I asked. 'This was for you as much as it was for me.'

He scratched his head, releasing strands of hair from his ponytail. They clung to his cheeks like wet seaweed. 'I'd love to have a girlfriend, but it's not easy. I don't get many opportunities to meet girls.'

'Obviously,' I said, glancing at his grandmother and frowning. 'Anyway, how's it going? Have you met anyone nice?'

'All the girls are lovely,' he said amiably. 'We've had some nice chats.'

'Can I see your card?' I asked, reaching across the table. 'I want to see who you ticked.'

'It's private,' he said, snatching it away before my fingers could make contact.

'Yes, but I need to find out—'

The rest of my sentence was lost in the clang of the organiser's bell. Our three minutes were up.

'See you in a bit, Lucy,' Archie said, jumping out of his chair. 'Only one date left.'

I glanced across at his grandmother, who was watching us through narrowed eyes. When she caught my eye she smiled, her thin lips almost disappearing into the grimace.

'Isn't this fun?' she said.

As it turned out, I didn't get chance to say more than five words to Archie for the rest of the evening.

'Grandmother's tired,' he said as I tried to collar him

for a quick chat after the event had finished. 'She wants to go home.'

Mrs Humphreys-Smythe was jabbering away to the organiser beside the bar, waving her hands around and touching him on the arm. She looked anything but tired and the organiser seemed to be scanning the crowd for the fastest escape route.

'Did you have fun, Archie?' I asked. 'Was it a good night?'

He smiled up at me. 'Well, I did enjoy one of my dates.'

'Which one was that, the one with your gran?'

'Oh, very droll,' he laughed.

'I'll see you at work tomorrow then?' I said, opening my arms for a hug. 'They put all the marks on the cards up on the Internet so you can see if you matched with someone you'd like to date again.'

Archie was just about to reply when his gran steered between us and angled him away.

'Goodbye, Miss Brown,' she said as she pushed Archie towards the door. 'I'd like to say it was nice to meet you, but that would be a lie.'

'I … I,' I stuttered, too shocked to think of a witty comeback.

I'll show you, I thought, as she disappeared into the night and I pulled on my coat and picked up my bag. You'll be smiling on the other side of your horrible, old face when I check Archie's matches tomorrow and find him the love of his life.

So there.

Chapter Twenty-three

Wednesday 8th May
Day Twelve

By 8.55 a.m. on Wednesday morning I was at my desk, my fingers a flurry over the keys. Please, I thought as I typed in the speed-dating URL, please let someone like Archie.

An instant message flashed up on the screen. *Could you come to my desk please? NOW.*

It was Graham. What did he want? He'd told me I had until Friday to get the website done.

Coming, I typed back, one eye on the speed-dating site that was loading infuriatingly slowly in the background.

I could make a lewd comment, Graham typed back immediately. *But someone might report me to the Equal Opportunities Commission.*

Ew!

'Graham,' I said, jumping out of my seat and rounding the corner to his little cubbyhole. 'You wanted to see me?'

My boss stopped clipping his fingernails into the bin

beside the desk and glanced up. 'Ah, yes. Maureen rang me last night to say there was a bit of a HR problem.'

I felt sick. I'd managed to blag Graham with my fake CV but what if Maureen, the accounts-cum-personnel woman, had checked up on me? What if she'd got me figured out as the big, dead fraud I actually was?

'A problem?' I asked, desperately trying to sound casual.

'Yes, no National Insurance number.'

'Sorry?'

Graham, who had transferred his attention to his cuticles and was gnawing them off in strips and spitting them at the bin, removed a finger from his mouth. 'You'll need to give us one if you're going to get paid at the end of this month.'

Shit, I'd forgotten about that. Not that I'd be around on pay day (I'd be a ghost by Dan's side with any luck), but I couldn't very well give them my real National Insurance number, could I? Maybe I could just make up a random sequence of numbers and letters and pass that off? Or steal someone else's? Another question for Brian.

'I can't remember it offhand,' I said. 'I'll have to go home and check.'

'Just get it to me by the end of the week.' Graham waved me away. 'Oh, Lucy ...'

I turned back.

'... how's the website going? I'm expecting great things you know.'

'It'll be brilliant,' I said, forcing a smile. 'Don't you worry.'

'Great. Oh and Lucy …'

'Yes?'

'Do you know what else is happening on Friday?'

'Um, no.'

'It's the annual work charity do.'

That sounded like a laugh. Maybe I could convince Archie to invite someone from the speed-dating event along. If anyone *wanted* to date him, that was.

'Is it a dinner?' I asked, imagining Archie in a tux. Maybe with a bit of a beard trim he'd look quite smart.

'No.' Graham shook his head. 'It's fancy dress at work day. The winner gets a prize and the person in the worst fancy dress has to do a forfeit. You have to dress up as your favourite thing.'

'So I should dress up as a karaoke machine?' I joked.

'If you like.'

'Oh.'

I hurried back to my seat and had just put my fingers to the keyboard when Nigel plonked himself into the seat next to me.

'Did I just hear Graham telling you about Fancy Friday?' he grinned.

There was a look in his eyes I couldn't quite read.

'Yes, he just mentioned it,' I replied.

'You're in for a treat.'

'What's that supposed to mean?'

'Just you wait and see.'

I raised an eyebrow and waited for him to tell me more, but he just winked at me and turned back to his screen. Fine. He could keep his geeky wind-ups to himself. I had more important things to do, like finding out whether I'd found Archie his soulmate or not.

My heart was thumping as I entered Archie's code into the speed-date-to-love website.

Yes! There were two ticks. Ohmigod. I'd done it! Two women were interested in him. I'd found him someone.

Hang on a sec.

One of the ticks was for 'friend'. That was me. OK, cool, no problem. That left one dating tick. *Someone* wanted to date Archie and her name was …

Jean Humphreys-Smythe.

No! It wasn't possible. I refreshed the screen and scanned it again but …nothing. No one wanted to date Archie, apart from his sick, twisted gran.

I spent most of the morning in the ladies' loo, alternately banging my head against the wall or holding it in my hands in despair. When I finally sloped back to my desk Nigel glanced at me out of the corner of his eye but said nothing. I sank back into my seat, grateful for his silence. Call it hope or desperation, but I couldn't stop myself logging back into the speed-dating website to re-check Archie's matches, just in case *someone* had changed their mind about him. But no, still just me and Gran. I was too depressed to even think of checking my own stats.

When lunchtime finally rolled around, an instant message flashed up on my screen.

Hi, Lucy.

It was Archie.

Thanks for taking me speed-dating last night. It was … interesting. Did anyone … er …

I waited for him to finish, but the cursor just flashed on the screen. Poor thing, he didn't have the guts to ask the question I was dreading answering.

I didn't think much of the girls who were there, I typed back. *You could do loads better.*

There was a pause.

So no one loved me? he typed.

Just me and your gran, I'm afraid.

Well, that's nice to know, anyway. Want to go for a drink at lunchtime? I'd like to talk some more about last night.

He wanted to know where he went wrong. That was good. In fact, it was better than good. It was great. I could give him some tips, maybe talk to him about his clothes sense and his personal grooming. All was not lost – I might be able to find him his soulmate after all!

I'd love to go for a drink, I typed back. *How about we go somewhere other than the pub so we're away from the rest of the boys.*

Sounds like a plan, he typed. *There's a nice little eatery round the corner that does tapas and beer. Fancy it?*

Sounds good. Meet you outside.

The tapas bar was busy, but it was cool and light and the menu looked delicious. Better than that, Archie and I managed to secure a table near the back of the restaurant, away from the prying eyes of any Computer Bitz boys who might walk by.

'So,' Archie said, holding out my chair and tucking me in, 'what do you fancy?'

'Anything tasty.'

'Well, there's plenty of that here,' he said. 'And, by the way, lunch is on me. Choose whatever you'd like. If it wasn't for you, I would have had another night in last night.'

'And instead, you had a night out with me, your grandmother and a roomful of desperate women.'

Archie grinned. 'Well, you have to start somewhere.'

'Thank you,' I said. 'For suggesting lunch. I really needed this.'

We browsed the menu, finally deciding on a potato dish, an olive dish, little pieces of salami, a mini-omelette and a big basket of bread. The waiter brought us a bottle of Spanish beer each, with a lime jammed into the top, and returned fifteen minutes later with a tray laden with dishes. He spread them on the table between us before hurrying off.

'So,' I said, dipping a chunk of bread into a dish of olive oil and balsamic vinegar, 'what do you think went wrong last night?'

'I'm not sure,' Archie said, looking puzzled. 'I thought it was going well. I actually talked quite a lot.'

I pushed the lime into my beer bottle and took a sip. 'What did you talk to the girls about?'

'Well, most of them asked me what my job was, and what my hobbies were, so I told them.'

I stared at him with alarm. 'You told them about LAN parties?'

'That and *Star Wars*. I've got all the original 1970s action figures you know, *and* they're all in their original boxes.'

I stared at him, open-mouthed, then started to laugh. It was either that or cry.

'I'll have you know that they're worth a lot of money on the open market,' Archie mumbled, stabbing a potato with his fork.

'Oh, Archie,' I said. 'I'm sorry. I didn't mean to laugh. It's just, well, it's just not a topic girls are likely to get excited by.'

'That's not my fault.'

He was right. It wasn't his fault. He genuinely didn't have a clue.

'So what kind of questions did you ask the girls?' I asked.

'I didn't. It took three minutes to tell them about the different types of Darth Vadar figures I've ...' He tailed off, looking dejected.

'Oh, Archie.'

He slumped in his seat and tossed the piece of bread he'd been nibbling on at his plate. 'I screwed up, didn't I? I was only trying to be polite and answer their questions.'

'It's OK, Archie,' I said, patting his hand, 'never mind.'

'So, what about you?' he asked miserably. 'I bet loads of guys wanted to date you.'

'There wasn't anyone there for me.'

Archie looked crestfallen. 'Oh.'

'I mean, obviously I ticked you as a friend but, other than that, no one.'

'You ticked friend?' he said, brightening a little. 'So, in your esteemed opinion, how might one go about persuading women that they want to date you, rather than be friends with them?'

I nibbled on my bottom lip. 'Could I be totally honest with you?'

'Of course. Be as honest as possible. I need all the help I can get.'

'Well, you could start by getting your hair cut and having a shave.'

'Do you really think that would do it?' he asked, pulling at his beard thoughtfully.

'That, and a clothes make-over.'

Archie looked down at his 'Gamer' T-shirt and stroked the logo. 'But I love this T-shirt.'

'Well, if you're not serious about this ...'

'I am. I am. So when is this miraculous make-over going to happen?'

I looked at my watch. It was five past two. Even if we hurried, we'd still be late back from lunch.

'Let's ring Graham,' I said, 'and tell him we developed food poisoning.'

Archie's eyebrows nearly disappeared into his hair-line. 'Skive work? I've never done that before.'

'There's a first time for everything,' I grinned. 'Give me your phone and I'll ring Graham. Archibald Humphreys-Smythe, prepare to become a super-hunk.'

Chapter Twenty-four

'Can I help you?' the receptionist asked, looking us up and down. He was dressed all in black and had scarily cool hair; long at the back, streaked red at the front and feathery layers at the sides. 'Hairdresser hair', Dan and I used to call it, the kind of style that only the truly trendy can get away with. On anyone else it would be a mullet, and a particularly ugly one at that.

'My friend would like a haircut and a shave,' I said as Archie looked from me to the hairdresser and back, a look of terror on his face. 'Do you have any free appointments now?'

'Michael's free,' the receptionist said, flicking through the book. 'Name?'

'Archie.'

He waved us away. 'OK, take a seat. Michael will be with you in a moment.'

We sat, side-by-side, in chairs near the door as the receptionist disappeared off into the back of the shop.

'Lucy,' Archie whispered, perching on the very edge of his seat and tapping the toes of his trainers on the floor. 'You don't want me to have hair like him, do you?'

I laughed. 'Absolutely not.'

'So no red streaks then?'

'No streaks at all. Just something a bit shorter at the back and sides, maybe a bit messy-ruffled-spiky at the front.'

'Lucy, ' Archie said, staring at the door. 'Can we go for a drink instead? There's something I'd like to talk to you—'

'How about something like this?' I suggested, plucking a magazine from the glass table in front of us and pointing to a very good-looking male model with exactly the kind of hairstyle I'd described. It was modern, it was short and, on the model, it was unbelievably sexy.

'Do you think it would suit me?' Archie asked uncertainly, twisting his long hair in his fingers as he stared at the picture.

I leaned back in my chair and looked at him, blurring my eyes. It was hard to imagine how he'd look with short hair, but the model's hairstyle would definitely be an improvement on what passed for his current hairstyle.

'I think you'd look great,' I said. 'Promise.'

'OK.' He looked me straight in the eye. 'If you think it'll look good, Lucy, I'm sure I'll like it too.'

'Here,' I said, tossing him another magazine. 'Read this and try to chill out. And stop trying to get out of it. We can go for a drink when we're done.'

Ten minutes later, Michael, a tall, skinny man with blonde, layered hair down to his shoulders, finally appeared. Archie was so jittery my chair was vibrating.

'Hello,' he squeaked, half-rising and holding out a limp hand as the man approached us. 'I'm Archibald.'

'What can I do for you today?' the hairdresser replied, ignoring the outstretched hand and instead rubbing a lock of Archie's hair between his thumb and finger. He raised an eyebrow at me. 'Have you *seen* these split ends?'

'I'd like my haircut to look like this,' Archie said, jerking his head away and pointing at the magazine, 'and I'd like my beard shaved off too please.'

Michael grinned at me and ran a hand through his own, perfectly groomed, hair. 'Girlfriend giving you a bit of a make-over, is she?'

'She's my friend,' Archie corrected, the back of his neck turning red.

'Is she now?' The hairdresser winked at me. 'OK, Archie, let's see what we can do.'

I tore the magazine from Archie's sweaty palms as he stood up and sloped after Michael to the sinks at the far end of the shop where an assistant promptly took over. She dressed him in a black robe, tucked a towel around his shoulders and gestured for him to sit back in the chair with his head over the sink. Archie clutched the chair arms and shut his eyes as she turned on the taps and bent over him. Anyone would have thought he was about to be electrocuted, not have his hair washed and conditioned.

I picked up a magazine, feeling just the teeniest bit guilty. Archie was obviously nervous, but it wasn't as though I was forcing him to have a make-over; he'd jumped at the suggestion. He wanted to meet someone and I was just helping him along. That was all.

When I looked up from the article I'd been reading, Archie had been transferred to a chair in front of one of the enormous mirrors opposite me, and Michael was combing his hair. It looked even longer when it was wet, and slithered down his back like black seaweed. Michael said something I couldn't hear, then gathered the wet hair into a ponytail and reached for his scissors. Archie glanced at me in the mirror, his eyes wide.

'It'll be OK,' I mouthed. 'I promise.'

Michael's scissors sliced through Archie's hair and a long, wet lock dropped to the floor. I looked away, too chicken to acknowledge the look of fear in Archie's eyes. When I glanced back up, Michael had already shaped the hair at the back of his neck and around his ears and was snipping away at the top. I smiled at Archie in the mirror. Even with the beard, he already looked loads better.

'It looks great,' I mouthed, and Archie smiled.

Half an hour later, trimmed, shaved and shaped, Michael span Archie round in his chair.

'Well?' he said. 'What does Madam think?'

I couldn't stop grinning. 'Archie, you look amazing!' I said, resisting the urge to give his new haircut and shave a round of applause.

'Sure?' Archie said, rubbing the back of his neck and looking at me from under his eyebrows.

'You look great,' I said.

He really did. He looked younger with the long hair

and beard gone; really fresh-faced and cute. He was a different man. A much, much cleaner, better-looking man.

After he'd paid, Archie shuffled towards me, head down. 'Are you sure you like it, Lucy?'

'I love it,' I said, standing up and patting him on the shoulder, 'and other women will, too. I guarantee it.'

Instead of looking pleased, he shoved his hands into his pockets and sighed. 'Can we go for that drink now, Lucy? Please? I really need to talk to—'

'Later,' I said, ushering him through the door. 'We need to go shopping first.'

'Shopping,' he said. 'Great.'

It took us hours to find Archie a couple of new outfits. Because he was so short and slim, all the trousers I picked out either dragged on the floor or bagged round his bum and his thighs. I'd only ever chosen clothes for Dan before and, to be honest, I had no idea how to dress someone who was so much shorter. Archie put up a bit of a fight too. He refused to wear a fantastic salmon-pink shirt I'd picked out and described the designer jeans I'd chosen as 'tragic'. After an hour spent traipsing from rack to rack (while Archie moaned that everything was ugly and his feet were hurting), we decided to split up and comb the store separately. He returned with an armful of faded, pale-blue jeans and ugly, bright T-shirts and I'd gathered smart trousers and tailored shirts. We looked at each other's offerings and laughed. We couldn't have picked out more differ-ent outfits if we'd tried.

In the end we reached a compromise – tailored combat-style trousers and long-sleeved T-shirts layered under regular T-shirts (with no crappy gamer logos on the front).

'Well?' Archie said, stepping out from behind the changing room curtain for the fifteenth time. 'How about this?'

'You look great,' I said. 'Really, really great.'

I meant it too. He really did look good. The layered tops made him look less skinny and the trousers and boots made his legs look longer and chunkier.

'Hooray,' he said as he disappeared back behind the curtain. 'Can we go for a drink now, Lucy. Please?'

'Fine,' I grinned, delighted with the result of my first ever make-over. 'Anything to shut you up.'

The trendy wine bar Archie suggested wasn't really my kind of place but I didn't put up a fight. We were celebrating my marvellous, magical make-over and it was the least I could do to thank him for being such a good sport about it all. I grabbed a table while Archie went to the bar and a few minutes later he returned with a large glass of wine for me and a pint of bitter for himself. I raised an eyebrow at the fact he wasn't drinking a half, but said nothing. Celebration called for more booze than normal, everyone knew that.

Archie sat down heavily in his chair and gulped at his drink while I stared at him, open-mouthed. He looked so different, like a completely new man.

He caught me looking and peered at me over the rim of his pint. 'Good?'

'You look great.'

'So, do you think women would want to date me, looking like this?'

'Oh God, yes.'

'I'm glad you joined Computer Bitz,' he said, setting his pint back down and picking up a beer mat.

'Me too,' I gushed. 'Although, I wasn't sure I was going to get the job, not after what happened with Graham Wellington during my interview.'

'I'm sorry you had to go through that,' he said, his grin slipping a little. 'Graham's a little eccentric, to say the least, and he takes some getting used to. He's not a bad person at heart, he's just ...'

'... a bit of a perve?'

Archie laughed. 'You don't know the half of it.'

'What I don't get,' I said, taking a sip of my wine, 'is why he'd employ me after I slapped him? He said someone had threatened to report him to the Equal Opportunities Commission, but I can't imagine anyone at Computer Bitz doing that.'

'I did,' Archie said softly, ripping the top layer off the bar mat and scrunching it into a ball.

'What?'

'I did.'

'No way! *You* threatened to report him?'

'Yes. There's only so much Graham should be allowed to get away with and anyway, you seemed nice.'

'I am nice,' I said, pretending to polish my halo. 'I'm the nicest person you'll ever meet. Ask anyone, ask ...' Archie was sitting up in his seat, staring into the mirror behind me, ruffling his hair. 'Ask ... ' He was totally destroying the messy, yet sculpted, look the hairdresser had created.

'Are you sure you like your new hair?' I asked, feeling confused. Hadn't he just got excited about the fact his new hairstyle made him more date-able? Wasn't that why he was drinking a full pint? To celebrate?

'I'll get used to it, I suppose.' He shrugged and flattened his hair trying, and failing, to brush it forward over his eyes.

'At least your gran will like it,' I joked, trying to lighten the mood. 'I'm sure she'll think you look like a very smart young man.'

Archie didn't laugh. Instead, he looked down and continued to rip at the beer mat, tearing it into tiny little pieces. I'd never seen anyone look so uncomfortable and self-conscious.

'You didn't really want to get your hair cut and your beard shaved off, did you?' I said, feeling a bit sick.

There was a pause that seemed to last for ever. Finally, Archie spoke. 'Not really.'

'Then why did you?'

'Because you thought it would be a good idea.'

'OK.'

'And because I love spending time with you.' He swallowed hard. 'And because ... because ...'

'Because?' I said, my mouth suddenly dry.

He covered his face with his hands and I held my breath.

'Because I've fallen in love with you,' he said.

Chapter Twenty-five

I froze, the wine glass pressed against my bottom lip. Had Archie just said what I thought he'd said? He couldn't have.

'Sorry, Archie, what did you just say?'

'I said …' He cleared his throat. 'I think I'm in love with you, Lucy.'

My stomach knotted so tightly I felt physically sick. Archie wasn't supposed to fall in love with me. I was supposed to find him his soulmate. He wasn't … couldn't … be in love with me. My wine glass trembled as I set it back on the table.

'Are you … you …' I forced a smile. 'You're joking, right?'

Archie shook his head, his eyes fixed on the pile of shredded beer mat in front of him, his expression pure misery. He couldn't be in love with me. He just couldn't.

'I'm sorry,' he mumbled, his cheeks scarlet. 'I just couldn't keep it to myself any longer. I felt like I was going to burst. I ticked 'date' on the speed-dating thing, but when you didn't say anything about that this morning I just had to tell you, no matter how you might feel about me and' – he paused for breath – 'from your reaction, I can tell you don't feel the same way ...' He hung his head, but now there was no long hair to fall into his face to mask the look in his eyes.

Something inside me cracked, and I felt like crying. This wasn't what I'd wanted. I'd wanted to build up Archie's confidence so he could find the right woman. The *right* woman, not me. I was trying to find my way back to Dan. Had I gone about my task the wrong way? Had I got too close to Archie? Given him the wrong signals?

'Archie,' I said, touching him on the elbow. 'Archie, look at me.'

'I can't,' he said, shaking his head. 'I shouldn't have said anything. I've made a total fool of myself.'

'You haven't.'

'I have.'

'Archie,' I said desperately, 'you can't be in love with me. We're friends.'

'I thought we were more than that,' he mumbled. 'Even Nige said he thought you were, er, how did he put it? Unusually interested in me.'

Oh God. How stupid was I? Of course he'd think I was interested in him. I'd pretended to be into LAN parties, chatted to him over lunch and stared at him at work. I'd even invited him out, to a speed-dating party admittedly, but if you looked at it impartially, I'd made all the first moves. I'd even taken an interest in the way he looked and given him a make-over. No wonder he was confused.

'I like you, Archie,' I said, fiddling with my empty wine glass. 'I like you a lot …'

'But?'

'But I see you as a … as a … little brother.'

'Brother?' He laughed tightly. 'Right. Thanks for that.'

'No,' I said, reaching for his hand. 'Don't be angry, please. I just wanted to help you meet someone.'

'Why would you do that, Lucy?' He snatched his hand away and left mine trailing alone on the table-cloth. 'You hardly know me.'

His cheeks were flushed and he was glaring at me, his hands clenched into tight, white fists. I'd never seen him look so angry and hurt. But what could I say? I couldn't tell him the real reason why I was trying to find him a soulmate.

'You looked lonely,' I said.

'No shit.'

'But, but,' I stuttered. 'I don't think you're in love with me, not really. Maybe you just like the way I make you feel about yourself.'

'Could you be any more patronising, Lucy?'

'What?'

'I'm not some kind of desperate lost cause, you know,' he said, leaning back in his chair, his eyes cold. 'I didn't ask you to take me under your wing and find me someone to love, did I? I was doing perfectly fine on my own, you know.'

'Were you?'

Archie opened his mouth to reply, then shut it again,

shaking his head. Then he was up, out of his chair and halfway to the door, before I knew what was happening.

'Archie,' I called. 'Archie, don't go. Please. Let's talk about this.'

He turned back and stared at me. 'Oh just fuck off, Lucy.'

And then he was gone.

I drank three large glasses of wine and then left the pub and started walking. Cars beeped and honked and frustrated commuters elbowed me out of the way, but I kept on going. I walked until the sun set and the street lamps flickered pools of amber light onto London's dark streets.

And then I stopped.

Outside 33, White Street. NW6. My old house.

I sat on a wall on the opposite side of the road and looked at my watch. It was just after eight, but all the lights were off in the house and the curtains were closed.

But I didn't need to look through the window to remember my house. I just had to shut my eyes.

The living room ... where Dan and I had made a bed on the floor using blankets and duvets while we waited for our new bed to be delivered. We didn't sleep a wink, but giggled like children playing at sleepovers until we only had four hours sleep before had to get up to work. The dining room ... I'd bought a gorgeous antique wooden table and eight matching chairs so we could have fancy dinner parties with cotton napkins, candles, starters, main courses and desserts. We only had one dinner party in the end because we all felt so awkward and silly, dressed up in our finery making polite chit-chat, that I moved everyone into the living room instead and we ate our meals on our knees in front of the TV, laughing like loons at how we'd never be proper 'grown-ups'. The kitchen ... our beautiful yellow kitchen. It was monochrome and steel, with white walls when we moved in, but I'd always dreamed of a yellow kitchen and I told Dan as much. One day I returned from work to discover he'd taken the afternoon off from his job at Creative Ink Advertising Agency to paint it the most beautiful primrose yellow. He hated it, he told me later, but it had been worth it just to see the look of delight on my face when I walked through the door ...

Someone coughed and my eyes flew open. Dan was standing beside me.

'You again!' he said, staring down at me, his eyes wide with surprise. 'If you're stalking me you need to start being a bit more subtle.'

I should have jumped up and run away, but I couldn't move. I stared up at him, my heart pounding in my chest. He was holding a black umbrella over his head while fat, wet droplets bounced on my cheeks and dripped off my jaw. I hadn't even noticed it was raining.

'Why are you staring at my house?' Dan perched on the wall beside me and my breathing quickened. I was hyperventilating with longing. 'There's nothing worth nicking, you know.'

It's our house, I wanted to say. Mine and yours. Why can't you tell that I'm sitting beside you? Why can't you sense it's me?

'You're shivering,' Dan said, holding the umbrella over my head. 'Look, I don't know who you are or what you want from me, but you've got to stop doing this. Otherwise I'll call the police or' – he looked me up and down and shook his head – 'social services.'

The skin below his eyes was crinkled with wrinkles but they weren't laughter lines, neither was the ridge between his brows. He looked worried and tired, but he still cared enough to keep me, his mute stalker, dry while the rain flattened his hair to his head.

I had to try and tell him what was going on. He had to understand.

'Dan,' I said. 'It's Lucy. I'm trying to get back to you but I think I've screwed it all up. The man I was supposed to find love for has fallen in love with me instead and I don't know what to do.'

He stared at my lips but said nothing. It was useless. He couldn't hear a thing. I was just about to get up when he rummaged in his bag and held up a notepad and pen.

'I can't hear what you're saying,' he said slowly and loudly, as though I were deaf. 'But if you write down what's wrong, I might be able to help. Call someone or something.'

He leaned towards me, the notebook in his hand,

and I caught the warm, musky tones of his aftershave. I inhaled the scent of him, temporarily lost in a thousand tender memories, then reached out my hand. His fingers brushed mine as I took the pad and pen and a million volts of electricity sparked up my arms.

This is Lucy, I scribbled desperately. *I love you so much, Dan, and I'm so sorry we argued before I died. I was just stressed about the wedding and I should have said I love you, too, but—'*

Dan touched my hand. I stopped writing and looked up at him. Oh my God. Oh my God. Had he … had he actually understood what I'd just writ—

'I'm sorry,' he said softly. 'But I've got no idea what that says. Is it Arabic? Hindi? I don't understand what you just wrote.'

My heart rate slowed to a dull thud. Every tiny speck of hope I'd clung to so desperately had just floated away and disappeared. I tore the page from the pad, crumpled it up, and threw it into the gutter.

'Come back,' Dan shouted as I turned and walked away. 'Let me help you.'

'You can't,' I whispered. 'Nobody can.'

Chapter Twenty-six

Claire was peering out of the hallway cupboard, the phone in her hand, as I trudged through the front door of the House of Wannabe Ghosts.

'Lucy,' she said. 'It's for you.'

My heart skipped a beat. There were only two people who knew my home telephone number and one of them was Archie.

'Is it Archie?' I mouthed as I hurried down the hall.

She shook her head. 'No, and I think you're going to get a bollocking.'

A bollocking? What for? Oh God. Was it Graham Wellington?

'Hello?' I said, snatching the phone from her hand.

'Hello, Lucy,' said a familiar voice. 'This is Saint Bob.'

I nearly dropped the phone. Saint Bob? Limbo could call the house? Why hadn't anyone told me?

'Lucy' – Bob's tone was officious – 'where have you been?'

'When?'

'Just now.'

I was tempted to lie, but I had the distinct impression

that lying to my celestial boss wouldn't do me any favours.

'I went to see my fiancé ... I did something wrong, didn't I?'

'Lucy – have you read the manual?'

'Parts of it.'

Bob sighed. 'Did you read the part about contacting people who knew you when you were alive?'

I swallowed. Oh shit. They definitely knew where I'd been.

'Yes,' I said.

'According to our records, Lucy, you have made two attempts to communicate with your fiancé. On the first occasion you attempted to speak to him and on the second, today, you attempted to speak to him *and* communicate with him through the written word.'

'I'm sorry, I was desperate,' I said. 'My task wasn't going well and I was going to give up and ...'

The thought hit me like a juggernaut in the face. I didn't want to give up. I didn't want Bob to whisk me back up to limbo and load me onto the up escalator. I wanted to pass my task, no matter what. If Archie loved me, I could make him *not* love me. I could make him hate me, if I had to. I just had to get back to Dan.

'Please,' I begged. 'Please don't force me to go up to heaven. I'm sorry. Just give me another chance. Please, Bob, please.'

'Lucy—'

'Please? I'm begging you. Please.'

'Lucy!'

'Yes?'

'This is your official warning, your only warning. We let the first offence go as it was your first day back on earth and you hadn't read the manual, but this time you blatantly broke the rules. You have one last chance—'

'Oh, thank you,' I gabbled. 'Thank you, thank you, thank you.'

'BUT,' Bob said, 'if you try anything like this again, you will immediately be returned to limbo and your task will be cancelled.'

'I won't,' I promised, twisting the phone cord round my finger. 'I won't try and communicate with anyone again.'

'Good.' Bob said. 'You might want to remind Claire of the rules. She's on her last warning too and we've noticed she's come perilously close to breaking it recently. Goodbye, Lucy—'

'Wait,' I said. I'd just remembered the last conversation I'd had with Claire. 'Can people find love in heaven? I mean, if someone didn't find love when they were alive, can they find love up there instead?'

'Of course they can.' Bob sighed. 'What kind of heaven do you think would let the loveless exist for eternity on their own?'

I'd only just set the phone back on its cradle when Brian poked his head round the door.

'Hi, Lucy,' he said. 'Sorry to burst in on you, but I was wondering if you were ready to help me with my task? You did say you'd help me today.'

I was one breath away from saying no, but the

desperate look on his face made me swallow my words.

'OK,' I said. 'I'll just go and change my clothes and then I'll be down.'

'Marvellous.' He beamed at me and scratched his mop of dark hair. 'I knew you wouldn't let me down.'

'Oh, Brian,' I said, as I climbed the stairs, 'could you grab two of your railway magazines? We're going to need them.'

'Magazines,' he repeated, looking confused. 'Right.'

Chapter Twenty-seven

It was still raining when we hopped off the tube at Tooting Broadway and traipsed down the deserted high street. Brian stormed ahead, a look of steadfast determination on his face.

'This is where Troy lives,' he said, pointing at nowhere in particular as I trotted behind him.

'OK,' I said, staring around nervously. Even the street lights looked scary. 'But is this a good idea? It's quite late and there's no one around. How will we find him?'

'We'll find him,' Brian said, glancing back at me. 'I know exactly where he'll be.'

I had no idea what a bunch of teenagers would be doing on a rainy May evening. Probably something they shouldn't, I thought cynically.

'OK,' he said, stopping suddenly in the middle of the street. 'We're here.'

'Where's here?' I replied, scowling as a man on a bike splashed through a puddle in the road and drenched my jeans.

Brian pointed to the glowing arches above the nearest shop.

'McDonald's?'

'Yes,' he said, pushing the door open. 'Fancy a burger?'

I traipsed in behind him, glad to get out of the rain, as he hurried to the counter. The place was packed. Everywhere I looked, teenagers were cramming chips into their mouths, slurping on milkshakes or slouching on the tables doing not very much at all.

'OK,' said Brian, waving a tray of stinky junk food under my nose, 'now we're here, how are you going to help me with my task?'

'Don't stress,' I said, reaching for a chip and popping it into my mouth. 'I'll come up with something, but you need to tell me where Troy is first.'

'See the two boys and the girl over by the door?' Brian inclined his head and I nodded. 'Troy is the boy in the grey hooded top, the black trousers and the white trainers.'

'OK then,' I said, nudging him, 'let's go and sit at the table next to them.'

Brian visibly paled. 'Tell me you're joking.'

'Brian,' I said, rolling my eyes, 'how are you supposed to start a conversation with someone unless they can hear what you're saying?'

'I was kind of hoping you'd come up with some kind of plan that didn't involve conversation.'

'What, like kidnapping him and tying him to the bridge at Paddington Station until he agrees to become a trainspotter?'

'Well …' Brian shrugged. 'Maybe not something quite so obviously violent, but —'

'Brian!'

'He called me a paedophile, Lucy. He'll run a mile if I try and talk to him again.'

'Oh, for God's sake, Brian,' I said, snatching the tray from him and heading towards the empty table. 'Let's just go and sit down and take it from there.'

'OK,' he mumbled. 'But if he calls me a kiddy-fiddler again, it's your fault.'

Troy looked up as we sat down, but he didn't scream, run or pull a gun on us. Which was a good start.

'See,' I whispered, pushing a bag of fries towards Brian. 'He doesn't even remember you.'

'Good.' He looked relieved. 'What now?'

'Take out those two magazines I asked you to bring.'

While I tried my best to look nonchalant, Brian foraged around in his bag and extracted two magazines, pristine in their clear plastic sleeves. I snatched one from him.

'Careful,' he hissed, jumping forward in his seat. 'They might be collector's editions one day.'

'Keep your wig on.' I wiped the ketchup from my fingers (and the plastic sleeve) and turned the first page. 'So, what's every railway enthusiast's wet dream?'

Brian gasped and almost fell off his seat. 'Sorry?'

'What's the one thing a railway enthusiast wants more than anything else in the world?'

'I always dreamed of building a station on an old track bed,' he said, his saggy face lighting up. 'No, buying two stations and reconstructing the line so a steam train could run between them.'

'Lovely.' I glanced at Troy, who was furtively checking out the cover of the magazine I was holding. 'Now, announce you've done just that. Say it loudly.'

'But I haven't,' he protested.

'Oh, for God's sake, Brian, just act. Weren't you ever in a play when you were a kid?'

'I was in the nativity.'

'Great start!'

'As a tree.'

'Just pretend your greatest dream has come true,' I explained, 'and I'm one of your railway enthusiast friends and you're telling me the news.'

'I've bought two stations,' Brian shouted at the top of his lungs. 'And I'm going to run a steam train between them.'

Troy stared at us. So did the rest of the restaurant.

'Fantastic,' I said, forcing a smile. 'I've, er …' I glanced down at my magazine and speed-read the first few words of an article. 'I've just come back from a trip to the Isle of Man Steam Railway.'

'I've been there too,' Brian bellowed. 'It's fantastic.'

Oh God.

Still, at least we had Troy's attention. But we had one major problem. He was sitting with two friends; two non-railway enthusiast friends. If we were going to get to Troy, we needed to get rid of them. And fast.

'So, Lucy,' Brian shouted. 'What did you like best about—'

'Brian, shhh.' I glared at him. 'I'm thinking.'

How could I get rid of Troy's mates? I could probably get the girl into the ladies' loos with some kind of women's problem (an urgent tampon request, maybe?), but that would leave the male friend behind. If I shouted 'fire!' everyone would leave the building (Troy included), so that was no good either.

I scanned the table next to us, desperate for an idea. The three teenagers had a cup of coke each, but no food. What else? They were all fiddling with their mobile phones. Two of them had the same make, but Troy's was different. That gave me a idea. A stupid one, perhaps, but it might just work.

'Brian,' I said loudly, but without shouting, 'how many people did you sign up for the Sony Ericsson free Big Mac promotion?'

He looked at me blankly, but I could tell I had the attention of the three kids on the next table. They'd stopped talking and were listening to me in that *über*-cool, 'I'm *so* not listening cos you're *so* sad' teenage way.

'I got a hundred,' I said quickly, before Brian had chance to put his foot in it. 'You only got ninety-eight, didn't you? You'll lose your job if you don't get two more. You'd think kids would snap up a free Big Mac meal like that' – I clicked my fingers together – 'wouldn't you?'

Brian continued to stare at me, open-mouthed. At

the table next to us, Troy's friend was kicking the girl under the table. I put on my most winning smile and turned towards them.

'I don't suppose any of you have a Sony Ericsson, do you? My friend here will lose his job tomorrow if he doesn't give out two more free Big Mac meals.'

'I've got one,' Troy's friend said, snatching up his mobile and thrusting it in front of my nose. 'What do I have to do? How do I get a free Big Mac?'

'Me too, me too,' squealed the girl, pushing her pink phone across the table.

'You don't have to do anything,' I said, grinning inanely. 'It's just a, er, survey we're doing in Tooting Broadway. And you've made Brian's day. Haven't they, Brian?'

Brian clenched his teeth into the most bizarre fake smile I'd ever seen.

'Why yes, they have, Lucy,' he said as I kicked him under the table. 'Yes indeed.'

'Well, get your wallet out then, and buy these two a Big Mac meal each.'

'Can I have a filet-o-fish meal?' asked the girl, patting her non-existent stomach. 'I don't wanna get fat, innit.'

'You can have whatever you like,' I said. 'That's part of the promotion. Off you go with Brian and choose.'

'Lucy ...' Brian said.

I kept the smile fixed to my lips. 'Just buy these helpful young people whatever they'd like.'

'OK,' he said, angling himself out of his chair and standing up. 'Buy food. Right.'

As Brian and his new best friends hurried up to the counter I glanced at Troy. He was flipping his mobile over in his hands and looked utterly dejected.

'I'm really sorry,' I said, picking up my copy of *Railway Enthusiast* magazine. 'You've got a great phone, but it's not one we represent.'

'Whatever.' He shrugged. 'I never get free shit.'

I flicked over a page and ooohed at a photo of a train.

'What's so special?' Troy asked, trying hard not to look interested.

'Oh,' I said. 'It's nothing. It's just a Shinkansen Bullet Train.'

'Top speed of 186 miles per hour.'

I scanned the page to check if he was right. He was.

'Are you a railway enthusiast, then?' I asked casually.

'Nah.' He pulled the hood of his sweatshirt up over his head and put his elbows on the table. 'That's just wrong.'

Damn. If Brian was going to pass his task he needed to get Troy to admit to his passion for trains. It wasn't looking good.

'Why's it wrong?' I turned over another page and tried to look nonchalant.

'It's for nerds. Check out your man over there.'

Over at the counter Brian was scratching his moustache and staring vacantly into space as Troy's friends pointed at the overhead menus and whispered to each other.

'Fair point,' I said. 'Brian might look like a bit of a nerd, but that doesn't mean we all are.'

Troy raised an eyebrow. 'You into trains then?'

'Absolutely.' I reached for my Diet Coke and sipped it thoughtfully. 'Brian's taught me loads about the railways. He's like a train genius.'

Troy looked from me to Brian and back. 'Is he your husband then?'

Diet Coke shot out of my nose and sprayed Brian's prize magazine.

'Housemate,' I said, dabbing the spattered page with a greasy napkin. 'We're friends.'

Over at the counter, Brian was fishing around in his wallet. I didn't have much time.

'Are your friends into trains?' I asked Troy.

'Nah.' He looked down at the table and batted his mobile from one hand to the other. 'They'd laugh, innit.'

What was the correct answer to that? I wasn't sure.

'Innit,' I ventured, nodding sagely.

'You what?' he said, peering at me from under his hoodie as though I was insane.

My cheeks burned and I glanced over my shoulder. Brian and his new friends were only seconds away from us. I had to be quick.

'Listen,' I said, leaning towards Troy. 'Me and Brian hang out at Paddington Station, up on the bridge. Do you know it?'

He nodded.

'We hang out there a lot, so if you want to come and hang out with us or just have a chat about trains or pick Brian's brains, you're welcome to join us.'

'Dunno, man. I'm pretty busy.'

'Is there a day when you're not busy?' I asked, crossing my fingers under the table.

He shrugged. 'Monday night, maybe?'

'Well, the offer's there,' I said, giving him my best friendly smile. 'It would be, er, wicked, if you showed up.'

'Right, yeah but—'

'S'up man?' interrupted his friend, rounding the table and sitting down. 'Getting fresh with the old bird?'

What? How rude. Since when was I—

'Shut up,' Troy said, reaching across the table. 'Give us a fry, man.'

'Lucy,' Brian hissed as he sat down opposite me. 'What happened? Why did you send me off to get those kids some food?'

I winked at him. 'I'll tell you on the way home.'

Chapter Twenty-eight

Thursday 9th May
Day Thirteen

My hand shook as I opened the door to the office. After the excitement of Brian's task the night before, it was time to get on with *my* task again. And it wasn't looking good. It was day thirteen, Archie was in love with me, and the last thing he'd said was 'Fuck off, Lucy.' Not good. Not good at all.

I took a deep breath and stepped into the office. Archie was curled over his screen, headphones jammed onto his ears. His hair was still short, but his jaw was dark with stubble and the Gamer T-shirt was back. Pissed off Archie: 1 point. Lucy make-over: nil.

'Morning, Archie,' I said, smiling nervously.

The muscles in his jaw clenched, but he didn't reply.

'Hello, SpongeBob,' I said, picking up the little plastic statue from the corner of his desk, determined not to give up. 'How are you?'

'I'm fine thank you, Lucy,' I squeaked in a silly voice, bouncing the cartoon figure in front of Archie's face.

'Don't you think Archie is looking smart toda—'

'Haven't you got some work to do?' he said, snapping off his headphones and glaring up at me.

'Yes,' I squeaked in the SpongeBob voice. 'I mean …' I switched back to my normal voice. '… yes, I do. I'm very busy, in fact. No time to chit-chat.'

I hurried away, weaving through the office until I reached my desk.

'Did you see Archibald?' Nigel said, nudging me the second I sat down.

I ignored him, switched on my computer, and flicked through my Javascript manual. Maybe if I looked studious he'd just go away.

'Hey.' He nudged me again. 'Did you see Archibald's hair?' He was grinning from ear to ear. Idiot. 'Did you see his hair, Lucy?'

'What about Archie's hair?' I snapped.

'Archie, is it now?' He raised an eyebrow. 'Well, *Archie* has only gone and cut all his hair off. The beard's gone too.'

'So?'

'He won't tell us why he did it. Do you know?'

'No idea.'

'Really?'

I slammed the book shut and glared at him. Geoff and Joe had both stopped typing and were, oh-so-casually, listening in to our conversation.

'Why are you so interested in Archie's hair, Nigel?'

He leaned back in his chair and looked from Geoff to Joe. 'Well, it's a bit weird, isn't it? You and Archibald both go off sick yesterday afternoon and then he comes back with a new hairstyle.'

'So what?'

'So ... something going on with you two, Lucy?'

'No. Nothing. Nothing's going on with me and Archie, got it?'

'Oooh!' He pulled a face and pretended to lift a handbag up to his chin. 'No need to be so touchy.'

'Then how about you shut up and let me get on with my work?'

I glared at Geoff and Joe until they withered under my stare and started typing again. Nigel just shrugged and turned back to his monitor. It was going to be a long day.

At lunchtime Nigel, Geoff, Joe and the rest of the office got up and pulled on their coats. They were obviously on their way to the pub but no one had mentioned it to me. Hardly surprising, considering the filthy mood I was in.

As they filed out of the office, Nigel leaned across Archie's desk, pulled back one of his headphones and said something I couldn't hear. Archie shook his head, glanced across at me, but looked away the second our eyes met.

'All right then,' I heard Nigel say. 'I'll see you later.'

And then the office was empty. Apart from Archibald and me.

OK, this was my chance. All I had to do was get up, go across to his desk and have a chat with him. What was the worst that could happen? He could never talk to me again and I'd fail my task? OK, better not think like that. Think on the bright side. Or not at all. Just GO!

'Archie,' I said softly as I approached his desk. 'Could we have a talk about what happened yesterday?'

He was just about to reply when the door to the office swung open.

'Afternoon, fellas,' said Sally, swinging her basket onto the edge of Archie's desk and knocking off his pot of pens. 'Oh, just the two of you, is it? Where's Archibald today?'

'Archibald?' I said, confused. 'What do you mean? He's just ther—'

'Want a sandwich, New Boy?' Sally asked, poking Archie's shoulder with an electric-blue fingernail.

'Sally,' he said, waving up at her. 'It's me!'

'Bloody hell.' Sally jumped so violently she nearly knocked her basket off the desk. 'What happened to you?'

Archie blushed, but said nothing.

'What's this?' she said, fingering his short crop as though it was infected. 'What happened to you?'

'A mistake,' he mumbled. 'A big mistake.'

'I should say. And why the hell would you shave off your beard too? You look weird.'

'Hey,' I said. 'There's no need to be rude.'

'What's it got to do with you, Lucy?' Sally clasped her fingers to her slim hips and stared up at me. For a small woman she could look bloody intimidating when she wanted to.

'I just think you should keep your opinions to yourself, that's all,' I said, taking a step backwards. 'You're making Archibald uncomfortable.'

'I'd say he looked pretty damned uncomfortable anyway.'

'How do you know?'

'Just look at him,' she said, passing her hand over his hair. 'He looks like he's been shorn.'

'Why do you care?'

'Why do you?'

'Stop it,' Archie shouted, jumping to his feet and holding out his hands. 'Stop it, both of you.'

We both stared at him in amazement. Sally even squealed in surprise.

'What is it with women?' Archie said, shaking his head. 'Why do you insist on interfering in my life? If it's not my gran, it's you, Lucy, and now you, Sally. Have I got loser printed on my forehead, or what?'

'You're not a loser, Archibald,' Sally said, quickly regaining her composure. 'But your hair and your beard were part of who you are and I can't understand why you'd want to change.' Her defiant expression had faded and she looked genuinely upset. 'I can't understand it at all.'

'Archie,' I said. 'Can we just talk? Please.'

He looked from me to Sally and back again, then rubbed his face in his hands. He looked exhausted.

'Would you mind leaving, Sally?' he asked. 'Lucy and I need to have a chat.'

'Fine,' she said, glaring at me and snatching her basket off the desk, 'but if she's responsible for your new look, Archibald, I suggest you ignore everything she says.'

The office door slammed shut and Archie and I stared at each other, neither of us saying a word.

Chapter Twenty-nine

Archie was the first to speak. 'Sit down, Lucy,' he said, gesturing to the empty chair at the nearest desk. I wheeled it towards me and sat down, feeling strangely nervous. It wasn't like him to be so forthright.

'Archie,' I said. 'I just wanted to tell you that—'

He held up a hand. 'Could I go first? Please, I'd like to.'

I shrugged. 'Sure.'

He leaned back in his chair and fiddled with his stapler, opening and shutting the lid over and over again. Click-click-click-click.

'I'd like to start by apologising for my behaviour yesterday,' he said. 'I have never sworn at a woman before, Lucy, and it was most unfair and ungentlemanly of me.'

'That's OK, Archie,' I said, digging my heels into the carpet, carving little half moon shapes into the pile.

'I was unusually emotional yesterday and I didn't know how to handle it.'

'Archie—'

'Please.' He held up a hand again. 'Let me finish. I think the reason I acted so unreasonably yesterday was because you touched a nerve when you said you thought I was lonely.'

I opened my mouth to speak, but changed my mind almost immediately and shut it again.

'I was, am, lonely,' Archie continued, 'and when you showed up here for your interview I liked you straightaway, but thought there was no way you'd ever like someone like me. I thought you were out of my league ...'

I wasn't out of anyone's league, especially not Archie's.

'... and then when you got the job and you showed an interest in me it seemed like fate. I thought I was going to be happy, for once. I really believed things were going to change ...'

I felt my mouth fill with saliva, the way it always does right before I cry, and I swallowed hard.

'... but maybe you were right, Lucy. Maybe I was in love with the way I felt when I was around you. I'm just an idiot who is in love with the idea of being in love.'

Archie's voice choked on the word 'love' and I looked up.

'Love is supposed to be a beautiful, amazing experience, Lucy, and I can't think of anything more cruel than falling in love with someone who doesn't love you back.'

That was it, the line that broke me. Tears rolled down my face, curved round my nose and dripped off my jaw. I cried for me, for Dan, and for Archie. I cried because he deserved someone special and he'd fallen in love with me instead. It was all so horribly unfair.

'Lucy,' Archie said softly. 'Lucy, please don't cry. I didn't mean to upset you.'

I shook my head. The lump in my throat was so large I couldn't speak.

'Here,' Archie said, passing me a clean, white handkerchief.

The tenderness of the gesture set me off again and I buried my head in my knees.

'Lucy, please say something. I feel horrible for making you cry.'

'Archie,' I said, swiping at my eyes. Thick, black lines of mascara streaked the handkerchief and I crumpled it up in my hand. I must have looked awful, but I really didn't care. 'You have to believe that I never meant to hurt you. I really, really didn't.'

'I believe you,' he whispered, reaching for my hand.

'And I wish I could tell you why I'm here, but I can't.'

He smiled. 'Because you work here, Lucy.'

'Yes, no, what I mean is ... Oh, I don't know. Archie, there's a reason I got to know you. I really do want to help you find love.'

He pulled away and frowned. 'Why?'

'Think of me as your guardian angel.'

'Now you're being ridiculous.'

'Well yes, kind of, but I can help you, Archie. I know I can.'

'I don't know, Lucy,' he sighed. 'This experience has made me think maybe I'm better off alone.'

'Archie,' I said. 'Can we be friends? Can we at least start there?'

'I'd rather have you as a friend,' he said, looking at me sadly, 'than not at all.'

'Then give me a hug,' I said, holding out my arms.

We wheeled our chairs together and hugged, awkwardly at first, and then more tightly.

'Oi, oi,' said a voice from the doorway. 'What's going on here, then?'

Nigel was an absolute bloody nightmare for the rest of the afternoon. Whenever I stretched, swivelled in my seat or stood up to go to the toilet, he stopped whatever he was doing and stared at me.

'What?' I snapped after the sixth or seventh time I caught him gawping at me.

'Nothing,' he said, feigning indifference. 'Just wondering when you're going to admit that you and Archibald are an item.'

'Read. My. Lips, Nigel. Archie and I are friends, nothing more.'

'So why the tears and hug earlier? Did you dump him? Or did he dump you?'

'Oh, for God's sake.' I sighed. 'Archie and I are not, and never have been, involved. Romantically, or any other way. We're just friends.'

'Then why were you crying?'

'That's none of your business.'

'So you and Archie aren't going to dress up as each other for the fancy dress party tomorrow?'

'What?'

He smirked. 'We have to dress up as our favourite things. Remember?'

'Oh fuck off, Nige.'

I turned back to my screen, desperately wishing I had my own set of headphones to jam onto my ears. Archie and I had agreed to be friends, which was a massive weight off my mind, but I still had plenty to worry about:

1) How I was going to spy on Dan and Anna during their dinner date that evening without being spotted

2) How the hell I was going to find love for Archie when I only had seven full days left

3) Would Troy admit he was a railway enthusiast so Brian could pass his task?

4) What to wear to the bloody fancy dress party

The most urgent thing on the list was spying on Dan and Anna's dinner date. Everything else would have to wait. Anna hadn't said what time they were meeting up, so my plan was to get to the restaurant as early as possible.

I looked around to check no one was watching and surreptitiously sniffed my armpits. Ew, the sprint into work had left me really stinky. There was no point hiding from Dan and Anna if they could smell me coming, I'd have to go home and get changed. I looked at my watch: 5.29 p.m. I'd have to be quick.

Chapter Thirty

I was standing in the shower, singing to myself and lathering my hair with shampoo when Brian's heavy footsteps reverberated on the stairs.

'Lucy,' he shouted, hammering on the bathroom door.

'Yes?' I mumbled, my ears full of suds.

'Sorry to interrupt you, but could I have a quick word?'

'Now? I'm having a shower. Can't it wait?'

'I'm afraid not. It's a bit of an emergency.'

I sighed, dipped my head back under the stream of water, then turned off the shower and stepped out of the tub, wrapping a towel around me.

'What is it?' I said, opening the bathroom door an inch. Cold water dripped down my back and I shivered.

'It's Claire,' Brian said, looking even more frazzled than normal. 'She just called. Apparently she's staging some kind of sit-down protest outside Keith's house. When he threatened to ring the police she snatched his mobile and refused to give it back.'

'You're kidding?'

'I'm afraid not. Claire decided to ring us for back-up when Keith went into his house to ring the police.'

'Back-up? What does she expect us to do?'

'I've got no idea, but we need to get over there ASAP.' Brian's gaze slipped to my cleavage and he coughed violently.

'Brian,' I said, pulling my towel more tightly around me. 'Why are you always so concerned about Claire? Do you fancy her or something?'

'I most certainly do not!' he spluttered. 'She's young and we're all she's got. If we don't help her, who will?'

'Good point.'

'So, are you coming?'

I glanced at his watch. It was already seven o'clock. What if Dan and Anna were already at the restaurant? I didn't want to miss them.

'Well?' Brian said. 'Are you coming or not, because we need to leave *now.*'

'OK,' I said finally. It would be cutting it a bit fine, but there was still a good chance I could get to the restaurant in Swiss Cottage for eight o'clock. 'Just give me a minute to put my clothes back on and dry my hair.'

'Righto,' he said, turning his back to me. 'Be quick.'

I slipped past him, hurried back to my bedroom and reached for my clothes. What on earth was Claire playing at? Saint Bob had told me she was on her last warning and now she was risking her whole task just to piss Keith off. We had to stop her from making an even bigger mistake.

'Brian,' I shouted as I pulled on my boots. 'I'm ready to go.'

Claire was sitting cross-legged on the weed-infested patio of an enormous house in Hampstead. It was bitterly cold and she was shivering, but she didn't take her eyes off the black front door for one second, not even when we crunched our way across the gravelled driveway towards her.

'Claire,' I said, crouching down beside her. 'Are you OK?'

She shook her head.

'Do you want my waterproof?' asked Brian, slipping an arm out of his coat. 'It's cold out here.'

Claire shook her head again, her eyes still fixed on the house. Thin curtains hung at the windows but you could make out the shapes of people moving around behind them.

'Why are you doing this?' I asked, easing myself onto the gravel. I gestured for Brian to sit down, but he shook his head.

'Because,' Claire said, inching away from me, 'there's no way I'm going to pass my task, so I thought I'd just take my revenge now, while I can.'

'How is this revenge? You're shivering your arse off and Keith is warm and cosy inside the house.'

'He's got a groupie in there with him,' she said, pulling her crocheted jumper over her fingers. 'She's been with him since last night, the slut. I'm waiting for her to come out.'

'You've been here since last night? Shit, Claire.'

'What do you care?'

'I thought we were past all that "I hate you" stuff now,' I said, resisting the urge to snap back at her. 'I thought we were friends.'

'Great friend you are.' She tucked an errant dreadlock behind her ear. 'I haven't seen you for days.'

She was right. What with everything that had been going on with my task and Brian's, I hadn't given her a second thought.

'I'm sorry,' I said, shoving my freezing fingers between my thighs. 'I had a lot on.'

'Of course you did.'

'So,' I said, ignoring her sarcastic tone, 'when did Keith discover you were out here?'

'About half an hour ago. His slut opened the door to the pizza delivery boy and noticed me sitting here.'

'Then what happened?'

'Keith came out,' she said, pulling her knees to her chest and tucking her hands under her armpits, 'and asked me why the hell I was sitting outside his house. When I didn't say anything he pulled his mobile out of his back pocket and said he was going to call the police. That's when I snatched it and called you guys.'

'Ahem.' Brian, who still had one arm in his jacket, the rest of it dangling behind him, had wandered over to the gate. 'Talking of police ...'

'Run,' Claire shouted, jumping up and dragging me after her. 'Run!'

*

245

We were all panting as we piled into the White Horse and draped ourselves over the bar.

'Dogs after you, are they?' asked the barman, raising an eyebrow.

'No.' Claire said. 'The police. Three pints of snake-bite, please.'

The barman nodded as though he'd heard it all before, and reached under the counter for three pint glasses. I was about to protest and ask for a white wine instead, but Brian nudged me and shook his head.

'Just drink it,' he mouthed.

'Did you really see a police car?' I whispered, leaning closer.

'No.' He grinned. 'But it got her moving, didn't it?'

Wily old fox. He was a lot more clued-up than I, or anyone else, gave him credit for.

'Come on,' Claire said, pushing a pint across the bar towards me. 'Let's sit down.'

We settled around a table in the corner of the room and slouched into our seats. Brian and I sipped at our revolting drinks but Claire ignored hers and stared into space, her face even paler than normal.

'Are you OK?' I asked, tentatively touching her shoulder, half-expecting her to bite my fingers, and then my head, right off.

'No,' she said in a small, croaky voice. 'No, I'm not.'

When she reached out for her pint, her fingers shook and her nails tap-tap-tapped against the glass. A single tear welled in her right eye and dripped down her cheek.

'Claire!' I said, horrified. I instinctively reached out and pulled her towards me. 'Oh, Claire, please don't cry.'

To my surprise, she didn't push me away or tell me to fuck off or anything. She just lay in my arms and let me hug her while she sobbed. Brian, who was still sipping his pint, looked everywhere but straight at us. He wasn't the only one weirded out by Claire's vulnerable side. I was in shock.

'It'll be OK, Claire,' I said, pushing her dreadlocks back from her face.

'It won't,' she mumbled, pulling away from me. 'I thought he'd miss me, but he didn't even notice I'd gone.'

'Who?'

'Keith, of course. Who did you think I meant?'

Oh God. She didn't just fancy Keith. She didn't just admire his musicianship or care about him because he was a sensitive poet who volunteered at a dog's home. She ...

'You love him.' I said. 'That's why you decided to do a task, isn't it? Not because you wanted revenge, but because you wanted to be near him.'

'Yes,' she said, pushing her hair back from her face and tying one of the extensions around the rest so they were all bundled together at the back of her head. With her make-up smudged, she looked impossibly young.

'But he was so awful to you,' I said. 'He slept with other women and laughed at you behind your back. How can you love a man like that?'

'Because he's the only man that's ever wanted me.'

'What do you mean?'

'Becoshewasonlymanislepwi',' she mumbled, hiding her face in her hands.

'What?' I leaned closer. 'You'll have to say that again. I didn't hear you.'

'Because he's the only man I've ever slept with.'

'Just going to the loo,' Brian said, standing up suddenly and spilling our pints all over the table.

I watched as he crashed through the drinkers congregated in the middle of the bar and disappeared into the Gents'.

'Claire,' I said, looking back at her, a smile on my face. 'I think you scared Brian off with the sex talk.'

Claire rubbed her face against her hands and sat back up. 'You can laugh at me now if you want.'

What was there to laugh about? She was eighteen years old. She'd slept with one person, fallen in love with him, and then killed herself because he'd slept with someone else. It was probably the most heart-breaking story I'd ever heard and, for the first time since I'd died, I realised that if there was a time machine that we could use to rewind to before we died, I'd put Claire in it, rather than me.

I was seventeen when I lost my virginity. I was so keen to get rid of it I practically threw it at the first bloke who showed an interest in me. He worked on the 'throw a dart, win a prize' stall on Brighton Pier and had called out, 'All right, gorgeous girl in the blue,' when I'd walked past with some friends. I'd automatically turned to my friends to see which one of them he was talking about, but then realised I was the only one wearing blue. I was only seventeen and no one had ever called me gorgeous before. He was in his twenties, dark-haired and handsome, and cocky with it so I wandered over to say hello. He told me he was a Sports Science student from the university and was just working the stall to make some money during the summer holidays. We didn't really go on any dates before we slept together, I just hung out at his stall in the evenings and chatted to him as he worked. After three weeks I was so desperate to kiss him and get rid of my wretched virginity, I happily agreed when he suggested we have 'a bit of a lie-down' on the pebbles under the pier. The act itself was over fairly quickly and, although he promised we'd go on a date the next day, he ignored me when I turned up at his stall the next evening. I returned the following day and he told me that he'd decided to go back to his parents' house in Leeds for the last few weeks of the holiday and that, while it was lovely to have spent time with me, he couldn't really see a relationship between a twenty-year-old and a seventeen-year-old working out long-term. I was heartbroken, of course, more by the rejection than anything else, but I got over it in time.

'No, Claire,' I said, shaking off the memory and smiling supportively at her. 'I'm not going to laugh at you. But why did you lose your virginity to Keith? Why him, of all men?'

She smiled and reached for the pint Brian was

holding out. He'd returned to the table with fresh drinks and was looking decidedly flushed. I strongly suspected he'd downed a couple of whiskies at the bar before coming back.

'I heard the Lust Boys on the radio one night when I was at college,' Claire said, taking a sip of her drink, 'and the lyrics really moved me. It was like they'd been written just for me, you know? They were about being lonely and isolated and I really felt like, if me and whoever wrote them ever met, we'd understand each other.'

'So what happened then?' asked Brian, looking much more comfortable now the conversation appeared to have switched from sex to personal passions.

'Well,' said Claire, fiddling with the silver skull ring on her right hand, 'there was a girl in the sixth form that I got on with, the only girl I got on with; she was a goth too, so I asked her if she'd be interested in going to a gig with me. She was, so we went along.'

'And then you met Keith?'

'No, not at that first gig, but seeing him in person was amazing. When he screamed out the lyrics to the song I'd heard on the radio, I felt like he was singing to me.'

'So when did you sleep together for the first time?' I asked.

She grinned. 'After the fourth gig I went to. I told my friend I wanted to hang around outside and wait for Keith to come out, but she didn't want to. We ended up having a massive argument and she stormed off, so

I had to wait on my own. After twenty minutes, one of the roadies came out, so I asked him if the band was still around. He just looked me up and down and grinned.'

'And?' I said.

'And' – Claire swigged back her drink – 'I said I'd give him twenty quid if he could arrange for me to meet Keith. He took the money, loaded a drum into the back of the white van that was parked outside the venue, and told me to wait inside.'

'The van?'

'Yeah.'

'You didn't get in, did you?' I stared at her in disbelief. 'Claire, he could have been some kind of twisted pervert.'

'I didn't care,' she said, shrugging. 'Anyway, after a bit the doors opened and there was Keith, swaying and grinning at me. He said, "I heard you wanted to meet me, young lady," and crawled into the van and shut the doors after him.'

'And then you had sex?'

'Toilet,' said Brian, fleeing his seat.

'No, not straightaway.' Claire paused to nibble her black nail varnish and then looked back up at me. 'First I told him how much his song had meant to me and then I started gushing about how lonely I was and how no one understood me, and Keith just kept stroking my hair and telling me how lovely I was. Then we just started kissing—'

'And one thing led to another?'

'Yeah.'

'Oh, Claire.'

'What? I wanted him to. OK, so we were in the back of a grubby old van and my head kept knocking against the drum case, but it was special to me. I didn't feel like fatty Claire. I felt beautiful and sexy. I was the woman the lead singer of one of London's biggest up-and-coming bands wanted to sleep with. It was amazing. I thought if I auditioned for the band, I could be part of his life …' She tailed off and stared wistfully across the room.

I stared down at the table and traced a finger through the spilt beer. It wasn't amazing, it was awful. I couldn't help thinking that if Claire had just felt a bond with someone other than Keith, if she'd lost her virginity to someone who really was sensitive and caring and didn't just put it on as an act to pull groupies, she'd still be alive.

'What are you going to do now?' I asked, reaching across the table and squeezing her hand.

Claire shrugged. 'Dunno. I had an argument with the girl I was supposed to be teaching the guitar to and she won't take my phone calls any more. Fat chance of getting her into a band now. That was my task, by the way, but I've failed it and no one's ever going to love me or miss me now.'

'That's not true,' I said, suddenly remembering the phone call I'd had with Saint Bob. 'You've still got a second chance to find someone special.'

'What do you mean?' she asked, her eyes wide.

'In heaven. When I spoke to Bob the other day he told me people fall in love up there too. Just because you're dead doesn't mean you have to spend eternity all on your own.'

Claire's face lit up like a child's on Christmas Day and we grinned inanely at each other for all of five seconds before she looked down and fiddled with the hem of her black jumper.

'I'm sorry,' she mumbled.

'What for?'

'For winding you up about Dan when you first got here. I was just jealous. I wanted what you've got.'

'Had, Claire,' I said sadly. 'What we had.'

'Yes. Anyway, I'm really sorry. I was a real bitch.'

I reached for my pint, my mind slightly foggy, and took a sip. Dan. She'd mentioned Dan's name and an alarm bell had gone off in my head. What was I supposed to be—

Shit.

Dan and Anna were meeting for dinner and I'd forgotten all about it. I glanced at my watch. It was half past nine.

'Claire,' I said, squeezing her hand quickly, then letting it go. 'I'm really sorry but I've got to leave. I'll explain it to you later, but there's something I have to do.'

'You go, Lucy,' she said, smiling across at me with genuine warmth. 'Really. Go. I can tell it's important. Don't worry. Brian will look after me.'

I stood up. I really, really needed to leave, but I was

still worried about her. 'Are you sure? You're not going to do anything stupid?'

'No,' she laughed. 'I promise. Now, bugger off, Toga Girl. And good luck.'

Good luck? I suddenly felt sick. I was only going to spy on Dan and Anna. What did I need good luck for? It was just two friends having dinner. Wasn't it?

Chapter Thirty-one

'Excuse me,' I said, bursting through the door of Kung Po's restaurant and grabbing the first waitress I saw. 'I'm here to meet friends – Dan Harding and Anna Cowan. Have they been in yet?'

'In a group or a table for two?' the waitress said, twisting her wrist out of my hand and glaring at me.

'Just the two of them.'

'No couple here now.' She held out her hands to show the empty seats all around us. 'Last one just left.'

'But—'

She dismissed me with a curt nod of her head and turned to go.

'Are there any couples booked for later this evening?' I darted in front of her, nearly knocking over the Chinese dragon that balanced precariously on a column in the middle of the room, and blocked her path to the kitchen. 'Please check. Please, it's important.'

'No couple,' she said, her black, beady eyes taking in my rain-damp hair and grubby shoes. 'Table for eight booked for ten and that's it.'

'Can you describe the people who left?' I asked

desperately. 'Was the man tall and dark-haired and the girl blonde?'

The waitress shrugged. 'Maybe. Maybe not. Many couple come and go. I'm waitress, not freakin' Colombo.'

She was as much help as a rice-paper umbrella, and talking to her was wasting valuable time.

'Thanks for your help,' I said, hurrying back out of the door, the bell tinkling behind me as I stepped onto the wet street.

Where had Dan and Anna gone? If I'd just missed them maybe I could catch them up. I looked left and right, searching for clues. The tube station was a couple of metres to the right of where I was standing and the bus stop was over the road. Anna lived near Baker Street underground and couldn't stand travelling by bus, so she'd have gone home by tube and Dan would have taken a bus, or maybe a cab. But what if they hadn't gone home at all? What if they'd gone on to a pub in the West End or something? I'd never find them. I was too late.

I pulled my thin jacket around me and shivered. The rain was getting heavier and I needed somewhere to gather my thoughts before I headed back to the House of Wannabe Ghosts. I sprinted across the road to the bus stop and squeezed against the mass of shivering students sheltering from the rain. Cars splashed through deep puddles, drenching anyone daring to walk on the pavement. People were hiding under anything and everything they could find. Even the entrance to the tube station was crowded, but one woman was determined to get out into the rain. I watched as she elbowed people out of her way and tottered down the street, her handbag held over her very straight, very blonde hair.

It was Anna!

And she was going into Kung Po's.

I sprinted back across the street, dodging cars and motorbikes, and hovered outside the clothes shop next door as my heart thumped in my chest. Why had Anna gone into the restaurant? Maybe the waitress had lied to me and there *was* a reservation for a couple at ten o'clock. Was Dan on his way too?

I was just about to slip into the restaurant when Kung Po's doorbell tinkled again and Anna stepped back out onto the street, her mobile clamped to her ear.

'Jess,' she was saying. 'Sorry I missed your call. I was out with Dan and I only went and bloody left my mobile on the table. I was halfway to Baker Street when I remembered.'

There was a pause as Jess answered.

'Hang on,' Anna interrupted. 'It's absolutely pissing down. Give me a sec, OK? Don't go anywhere. I've got so much to tell you.'

She hurried off, her high heels clattering on the wet pavement and I followed behind, my head down. When I passed a bin stuffed full with free newspapers, I grabbed one and held it in front of my face, angling it so I could still see Anna's pencil-thin heels striding ahead of me as she walked into Swiss Cottage tube station and leaned up against a wall. I squeezed myself between two ticket machines, close enough to hear the conversation Anna had resumed with Jess, but far enough away that she wouldn't immediately notice the dripping wet girl standing in a puddle of rainwater with her nose in a discarded newspaper.

'Yes,' Anna was saying. 'Actually, Dan seemed much chirpier than the last time I saw him and he seemed genuinely interested in what I had to say ... No, he didn't mention Lucy ...'

My heart sunk. Dan didn't mention me once during a meal? Not once?

'Yeah,' Anna said. 'I think that's a good sign too. Jess, if I tell you something, do you promise you won't over-react? Promise? I think Dan was flirting with me ...'

I nearly dropped my newspaper. What?! WHAT?!

'When I tried to top up his wine glass he put his hand on mine to stop me pouring so much. I protested, of course, and he gave me this look .... Yes, *that kind* of look and he didn't look away ... I actually had butterflies, Jess.'

I lowered my newspaper and glared at her. What the hell was she playing at? Any look Dan may have given her would have been a 'stop trying to get me as pissed as you' look. We both used to laugh at how drunk Anna liked to get. The only thing was, she didn't like getting pissed on her own. Everyone else had to join in, whether they liked it or not.

'Why did I have butterflies?' she continued. 'Because

258

Dan's Lucy's fiancé, *was* Lucy's fiancé, and I couldn't understand what was he doing flirting with me, but there was a spark between us, Jess, a real connection …Yes I did flirt back … No, no, it's not like that, Jess. I didn't want anything like this to happen, honestly, you know that … Jess, hang on a minute, let me speak … I only met up with Dan because I was trying to comfort him. I didn't have any ulterior motives.'

She fell silent as, I assumed, Jess asked her what the hell she thought she was playing at. I couldn't see Anna's reaction because her back was to me, but her shoulders slumped and she looked like she was sighing. Sighing? She didn't have a reason to sigh. She'd been flirting with my boyfriend. Where was her loyalty to me? She was supposed to be my best friend.

'Jess,' she said. 'Jess, don't be angry with me, but I think I'm falling in love with Dan and I'm pretty sure he feels the same way. I want him to be the father of my child.'

Something inside me snapped. All I could feel was blind rage and a pain in my chest as I charged up to Anna and shoved her with all of my strength. She gasped and stumbled backwards, grabbing at the wall. I pushed her again and she fell to the floor, her mobile clattering beside her.

'What's your fucking problem?' she shouted, grabbing her mobile and bag from the grubby tube floor and scrabbling to her feet.

I opened my mouth to reply, then shut it again, Saint Bob's warning ringing in my ears. If I said even one word to Anna, my task would be cancelled.

'I know who you are,' she said, looking me up and down. She was smiling, but her eyes were cold. 'You're that mute freak that's been stalking Dan. I don't know if you've taken a look in the mirror recently, darling, but he's way out of your league. Oh, and your line in conversation is a little … how can I put it? Lacking.'

I raised my arm to slap her, but she grabbed my wrist.

'I wouldn't,' she said, pushing the hair out of her eyes. 'I think you've done enough damage already, don't you? Now, do excuse me while I go and see Dan and tell him what a freak you are.' She smirked. 'Game over, loser. I win.'

I watched helplessly as she tossed her bag over her shoulder and sashayed towards the exit. 'By the way,' she said, turning back, 'he's a fantastic shag.'

Chapter Thirty-two

Friday 10th May
Day Fourteen

'Lucy … Lucy … Lucy … wake up,' said a gentle male voice.

I rolled over and pulled the duvet over my head. 'Go away, Dan. I hate you.'

'Lucy,' the voice said, more insistently. 'It's nine o'clock. You're supposed to be at work.'

'And you're supposed to be in love with me, you bastard.'

I felt the duvet being pulled from my head and I lashed out. 'Fuck off.'

'Fuck off yourself, Lucy,' said a woman's voice. 'We're only trying to help.'

Who the hell was in my bedroom?

I rolled over and opened one eye a crack. My house-mates were standing beside my bed; Brian was rubbing his moustache, Claire was twisting one of her dreads round and round her finger.

'You OK, Lucy?' she said, looking at me with concern.

I put a hand to my head. It felt like someone was chiselling away at the left side of my skull.

'My head hurts,' I said.

Claire raised her eyebrows. 'I'm not surprised. Your arse probably hurts too.'

'What?' I reached under the covers, pressed one of my bum cheeks and gasped with pain. 'What happened to me?'

'You were very, very drunk when you came home,' Brian said, releasing his moustache and crossing his arms. 'You could hardly stand.'

'And you fell down the stairs,' Claire added. 'Twice.'

I rubbed my eyes. They felt swollen and sore and, no matter how hard I tried, I couldn't open them more than a few millimetres.

'Did I fall on my eyes as well?'

'No,' Claire said, 'but you did cry, a lot.'

I swallowed. My throat felt as though I'd gargled sand. 'Did I shout a lot too?'

Claire and Brian looked at each other. 'Yes,' they said in unison. 'A lot.'

'You were very, very pissed off with some woman called Anna,' Claire added.

Anna? What had she ... the memory of the night before rushed back in a flash; the rain, Anna's phone call, her revelation, our fight, and the evil look in her eyes when she'd told me Dan was a great shag. Dan. My Dan. A great shag. My eyes filled with hot, angry tears. How could he have done that to me? HOW?

He'd claimed he'd be devastated if anything happened to me, but I'd only been dead for five minutes and he was already sleeping with one of my best friends. I'd never have shagged one of his mates if things were reversed and he'd died first. Never. What the hell was he thinking?

I'd gone straight to the pub after my fight with Anna, not the White Lion (I didn't want to risk running into anyone I knew), but to the first pub I found. I must have downed three or four foul-coloured shots of God-knows-what, before I ordered a bottle of wine and sat in a corner and drank it all by myself. I couldn't remember anything after that. I couldn't remember making my way home, letting myself in, or anything Claire and Brian had just described. I felt suddenly, horribly, nauseous.

'Here,' Brian said, whipping a bucket out from under the bed. 'You might need this, again.'

'Oh God,' said Claire, jumping back and wrinkling her nose. 'Please don't.'

I gripped the bucket and heaved but nothing came out.

'Did I tell you what happened?' I asked as I placed it back on the floor.

'Yes,' they said in unison. 'Several times.'

I grimaced. 'Sorry.'

'Are you going to work today?' Brian said, glancing at his watch. 'Or would you like us to call in sick for you?'

'No thanks,' I said, rubbing my aching head. ' I have

to go in. I'm going to find love for Archie if it kills me, no pun intended. There is no way I'm going to let Anna get her claws into Dan. No fucking way.'

Brian raised his eyebrows. He'd heard me swear more in the last five minutes than in the previous two weeks, but I really didn't care.

'Lucy.' Claire perched on the edge of the bed and tapped me on the leg. 'If there's anything you need us to do to help, we'll be here for you. Both of us.'

Brian nodded vigorously. 'Absolutely.'

'Thanks, guys.' I smiled up at the two of them.

'Oh,' said Claire, handing me a plastic bag full of what looked like netting and lace. 'Don't forget to take this to work with you.'

'What is it?' I asked, peering inside.

'Just a few of my things. When you weren't screaming about Anna last night, you were ranting on about some work thing that's happening today?'

'What work thing?'

'No idea,' Claire said. 'All you kept saying was, "I have to be Madonna. I have to be Madonna."'

I looked at her blankly. Why would I want to be Madonna?

Archie welcomed me to work with a massive smile. 'Afternoon. Nice of you to join us. You're a very radiant shade of green, if I may say so.'

I squeezed out a smile. 'I think I drank my body weight in alcohol last night.'

'You didn't get drunk because of what happened between us, did you?' Archie said, his smile slipping.

'No, no.' I shook my head. 'Nothing to do with that.'

'I'm glad, because I really do want us to be friends.'

'We are friends, Archie. Only my friends can get away with telling me how rough I look without being swiped round the head.'

He grinned. 'Good, because you look dog-awful.'

I pretended to clip him round the head, but my stomach lurched horribly. I needed to sit down quickly or risk throwing up over Archie's ultra-neat desk.

'See you later,' I said as I staggered across the office. 'Mine's a strong coffee.'

It was only when I slumped into my chair that I noticed Nigel wasn't wearing his normal jeans and T-shirt uniform. He was dressed in a thick, brown cloak with a hood almost obscuring his face.

I nudged him. 'Why are you dressed up like Friar Tuck?'

'Obi-Wan,' he said, peering at his monitor.

'Huh? Who won what?'

'Lucy,' he said, looking at me like I was the thickest person on the planet, 'I. Am. Dressed. Up. As. Obi -Wan Kenobi. From *Star Wars*? Fancy dress day. Remember?'

I looked down at the bag on my lap and pulled out a couple of raggy pieces of lace. One of them looked like a top, another was a pair of fishnets. In the bottom was my denim miniskirt and several rosaries and crucifixes that definitely didn't belong to me. Of course, it was fancy dress day. Other than karaoke, my favourite thing in the world was Madonna, circa 1987. Good old Claire.

'You might want to get changed into your hooker outfit now,' Nigel said. 'Graham will have a spazz if he notices you haven't got changed.'

'What about Graham and Archie?' I said, ignoring the hooker comment. 'They're wearing their normal clothes.'

Nigel shrugged. 'Graham will get changed later. He always leaves it until the last minute, but Archie had better get changed ASAP. He knows the consequences.'

'Which are?'

'You'll find out later. Now, go and get changed.'

Getting changed in the stuffy ladies' loos was such a bad idea. I was sick twice and took deep breaths as I tottered back to my desk in my ridiculously high, black ankle boots, crucifixes clanking around my neck and the lacy vest top slipping off my shoulder.

'Looking very slutty there, Miss Brown,' Nigel said as I sat down.

'Actually, I'm supposed to be Madonna, you ignoramus.'

'Yeah? In which gothic universe?'

'Oh shut up, Cape Head,' I said, swiping at his head. 'What would you know?'

I peered at my screen and started to type, but was distracted by the feeling that someone was staring me.

I swivelled round in my seat. Archie grinned at me from across the room.

'What?' I mouthed.

'Nothing,' he said and shook his head.

I was relieved we'd sorted things out after our little chat the day before. Archie seemed more comfortable around me and had stopped gazing at me with a woeful 'I think I love you' look. But there was still one major problem – I only had six days left to find him love.

I stared at my monitor, my finger poised over the mouse. Now what? Dating sites were out. It would take at least a week to register, write Archie's profile, wait for someone to show an interest in him, swap emails and arrange a date. And we didn't have a week! I typed 'dating in London' into the browser and examined the possibilities.

Find love in your lunch hour? No, it sounded a bit like speed-dating and look how well that went last time!

Gay and Lesbian dating? No.

London Escorts? Absolutely not. I needed to find Archie love, not a quick leg-over.

Webcam dating? No, Archie would be too shy (and there was a danger he'd bore his date to death talking about the technical specifications of her webcam).

What I needed was to find somewhere where Archie would feel at ease and fit in. I clicked from site to site, scanning the pages until, finally, something caught my eye – *DJ Kirk's dating party*.

Kirk ... my mind starting racing. Why did Kirk ring a bell? No, not a bell, more of a whooshing sound. A sci fi whooshing sound. Aha! Captain Kirk. From *Star Trek*. Of course. Archie had told me he loved that programme. Maybe it was something to do with *Star Trek* that he could get involved in? There were bound to be female fans of *Star Trek*. In fact, Jess had once drunkenly admitted to having a bit of a crush on Jean Luc Picard. I'd ribbed her mercilessly about it for weeks.

I typed 'Star Trek convention' into Google and crossed my fingers. My eyes scanned the page and ... Yes! ... there was one and it was scheduled for the weekend. It had to be fate.

Archie grinned at me as I sauntered up to his desk, my crucifixes clanging like church bells.

'Nice outfit, Lucy,' he said, raising an eyebrow. 'Are you supposed to be a hook —'

'I'm Madonna.'

'Right. Of course. Silly me.'

'So where's your costume?'

He shrugged. 'I haven't got one.'

'Why not?' I lowered my voice to a whisper. 'You know there's a forfeit for worst or no costume, don't you?'

'Of course I know,' Archie said, not looking the slightest bit bothered. 'I've worked here for three years. I'm just tired of people telling me what to do.'

I hoped that wasn't a dig about me giving him a make-over.

'No, no,' he said immediately, reading the expression on my face. 'I'm not talking about you. I've just realised that I need to learn to stand up for myself and take responsibility for my own life.'

'Well, good on you,' I said, approving of my friend's new, feisty attitude. 'By the way, what are you up to this weekend?'

'Nothing in particular,' he said, shaking his head. 'Why?'

'It's a surprise, but you'll love it. Trust me.'

'I trusted you once before, remember.' Archie ran a hand through his hair and winked at me. 'And I ended up getting shorn like a sheep.'

I picked a paperclip up off the desk and threw it at him. 'It's better than the scraggy mess you had before. Anyway, you'll love what I've got planned for tomorrow. Meet me at Edgware Road at 10 a.m.'

'Edgware Road tube at 10 a.m.' he said, tapping the information into his personal organiser. 'You're on.'

I grinned at him and tottered back to my desk feeling very pleased with myself. I just knew he was going to love the *Star Wars* convention.

'Sandwich?' said a chirpy voice in my ear.

I jumped and typed s*dlsflkds* into the *Star Trek* convention booking form.

'Sandwich, Miss Brown?' the voice said again and I looked up.

Sally was standing beside my desk, looking particularly eye-catching in her brightly embroidered jeans, blue tutu, pink trainers and tight pink vest top with a butterfly on the front. She also had a pair of fairy wings strapped to her back.

'What do you want?' she asked, waving her basket dangerously close to my head.

'Cheese and ham baguette please, if you've got one left,' I said, hitting the delete button and typing mine and Archie's names into the form.

'Are you and Archie going to a *Star Trek* convention?' Sally said, peering over my shoulder.

I shot her a look. 'Yes, and keep your bloody voice down, it's supposed to be a surprise.'

'So what is it?' she asking, putting my sandwich on the desk and holding out her hand for the money. 'Some kind of penance for cutting off all his hair?'

'Oh ha ha.' I placed two pounds fifty in her palm, fervently wishing she'd flutter her little fairy wings and fly off.

'Thanks.' She turned to go, then glanced back, looked me up and down and wrinkled her nose. 'Why are you dressed as a stripper, Lucy?'

I rolled my eyes. Was everyone in the office too young to remember Madonna in her pre-disco days?

'Because,' I sighed, 'my very favourite things in the world are strippers.'

'Each to their own.' She shrugged. 'Can you guess what I am?'

'Some girl band member?' I ventured.

'No.'

'A fairy?'

'Close but no.'

270

'I give up. What are you?'

'I'm a bratz.'

Wow. That was brave, admitting she was a brat. Maybe I should have dressed as an undead, completely crap matchmaker. Then I could have just turned up in my own clothes.

'I don't think you're a brat,' I said. 'A little bit loud, maybe, but not a brat.'

'A Bratz, you idiot,' Sally said, stamping one of her big pink trainers on the grey carpet. 'Jade in her Fashion Pixies look, if you must know.'

'Oh, right.' I still had no idea what she was on about. 'You look great.'

'Do I look sexy?' She grinned and shimmied on the spot. The fairy wings on her back sparkled as they wobbled from side to side.

'Um, sure.'

'Great. That's what I was hoping,' she squealed, then skipped across the room and smacked her basket against the head of her next sandwich victim.

I turned back to my form, freaking out when I realised that they only accepted online credit card bookings. All my bank cards had mysteriously disappeared from my purse when I'd arrived in the House of Wannabe Ghosts, but I still had plenty of cash left (another two hundred pounds magically reappeared every time I got down to my last pound). I'd have to ring the hotline.

'Hello,' I whispered. 'I really want tickets for the *Star Trek* convention this weekend, but there's a problem with my bank card. Can I pay by cash instead?'

'Yes,' the helpline guy hissed, as though he'd answered the same question a million times before. 'If you come to the box office before six o'clock today. Any later and you miss out.'

'Right,' I said. 'By six o'clock. OK, no problem.'

I put the phone down and looked at my watch. It was half past one and it didn't look like the fancy dress party was going to start any time soon. But it didn't matter. I had to get those tickets, no matter what.

At 2 p.m. the office suddenly went dark. I glanced at Nigel but he didn't look the slightest bit perturbed.

'Why have the lights gone off?' I hissed. 'I can't see a thing.'

He removed his headphones. 'Were you talking to me?'

'Yes,' I sighed, 'that's why I was looking at you and my lips were moving. Why have the lights gone off?'

'Office fancy dress party is about to begin.'

'In the dark?'

'There will be light.' He smirked. 'Don't you worry.'

I stared around the room, half-expecting my co-workers to jump up and explode party poppers, but everyone was still attached to their computers, their fingers frantically tapping away at their keyboards, eyes fixed to the screen. The only sign it wasn't a normal working day were the outfits. I was particularly impressed by the guy across the room who was dressed as a kebab with chilli sauce dripping down his face (either that or he'd been in a terrible road traffic accident on the way to work). But even he was flicking through a book, casually picking his nose.

I looked back at Nigel, but he'd put his headphones back on.

'Nige,' I said, poking him in the side with a ruler until he took them off again. 'We're having a party and no one's excited. I don't get it.'

He sighed. 'When you've worked here as long as we have, Lucy, you don't look forward to the annual fancy dress party, you fear it.'

I pulled a face at him. How bad could a party be, for God's sake? Anything had to be better than slogging away at a computer all day, surely? I was just about to tell Nigel as much when the room suddenly flashed orange, red, blue and green. Disco lights had magically appeared on Graham's desk and cheesy house music exploded from a very expensive-looking stereo beside them. Graham himself was standing behind his desk, grinning from ear to ear.

'Gentlemen and ladies,' he shouted, turning the music down and clapping his hands.

Ladies? There was only me, wasn't there? Ah, maybe not. Sally was squatting down next to Archie's desk, chatting animatedly and waving her hands around.

'Ladies and gentlemen,' Graham said again, 'the party will begin in precisely five to ten minutes, once I've changed into my outfit. Then we'll party and I'll judge who is wearing the best and worst outfits. Joe will now circulate through the office with the charity bucket. Please give generously.'

When no one said anything he turned the music back up and strode out of the office. Joe, who was dressed as Dracula, eased himself out of his seat and dangled a yellow bucket in front of my face.

'Contribution please, Lucy,' he sighed. 'Five pound minimum for getting to dress like a twat for a day.'

'If you all hate it so much,' I said, dropping a handful of coins into the bucket, 'why don't you say something?'

'Graham owns the company, Lucy,' Nigel said, reaching into his wallet. 'What he says goes. If you don't like it, you're out. Simple as that.'

I turned off my monitor. Crap party or no crap party, I wasn't going to do any more work. 'But he can't fire you for objecting to a fancy dress party, that's not—'

There was a loud knock at the door to the office.

'That'll be Graham,' Nigel said. 'You should stand up, Lucy. You'll want a good look at this.'

I eased myself out of my seat and looked warily in the direction of the office door as it swung open.

OH MY BLOODY GOD.

Graham Wellington, at least I was fairly certain it was him, was leaning up against the doorway. He was wearing a black leather choker, a pair of black rubber shorts, a pair of biker boots, a chain mail vest that revealed his very pert, very pierced, nipples and a mass of ginger chest hair, and … I swallowed hard … a black rubber mask covering his entire head.

And he wasn't alone.

He was holding a leather dog lead in his hand. It was attached to a collar worn by a short, slim, heavily made-up woman with waist-length black hair. She tot-tered into the room in a pair of impossibly high heels, a red and black basque and red knickers.

I turned to look at Nigel, my mouth opening and closing like a hooked fish.

'What ... the ... hell ... is ... that?' I squealed.

'That, Miss Brown,' Nigel grinned, 'is your boss demonstrating his favourite thing.'

'Making me throw up into my own mouth?'

Nigel laughed. 'S&M. He wore a similar outfit last year, but the woman on a lead – that's new.'

'Who is she?'

'God knows.'

I watched, fascinated and horrified at the same time, as Graham strutted into the centre of the office and gestured to Joe to turn the music down. Dog Lead Woman grinned and tottered after him as though being led into an office on a leash was the most normal thing in the world. It was the singularly most bizarre thing I'd ever seen in my life. And death.

'So,' Graham bellowed, the rubber on his face stretching and distorting as he opened his mouth. 'Time for the vote for best costume. To be quite honest, the majority of you have made sod-all effort. That said, I think there are three contenders for the crown. First, I'd like to nominate Mark for his kebab, at least I think it's a kebab and not a giant vagina. Secondly, I'd like to nominate myself. And thirdly, I'd like to nominate Miss Lucy Brown for her splendidly slutty outfit.'

I gasped and clutched at my crucifixes. Nigel sniggered.

'Anyone have any alternative nominations?' Graham asked.

No one said a word.

'Nominations for worst outfit then?' he continued. 'I nominate Archibald for making no bloody effort whatsoever. Anyone else?'

Again, no one said a word. Archie, standing next to Sally by the door, looked at his feet.

'OK,' Graham said. 'Time to vote. Who votes for Mark?'

Mark and the guy who sat next to him raised their hands.

'So that's two for Mark's vagina kebab. Who votes for Lucy Sluttypants?'

Archie, Sally, Nigel, Joe and Geoff all raised their hands. So did a couple of guys on the other side of the office. I glared at them.

'And votes for me and the lovely Miss Whiplash here?'

My hand shot into the air, as did pretty much everyone else's. I crossed my fingers and did a quick head count. Please let there be more for him than me, please, please.

Graham counted hands and unleashed a dazzling smile. 'I win. Ha!'

'No surprise there,' Nigel whispered. 'He wins every year.'

'Because I'm such a nice man,' Graham said,

scratching one of his exposed nipples, 'I'm going to share the prize with you. Six bottles of champagne. Bring out the plastic cups please. The loser will do his forfeit later on this afternoon.'

Shit. I'd missed out on six bottles of quality champagne. I should have been encouraging people to vote for me, not glaring at them, but Nigel had made such a big deal out of the forfeit for the loser that I'd assumed the winner's prize would be awful too. I turned to Nigel to tell him as much, but was immediately drowned out by the thump-thump-thump of the music Graham had just turned back up.

'Champagne?' asked Kebab-Mark, proffering a plastic cup.

I snatched it gratefully. 'Fill it up!'

By four-thirty I was drunk and talking to anyone who'd hang around long enough to listen. Most of the guys were speculating about who Miss Whiplash might be. Geoff thought it might be Graham's wife (I pointed out that he wasn't married), Joe thought she might be a professional S&M model and the more pissed he became, the more Nigel became convinced that she was a professional of a different kind. That made sense. I couldn't see any woman agreeing to be Graham's 'doggy', unless she was being paid.

I was just about to suggest we replace Graham's awful CD with something less offensive, when he turned the music off again. 'OK, people,' he bellowed. 'Time for the loser's forfeit.'

Several of the guys whooped and hollered. Archie, still in the corner of the room with Sally, stepped closer to the door.

'Oh no you don't,' bellowed Graham, stumbling towards Archie. 'In the centre of the room please, Mr Humphreys-Smythe.'

Archie folded his arms and glowered at Graham. No one said a word.

'Come on,' Graham slurred, grabbing his arm. 'Miss Whiplash over there is going to give you a spanking.'

Almost on cue, Miss Whiplash held a piece of wood shaped like a table tennis bat over her head and pirouetted. Geoff cheered and then hiccupped.

'Graham,' Archie said, taking a step back. 'You're drunk.'

'Drunk shmunk, you're a killjoy and you will be spanked,' Graham said, yanking Archie's arm and pulling him across the room towards Miss Whiplash.

Archie, half a foot shorter and six or seven stone lighter than his assailant, twisted and pulled, but failed to extricate himself from Graham's iron grip.

'Bend over,' Graham said, pushing the back of Archie's neck so his knees buckled.

'Fuck off, Graham!' he shouted, lashing out with his arms and wriggling.

The entire office was silent. Even Nigel was lost for words. We were all rooted to the spot, gawping at what was happening at the far end of the room.

'Spank him, Miss Whiplash,' Graham said, raising one hand in the air and beckoning with his index finger.

'Archie has been a very naughty boy and deserves to be punished.'

Miss Whiplash tottered towards Archie and raised her paddle. 'Prepare to be—'

A pink blur flashed through the air and knocked her to the ground. Several people gasped.

'Graham!' Miss Whiplash squealed, her spiky heels pedalling the air, her black wig askew. 'Graham, help me.'

But Graham was otherwise engaged. The pink blur had moved on and was kicking him in the shins, hard.

'Get off him, you perve!' it screamed, hanging onto his chain mail vest and ripping off his gimp mask. 'Get your filthy hands off him.'

It was Sally, her pink trainers pummelling Graham's legs, her eyes wide, cheeks flushed and fairy wings distinctly skew-whiff. Graham pushed Archie away and turned to face his unknown attacker.

'Go on then,' Sally said, jumping off him, shoulders back, her stance wide. 'Spank me and see what happens then. I dare you.'

Graham visibly paled. 'Get out,' he said quietly. 'Get out, both of you. Now.'

Archie picked himself up off the floor and tapped Graham on the shoulder.

'I quit,' he said, his fist flying through the air and smacking Graham straight on the chin.

The whole room gasped and then they were gone – Sally and Archie – straight out of the door.

'What are you lot looking at?' Graham said, rubbing

his jaw as we all stared at him, open-mouthed. 'Get out before I sack the lot of you. Out. Now.'

I looked at my watch. It was five-fifteen. Should I go after Sally and Archie or to the *Star Trek* box office? I only had forty-five minutes before it closed. My heart hammered in my chest. What should I do? What should I do?

Chapter Thirty-three

Saturday 11th May
Day Fifteen

I hopped from foot to foot outside Edgware tube, clutching the tickets in my sweaty palm. It was Saturday morning and I had absolutely no idea whether Archie was going to show up for the *Star Trek* convention or not. Or even if he was still speaking to me. It wasn't until after I'd bought the tickets that I'd started to regret my decision. I'd watched him get publicly humiliated by our perverted boss and just stood by and cringed. If it wasn't for Sally, God knows what would have happened. It didn't bear thinking about. I hadn't even run after them to check if Archie was OK. If I was him I don't think *I'd* speak to me, either.

'Cheer up,' said a cheery voice just behind me. 'It might never happen.'

It was Archie. His hair was ruffled, his chin was rough with stubble, and he had dark circles under his eyes, but he was smiling.

'I didn't think you'd come,' I said, feeling excited and nervous at the same time.

'Why not?' he said, looking bemused. 'It's not every day you get invited out for a surprise excursion.'

'I just thought … I mean … after what happened yesterday,' I garbled, twisting the tickets in my hands. 'What I mean is, are you OK, Archie?'

He shrugged. 'Sure, never been better. I'm jobless, girlfriendless, and I was woken up at 7 a.m. by Grandmother, who wanted me to pop to the corner shop because she fancied some kippers on toast for breakfast.'

'Oh for God's sake,' I said. 'Why didn't she just go herself? She looked nimble enough at the speed-dating event.'

Archie gave me a disapproving look. 'Lucy …'

'OK, OK.' I held out my hands. 'I'll keep my opinions to myself. Let's go.'

'Great.' Archie grinned. 'I've been looking forward to this.'

We strolled down the street towards the conference centre, nattering on about nothing in particular as we walked. Whenever there was a pause in conversation I filled it with random comments about the weather or the people we passed and made Archie laugh with my descriptions of Brian and Claire's weirder habits, even though he hadn't met them. If I kept talking, I reasoned, he wouldn't get chance to admonish me for doing nothing when he was nearly publicly spanked the day before.

'Stop,' I said, just as we were about to turn the corner to the conference centre. 'I need to cover your eyes.'

There was an enormous poster of Spock, Captain Kirk and the plastic-looking robot guy hanging over the entrance, and I wanted to see the look on Archie's face when I unveiled his treat.

'Are you ready?' I asked as we stumbled to a halt in front of the building.

'Yes.' Archie's cheeks bulged under my fingers as he grinned. 'Quite ready, Miss Brown.'

'OK then, ready, steady ... look!'

I pulled my hands from his eyes and peered at his face, waiting for a look of delight to appear.

'It's *Star Trek*,' I chirped. 'Your favourite.'

He looked from the sign to me, and back again.

'What?' I said.

'Nothing,' Archie said, then burst out laughing.

I stared at him, utterly perplexed as he rocked back and forth, clutching his stomach. Wow. I'd never seen someone laugh with such happiness before. It was extraordinary, and ever so slightly scary. I'd never seen Archie get quite so hysterical.

'Oh, Lucy, you are funny,' he said, wiping his eyes with the back of his hand.

'Huh?'

'I said I liked *Star Wars*. Not *Star Trek*.'

'What!' Now it was my turn to stare from the con-ference centre to Archie and back. 'No! Tell me you're kidding? Please.'

He shook his head. 'I'm afraid not. There's a big difference between *Star Wars* fans and Trekkers, Lucy. A *very* big difference. It's like, um, I don't know. You liking Gucci handbags and me buying you one from Primark instead. Not that *Star Trek* is cheap, per se, it's just ...' He tailed off.

I stared at the tickets in my hand. Four letters, that was all I'd got wrong, four letters. Wars instead of Trek. How could I have been so stupid?

'I'll take them back,' I said, folding them up. 'I'm sure they'll give me a refund and then we can do something else.'

'No, let's go in anyway,' Archie said, nudging me playfully. 'Who knows, it might be fun. We can laugh at all the geeks in there.'

That made me grin, him calling other people geeks. I was still disappointed though. I'd felt sure he'd meet his soulmate at the convention and there was no chance of that now. Not unless he wanted a 'Primark' girlfriend. I'd have to have another re-think. And I only had five full days left to find him the love of his life. Shit.

'Come on, you,' Archie said, linking his arm through mine. 'Stop looking so miserable. It'll be fun, honestly.'

Yeah right.

An overly smiley man in a *Star Trek* outfit took our tickets as we walked into the conference centre and handed us a programme each.

'Have a good day,' he said in a fake American accent.

'Live long and prosper,' replied Archie. He made some kind of weird shape with his hand and burst into laughter again as he walked away.

I just stared at him. Great, another geek joke I didn't get.

'Come on,' he said, pulling on my arm and dragging me into the main hall. 'What do you want to see first?'

It was an enormous venue, absolutely stuffed with people and geeky delights. There was stall after stall, each one crammed with Star Trek memorabilia, along the wall to our left and fast food outlets along the wall to our right. I sniffed the air. Hot dogs and chips mostly.

'Look,' Archie said, pointing upwards. 'There are spaceships hanging from the ceiling.'

'Right,' I said, looking from one piece of grey plastic to another. 'Very interesting. Oh look, isn't that the room where Captain Kirk sits in his chair and drives the spaceship?'

Archie looked towards the centre of the room where models of various characters in different uniforms and costumes were arranged into unusual poses.

'I think you'll find that's called the bridge of the *Enterprise*,' he said.

The only thing I was vaguely interested in was the stalls – they were the closest thing to shopping, after all. I drifted towards them and picked up a teddy bear in a *Star Trek* outfit.

'Which talk are you looking forward to more?' Archie asked, holding the programme in front of my face and pointing at the various 'events'. 'The Physics of *Star Trek* or The Soul of *Star Trek*: the Prime Directive and Beyond?'

I laughed and put the teddy back down. 'You may take the piss, Mr Humphreys-Smythe, but I bet you've really been to hundreds of geeky conventions in your time. You're probably an old hand at this kind of thing.'

'Actually,' Archie said, looking a bit huffy, 'I haven't been to a single convention in my life. I think they're a bit sad.'

'Really?' I picked up a model of some kind of alien that looked like a fish head on a belly dancer's body. 'But you said you liked *Star Wars*.'

'I do, but I'm not obsessive about it. You like karaoke. Have you been to a karaoke convention?'

'No. Of course not.' I put the fish head alien back down. *Star Trek* shopping was rubbish.

'Well then.'

He had a point, I thought, as I let him drag me towards the replica of the bridge of the *Enterprise*.

'Hey,' I said, pointing at my programme. 'William Shatner's going to give a talk.'

Archie grinned at me. 'And?'

'Want to hear it?'

He raised his eyebrows. 'Now who's the geek?'

'I just liked his cover of Pulp's "Common People", that's all,' I said, my cheeks growing hot. 'You know the one, it goes ...'

I was just about to start singing when Archie lunged towards me and grabbed my shoulders.

'Don't freak out, and don't look round,' he whispered. 'But I think we're being followed.'

I immediately looked round.

'I said, don't look round!' Archie hissed, turning me back.

'But who's following us?'

I tried to turn round again but he grabbed my arm. 'A Klingon.'

'What's a Klingon?' I asked. 'Something you stick in your pants when you're old and coughing makes a bit of wee come out?'

Archie pulled a face. 'Delightful. No, it's one of the alien races in *Star Trek*. They've got big ridges on their foreheads, a receding hairline and long, dark hair.'

'Sounds like the guy I lost my virginity to.'

'Lucy, I'm not kidding,' he said, running his hand through his hair. 'Someone has been following us since we came in.'

My heart sunk.

'Is it your gran?' I asked, clutching his arm. 'Please say it's not your gran.'

'Of course it's not my gran.' He rolled his eyes. 'For one thing, she's gone shopping in the West End and two, why would my gran wear a Klingon oufit?'

I grinned. 'Well, you had to inherit your geek tendencies from someone.'

'Me a geek?' He pointed to his chest. 'You're the one who wants to listen to William Shatner's talk.'

'And you're the one whose idea of a party is sitting in a dark room with two other guys.'

'*Touché.*'

'So, where's our stalker then?' There was an ageing

rocker in a 'Spock is God' T-shirt directly behind us, his greasy hair spread over his shoulders, but that was it for long-haired freaks. 'I can't see any Klingons.'

'That's because she's disappeared,' Archie said, pulling on my arm. 'I think she knows we're onto her.'

'What makes you think it's a her?'

'It was a very, very short Klingon.'

I shrugged. 'Maybe it was just a kid having a laugh.'

Archie didn't look convinced. 'Let's just carry on wandering around. If we are being followed we'll soon find out.'

I looped my arm through his and we strolled towards the nearest mannequin. It was a woman with fair hair pinned up into a french pleat and a piece of metal shaped like a lizard curved over her left eyebrow. She was dressed in a silver catsuit with a triangular badge pinned above her ludicrously large breasts.

'Stop here,' Archie whispered as we approached her. 'Pretend to look interested.'

I stared at the mannequin's boobs. They were hard to miss. 'Who is she?'

'Seven of Nine,' Archie said. 'She's a bit of a *Star Trek* fantasy figure.'

'For someone who claims not to be into *Star Trek*,' I said, raising an eyebrow, 'you seem to know a hell of a lot about it.'

'Everyone knows Seven of Nine is fit,' he said, gazing up at her. 'I am male, you know. Oh, hang on. I think our stalker is back. Have a look but, for God's sake, be subtle about it, Lucy.'

I hid behind the mannequin and peered through the crook of her elbow. A small person with a massively bumpy forehead, long, wiry hair and thick bushy eyebrows, was staring up at one of the model ships hanging from the ceiling. She was wearing a figure-hugging black and metal costume, but there was something about her outfit that wasn't quite right.

'Archie,' I hissed, hiding my massive grin behind my hand. 'Who do we know who wears pink trainers with stacked heels?'

'No idea,' he said, scratching his head.

God, men were so unobservant sometimes.

'Sally,' I said. 'Sally wears trainers like that.'

'But ... but.' He looked confused. 'Why would Sally come here and follow us around?'

'Because she's not following *us*,' I said, my mind slowly unpicking the events of the last few weeks. 'She's following you.'

It all made sense – Sally's reaction to Archie's haircut, her hostility towards me, the way she spent the whole of the work party glued to Archie's side, and then jumped to his defence when Graham picked on him.

'What? Me?' Archie looked at me as though I was mad. 'Why would she follow me?'

'I'm not one hundred percent sure,' I said, careful not to tempt fate or freak Archie out, 'but I suspect Sally may have a crush on you.'

'What?' he said, swaying and grabbing hold of Seven of Nine's arm.

I glanced over my shoulder. Our Klingon stalker caught my eye and looked back up at the ceiling.

'I think she really likes you, Archie.'

'If this is your idea of a wind-up, Lucy,' he said, looking a tad green, 'I don't think it's very funny.'

Someone behind me cleared their throat.

'Yes?' I said, looking round.

It was greasy rocker boy. He was sweating profusely and mopping his forehead with a crumpled-up tissue that had seen cleaner days. Beside him stood a tiny slip of a woman wearing a T-shirt that said 'My other boyfriend is Jean Luc Picard.' She glared at me.

'Would you mind moving?' Greasy Rocker said. 'I've been waiting to have my photo taken with Seven for several minutes now.'

'She's all yours,' I said, moving out of the way. 'We were just going. Weren't we, Archie?'

He jumped as I grabbed his arm and yanked him towards the next mannequin.

'I'm not winding you up, Archie,' I said, trying to work out if I was looking at a *Star Trek* alien with big ears, a big nose, and a wrinkly forehead or a model of Bruce Forsyth. 'I think Sally really does like you. The big question is – do you like *her*?'

'I don't know,' Archie stammered, the tips of his ears turning pink. 'There's no doubt that she's a very attractive girl and she did save me from Graham yesterday. Which, I hasten to add, I was extraordinarily grateful for—'

'About that,' I interrupted. 'I'm really sorry I—'

'And we had a really interesting chat about music on the way to the tube after we ran off,' he continued, totally oblivious to the fact I'd just spoken. 'Sally's into rap and hip-hop as well, you know. Did you know that?'

I shook my head. 'No, I—'

'I never, for one second, thought she might like me in the way you mention, Lucy. And besides, it wasn't so long ago that I thought I was in love with ...' He looked down, unable to finish his sentence.

I peered round the corner, too embarrassed to look at Archie. Sally the Klingon was standing near the Seven of Nine statue. Greasy Rocker was posing for a photo; one hand on Seven's boob, the other clutching a burger. It gave me an idea.

'Archie,' I whispered. 'Would you like to go out for dinner tomorrow?'

He frowned. 'What? I mean, pardon. I thought we were talking about Sally.'

'We were. Now I'm asking if you'd like to go out to dinner tomorrow.'

'I don't know,' he said, scratching his head.

'Please say you'll come,' I begged. 'Kung Po in Swiss Cottage at 8 p.m. Say you'll be there.'

He shrugged. 'I'll see what I can do, but I can't promise anything.'

'Great,' I said, holding up a hand. 'Now, stay there for a minute. Promise not to come after me.'

'Whatever you say, Lucy,' Archie said. The poor thing looked totally bewildered.

Sally didn't notice me creep up behind her.

'Hi, Sally,' I shouted in her ear.

She jumped, spun round, and elbowed me in the side of the head.

'Lucy!' she squealed as I toppled onto the conference centre floor. 'Fancy seeing you here. How did you know it was me?'

'Something gave you away,' I said, scrabbling back to my feet and pointing down at her trainers.

'Oh,' she said, looking down and rocking back on her heels. 'I did try wearing plain black boots, but I love these trainers. I just don't feel myself without them.'

'So, what brings you here?' I asked. 'I didn't have you down as a *Star Trek* fan.'

'Oh I am,' she said unconvincingly, smoothing down her uniform. 'I've loved them for, like, for ever.'

'I see.'

'Archie not with you?' she asked, standing on tiptoes and peering over my shoulder.

'Why, were you hoping to run into him?'

'No, not especially.' She fiddled with the silver cuffs around her wrists. 'I was just wondering where he was, that's all. You did say you bought the tickets for him.'

Time to put her out of her misery. I'd teased her enough.

'He's just round the corner,' I said, pointing across the room. 'I think he's looking at one of the exhibitions. Shall we go and join him?'

'That would be nice,' she said excitedly, almost bouncing on the spot.

We weaved in between a crowd of people all gawping at a life-sized replica of some kind of red, rocky planet. You could barely see for all the camera flashes going off.

'Sally,' I said, shielding my eyes. 'Would you like to go out for dinner tomorrow?'

She paused and looked up at me.

'Me?' she said, pointing at her chest.

'Yes, you.'

'With you?' She looked vaguely terrified.

'Not just me. Archie will be there too.'

'I'd love to go to dinner,' she grinned. 'I'd totally love it.'

'I thought you might,' I said as we rounded the corner and approached a nervous-looking Archie. 'I *totally* thought you might.'

Chapter Thirty-four

It was going to be the best Sunday of my life (or death, whatever), I just knew it. The *Star Trek* convention had been a brilliant idea. Talk about inspired. So Archie wasn't actually a fan of the programme, so what? That hadn't stopped it from being a fantastic day. As soon as I'd spotted Sally in her Klingon outfit I knew my luck had changed. I'd been searching the Internet for Archie's soulmate and she was under my nose the whole time. OK, so Archie had spent most of the day blushing furiously and laughing at my Captain Kirk impressions, but that was what the restaurant date was about: getting him to talk to Sally in a more normal environment. Task, schmask. I was practically home and dry.

I was the first one to take my seat at Kung Po's, shortly followed by a very sweaty Archie.

'Am I late?' he said, hurrying to the table and looking at his watch. 'Sorry, Grandmother had one of her turns before I left. I nearly didn't make it at all, but I couldn't bear to think of you sitting here all on your own, assuming I'd stood you up. You really should get a mobile phone you know, Lucy.'

'Yeah, yeah,' I said as he pulled off his jacket and sat down. 'Breathe, Archie, breathe.'

I poured wine into his glass and he nodded gratefully.

'Sorry, Lucy, I'm just a bit stressed at the moment. I spent hours looking for a job on the net last night. There are loads out there but the application forms take for ever to fill out and I need to find something ASAP. It's not just me I need to support.'

'So you're definitely not going back to Computer Bitz?' I asked.

He spluttered on his wine. 'You're kidding me, right?'

'Sorry,' I said. 'I wasn't implying that you should. Of course you shouldn't. I was just checking.'

If Archie wasn't going back to work on Monday, there was no point me going either. I had his mobile number and he had my landline, so we could easily stay in touch. The big problem was Sally. As far as I knew, they hadn't exchanged numbers and without their little chats when she brought in the sandwiches each day, they'd quickly lose touch. That's why the restaurant date was so important. Talking of Sally, where was she? I looked at my watch.

'Should we order?' Archie asked, picking up his menu. 'Oh, they've got prawn toast. My favourite.'

'Actually, we're waiting for someone else to join us,' I said, glancing at the door.

'We are?' He peered at me over the top of his menu.

I'd kept quiet about inviting Sally because I didn't want to scare him off. She was obviously into him, but I wasn't one hundred percent sure how he felt about her. And there was the not so small matter of him being in love with me.

'I invited Sally along too,' I said casually, reaching for my menu. 'I hope you don't mind.'

'Sally.' Archie frowned. 'What are you up to, Lucy?'

'Nothing,' I lied. 'I just thought it would be nice to go out to dinner together. I know Sally and I have had our disagreements, but she was great fun at the convention yesterday, so I thought I'd invite her along.'

'You might have told me,' Archie said, dabbing the beads of sweat on his forehead. 'If I'd known Sally was coming too, I wouldn't have been so worried about you being here on your own.'

'Sorry,' I said. 'It was a last-minute decision and anyway, she's not here yet, is she? I'd still have been on my own.'

Archie didn't answer. Instead he slammed his menu shut, crossed his arms and stared at the ceiling. Oh great. Now he was pissed off with me. I stared at the door, willing Sally to walk through it. I needed her more than ever. To lift the mood, if nothing else.

I was reaching for the last complimentary prawn cracker when she finally walked into the restaurant.

'Wow,' I gasped, dropping the cracker.

Sally looked absolutely astonishing, a vision in

black and silver. She was wearing a tiny little dress that skimmed the top of her thighs and a pair of black strappy high-heeled shoes with tiny diamantés on the straps. Her hair was piled on top of her head and she'd lined her eyes with kohl and painted her lips a deep red. Her beaming smile faded as she tottered towards us.

'Hi, Sally,' I said, standing to kiss her on the cheek. 'You look amazing.'

Archie stared up at her open-mouthed, a prawn cracker crumb resting on his lower lip.

'Sorry, sorry,' he said, swiping at his mouth with the napkin as he stood up. 'I forgot my manners. Sally, you look absolutely stunning.'

She smiled nervously and lowered herself into the chair Archie had pulled out for her.

'I feel silly,' she said as he pushed the chair in. 'You two are wearing casual clothes and I'm done up like a dog's dinner.'

'You look beautiful,' I said. 'Honestly. I'm the slob for turning up for dinner in my jeans.'

Archie gazed across at Sally, his menu limp in his hand, and then turned to look at me.

'I think you both look lovely,' he said. I couldn't read the look in his eyes.

'So do you, Archie,' said Sally. 'Blue really suits you.'

Archie blushed and stared at the table cloth.

'Wine, Sally?' I asked, gesturing at her empty glass with the bottle.

We were halfway through our starter of prawn toast, chicken satay and sticky ribs when Archie's phone rang. Sally had been teaching us how to swear in Cantonese and she was laughing hysterically at our pronunciation.

'Sorry, ladies,' Archie said, placing his nibbled prawn toast on his plate. 'I'll have to get that. Do excuse me.'

Sally and I stopped laughing and watched as he scrabbled around in his record bag for his phone.

'Hello, Grandmother,' he said.

I felt my heart sink.

'Yes, Grandmother,' he said again.

I could hear her plummy tones from across the table, but couldn't make out what she was saying.

'There's a torch in my bedroom,' Archie said. 'Sorry? OK, I completely understand … no, of course … absolutely … I'll see you in about half an hour. OK, see you then. Bye.' He frowned as he removed the phone from his ear and slipped it back into his bag.

'What's up?' I asked, trying desperately to look nonchalant.

'It's Grandmother,' he said, pushing his plate away. 'The lights have gone out, and she doesn't want to check the fuse box in case she electrocutes herself.'

What? Even *I* knew flicking the fuse switch back on couldn't hurt you.

'You're kidding?' I said.

Archie shook his head. 'I'm afraid not. The stairs to the bathroom are pitch-black and she's been crossing her legs for the last half hour. She said she can't hang on much longer.'

'Are you going to come back afterwards?' Sally asked. She was still smiling.

'Probably not,' Archie said, looking at his watch. 'By the time I get there, flick the switch and come back, it'll be ten o'clock and the main course will have been served.'

Sally's face fell. 'Couldn't you join us for a dessert or coffee?'

'I'm really sorry,' Archie said, standing up and wriggling into his jacket. He took a couple of notes out of his wallet and placed them beside his plate. 'Maybe we could do this again sometime.'

'Love to.' Sally stood up and kissed him on the cheek. 'Maybe the same time next week? Lucy? Is that OK with you?'

I reached for my glass of wine and knocked it back. I didn't have a week. If Archie didn't realise Sally was his soulmate by the end of Friday, it was all over for me. I'd be whisked off to heaven, whether I liked it or not, and I'd never see Dan again. Anna would get her claws into him and I'd become a distant memory. Lucy, Lucy who? Oh, that girl I went out with once …

'Lucy,' Archie said as I poured myself another glass of wine. 'Are you OK?'

I shook my head. 'Get back to your grandmother, Archie. She needs you. I'll call you next week, OK?'

'Thanks for being so understanding, Lucy.' He rounded the table and kissed me on the cheek.

'Can I just ask you one thing?' I said as he headed towards the door.

'Of course,' he said, turning back.

'Did your grandmother know you were coming out with me tonight?'

He smiled. 'Of course.'

I figured as much.

'What was that all about?' Sally asked as the bell above the front door tinkled and Archie disappeared down the street. 'Why were you so pissed off that Archie had to go back to his grandmother's? It's no big deal. We can have dinner next week instead.'

'I was just looking forward to tonight,' I said, pushing my plate away from me, my appetite ruined, 'that's all.'

Sally fiddled with her butterfly clip, reached for her wine glass, put it back down and then chewed on her thumbnail.

'Can I ask you something, Lucy?' she asked, looking at me from beneath her false eyelashes.

'Of course.'

'Are you and Archie in love?'

I laughed. 'Of course not! What gave you that idea?'

Her fingers went back into her mouth. 'Because you two have been inseparable since you joined Computer Bitz,' she mumbled. 'Everyone thinks you're an item.'

'Well we're not. We're just friends.'

'Oh, thank goodness.' She sighed and slumped back

in her chair. 'You have no idea how relieved I am.'

'Sally, are you—?'

The waiter appeared, raised his eyebrows at the amount of food we'd left and swiftly cleared the table. When he'd strutted off with our plates I tried again.

'Sally, are you in love with Archie?'

'Yeah.' She nibbled at her lip, leaving teeth marks in her red lipstick. 'I've been in love with him since I started doing my sandwich rounds at Computer Bitz.'

'Oh, Sally,' I said, reaching across the table to touch her hand. 'I think that's lovely. Why haven't you told him how you feel?'

She shrugged. 'I know I come across as some kind of badass, but—'

I laughed. Loud, boisterous and friendly maybe, but a badass? Definitely not.

'But I'm actually quite shy when it comes to men,' she said ruefully. 'I like them to make the first move. I'm kind of old-fashioned like that.'

'Archie's old-fashioned too,' I said brightly.

'I know, and I really like that about him, but I'm not an idiot, Lucy, I know he's into you.'

'No he's not.'

'He is,' she said, sitting up in her seat and leaning towards me. 'He shaved off his beard for you. He even cut off all his lovely hair. That's why I was so pissed off with you that day. He did it because he thought it would make you like him more.'

'That's not true,' I lied. 'Archie told me he was lonely and I was just trying to help him meet someone. I thought if I tidied him up a bit more, women would find him attractive.'

'But I found him attractive just as he was.'

'I didn't know that, Sally. I wish I had.'

The waiter appeared again, this time bringing the main courses. He looked quizzically at Archie's empty chair, but placed a bowl of prawn chow mein at his setting anyway. Sally prodded her Schezuan chicken with a chopstick and sighed.

'It doesn't matter,' she said. 'Archie doesn't like me like I like him. He only sees me as the chatterbox sandwich girl.'

I skewered a mushroom with my chopstick, popped it into my mouth and chewed it slowly as a hundred thoughts swirled around my head. 'I think he does like you like that,' I said. 'He just hasn't realised it yet.'

'Really?' Sally stared at me, her eyes wide. 'You're not just saying that?'

'No, I think he really does like you. He just needs to realise how much.'

And he needs to fall out of love with me, I thought, but didn't say.

'How?' Sally asked excitedly. 'How can we make that happen?'

I shook my head. I had absolutely no idea.

Chapter Thirty-five

Monday 13th May
Day Seventeen

Possible ways to make Archie fall out of love with me:

1) Gorge on cream cakes until grossly obese, then sit on him

2) Cut off all my hair, including eyelashes and eyebrows. Grow leg hair and ask him to stroke it

3) Laugh hysterically at everything he says, including sad stories

4) Rub myself up against Brian at every possible opportunity so I smell of BO too

5) Umm ...

I threw down my pen and paper and leaned back on my pillows. All of my suggestions were rubbish. Worse than rubbish, they were stupid and totally impractical. For one, I didn't have enough time to become grossly obese or grow my leg hair, and the thought of rubbing up against Brian ...

Still, it wasn't as though I didn't have time to work on a plan. It was Monday morning, but I didn't have to go to work. If Archie wasn't going back to Computer

Bitz, neither was I! I swung my legs off the bed and stretched. What I needed was a nice cup of hot coffee to zing my brain cells back into action. That might help.

I padded down to the kitchen and opened the door.

What the hell? Were my housemates actually *cleaning*?

Claire, her dreads piled up on her head like a pineapple, was kneeling on the floor scrubbing the lino while Brian, looking not entirely uncomfortable in a blue and white checked apron, was washing up.

I hovered in the doorway and rubbed my eyes. 'What's going on?'

'It's my last day,' said Brian, looking up from the foaming pile of dishes in front of him. 'And, one way or another, I'm not going to be here tomorrow, so I thought a bit of a clean-up was in order.'

Claire smiled up at me. 'I wasn't going to help, but I had nothing better to do.'

'Wow,' I said. 'Anything I can do?'

'You can put the kettle on,' said Claire, swiping her forehead with her forearm. 'I think we're due a break.'

I tiptoed over her freshly washed floor and picked up the kettle. The whole situation was so utterly surreal I felt unnerved. My housemates were happier than I'd ever seen them, *and* they were cleaning!

'Are you OK?' I asked Brian. 'I thought you'd be nervous today.'

He shrugged. 'The situation's out of my hands now. What will be, will be.'

'So if Troy doesn't show up tonight, you won't be gutted about going to heaven?'

'I'd be lying if I said I wouldn't be disappointed,' he said, swirling a cup under the tap, 'but if I don't pass my task I have to accept my fate.'

Gosh. I couldn't believe how philosophical he was being. The only reason I'd gone with him to meet Troy was because I thought he'd be devastated if he didn't become a ghost. Trains were his Dan, he'd said.

'Have you been back to Tooting since I went there with you?' I asked, reaching into the cupboard for cups.

He nodded. 'A couple of times. The first time I went to McDonald's, Troy wasn't there, but the next time he turned up on his own. I just sat and read my magazine and pretended I hadn't seen him.'

I grinned. 'Brian, were you playing hard to get?'

'So to speak.' He leaned out of the way so I could grab the box of teabags. 'After half an hour he sidled up to me and asked about the different rail journeys I'd done. We talked for ages, well, until his friends walked in. Then he called me a paedophile and jumped away.'

'Did he say anything about meeting us at Paddington tonight?' I asked casually.

Brian rinsed a plate under the tap and stacked it on the drainer. 'No.'

'Oh.'

'I can but hope, Lucy.'

'Hope's always a good thing,' I said, dropping the teabags into the cups. But I wasn't sure if it was Brian I was reassuring, or myself.

At seven o'clock I poked my head round Brian's door. He was sitting on the edge of his bed, his hands pressed between his knees. Unlike the kitchen, his room hadn't changed a bit; his train posters were still on the walls, his grubby rug in the middle of the room, books and magazines piled up neatly beside his bed.

'Aren't you going to pack or something?' I asked, picking up a book and flicking through it.

Brian shook his head. 'No need. Whatever happens next, the contents of this room will still disappear.'

'Really?'

'Yes, it'll be like I was never here.'

'That's really sad,' I said, and I meant it. Our undead rooms reflected our personalities, they were filled with the things we loved. Someone, somewhere, had already cleared out the flat Brian had lived in when he was alive. There might be a photo of him on someone's sideboard or mantelpiece, but when his things vanished from the House of Wannabe Ghosts, all trace of his personality would disappear too. He'd really be gone.

I knew from peering through the window that Dan had kept the house exactly as I'd left it. My cushions still littered the sofa, the rug we'd chosen together lay on the floor and my books were nestled between Dan's on the shelf. But one day that would change. My things would disappear. And if Anna got her claws into Dan, it would happen much sooner than I wanted it to.

'Are you ready to go, Brian?' I asked, trying to sound cheery.

He stood up slowly and wandered around the room, picking up his framed pictures and models of trains one by one, looking at them and setting them down again. He even opened the door to his wardrobe and smiled down at his neatly lined-up sandals.

'I've said my goodbyes,' he said softly. 'It's time to move on.'

'Would you mind waiting for me at the front door?' I asked. 'I just need to have a quick word with Claire.'

'Come in,' she called, as I tapped on the door to her room.

She was sitting cross-legged on her bed, strumming her guitar. She still hadn't put on any make-up and looked fresh-faced and glowing.

'Brian's about to go,' I said, 'if you'd like to say good-bye.'

She sighed and placed her guitar on the duvet beside her.

'It's weird,' she said. 'I couldn't stand the sight of Brian when I first met him … never mind the smell …'

I giggled.

'But I'm going to miss him.' She slid off the bed and padded towards me. 'It feels weird to say goodbye.'

'Claire.' I put my hand on her shoulder. 'Could I ask you a favour? There's something I need you to do for me while I go to Paddington with Brian.'

She listened patiently as I explained that Anna and Jess were going to be meeting up in the White Horse pub as usual. I described them both and how to get to the pub, and asked her if she'd mind listening in on their conversation.

'Sure,' she said, opening the bedroom door. 'No problem. But I've got a bit of a crap memory so I won't be able to remember everything.'

'That's not important,' I said. 'I just need to know what Anna says about Dan.'

Claire paused in the hallway and looked back. 'Isn't that your fiancé? Is there something wrong with him?'

'It's not Dan I'm worried about,' I said, giving her a pointed look, 'it's Anna.'

'What's wrong with her?'

'Nothing a sharp slap round the face wouldn't solve.'

'I see.' She grinned and I caught a glimpse of the old Claire again, the Claire that would rugby-tackle a skanky blonde to the floor as soon as look at her.

'Not that I'm suggesting you should slap her,' I said hastily, glancing at my watch. It was quarter past seven and Brian and I really needed to get a move on. 'Just listen to what they talk about and I'll explain everything when I get back. I promise.'

'No problem,' Claire said, squeezing my hand. 'I'll just say goodbye to Mr Smelly.'

I watched as Claire walked down the stairs and launched herself at a surprised-looking Brian.

'I'm really going to miss you,' she said, squeezing him tightly. 'Promise me you'll be happy, whatever happens.'

'You too, Claire, you too,' Brian said, wrapping his

arms around her and rubbing her back. 'I really am very fond of you, you know. Beneath the attitude and the make-up, you're a truly lovely girl and you deserve to be happy.'

I hung onto the banister at the bottom of the stairs, my eyes full of tears. When Saint Bob had told me people got too attached to their lives in the House of Wannabe Ghosts, I hadn't believed him. I should have. Watching Claire and Brian hang onto each other was heart-breaking. They were so mismatched; Brian tall and gangly with his wild, frizzy hair and moustache, and Claire, shorter and squatter, dressed head to toe in black, her woolly hair wrapped around his fingers, but they were the only people in the world who knew what I was going through and how difficult it was. And I would have done anything to make them happy. Anything at all.

Claire stifled a sob as Brian gently pulled away from her. There were tears running down both their cheeks.

'Are you ready to go, Brian?' I asked.

He wiped his face on his sleeve and nodded.

'Are you still OK to go and spy on Anna and Jess?' I whispered as I gave Claire a hug goodbye.

She nodded into my shoulder. 'Of course.'

'Thank you,' I said, squeezing her tightly. 'And don't worry about Brian. I'll look after him. I promise.'

The escalator popped us out in the middle of Paddington Station.

'Brian,' I said. 'How are you feelin—'

He didn't reply. Instead he picked up his pace and stormed towards the bridge, head down, hands deep in his pockets.

'How are you feeling?' I asked again, hurrying to keep up with him.

'Whatever will be, will be,' he mumbled, staring at the ground.

'Yes, but—'

'Whatever will be, will be, Lucy.'

By the time we reached the bridge I was about ready to thump him. Instead I paced from one side to the other while Brian stood in the middle, arms crossed, gazing at the trains that slowly chug-chugged into the station.

'So Troy definitely said he'd come,' I said as I passed Brian for the fourth time.

'Nothing's for definite, Lucy,' he replied calmly.

'But he sounded enthusiastic, right?' I glanced at my watch. It was eight o'clock. Where the hell was Troy?

'What does enthusiasm sound like?' Brian replied, shrugging his shoulders.

Good God. Was he deliberately trying to wind me up? Why wasn't he showing any emotion? If I was about to find out if I'd passed my task or not, I'd be pulling my hair out and going mental.

I looked at my watch again. It was ten past eight and there was still no sign of Troy. The more I thought about it, the more unlikely it seemed that he'd actually show up. I turned round at the sound of footsteps behind us.

'Brian,' I said softly, tapping him on the shoulder. 'Troy's here.'

He whipped round so quickly my hand flew off his shoulder and smacked against the bridge.

'Troy,' he said, holding out a shaking hand. 'So glad you could make it.'

Troy, his dark-blue hoodie pulled over his head, merely nodded at Brian's outstretched hand. 'All right, man.'

'I'm very good, thank you,' said Brian, his hand slowly drifting back to his side.

Troy looked me up and down. 'All right?'

I nodded. 'Good thanks.'

There was an awkward pause as we all stared at each other, unsure what was supposed to happen next.

'So I read that magazine you gave me, man,' Troy said, finally breaking the silence. 'Had to hide it behind *Loaded* like, so my mum didn't clock it, but yeah, I read it all.'

Brian raised his eyebrows. 'What did you think?'

'Some good stuff in there, man,' Troy said, nodding enthusiastically, his hoodie slipping even further over his eyes. 'I was reading all about trains in Peru. Apparently there are five switchbacks on the Cuzco to Machu Picchu route.'

'El Zigzag,' Brian beamed. 'I've been on it.'

Troy's mouth fell open. 'You're kidding?'

'I went ten years ago. The view on the return journey from Machu Picchu was spectacular. At night the whole city was illuminated.'

'Oh, man. I'd love to check that.'

They continued to discuss trains, their hands a blur as they talked. I couldn't help but grin. After a couple of minutes I left them to it and wandered back through the station and sat down in a café. I flicked through the pages of a magazine that had been left on my table but I couldn't concentrate. My head was full of questions. Would Troy admit to being a trainspotter? What would Claire overhear? Were Dan and Anna a couple? Was I too late? By nine o'clock I couldn't bear it any more. I deserted my coffee and headed back towards the bridge. Brian and Troy hadn't moved an inch and were still deep in conversation. Neither of them noticed me as I inched nearer.

'So,' Brian said, in an unusually high voice, his hands in his pockets. 'Would you say you were a railway enthusiast then?'

I stopped walking and stood completely still, still a good couple of feet away from them. Troy shifted from one foot to the other. The bridge was completely empty apart from the three of us. I held my breath. Please say you are, I prayed. Please say you are.

Troy cleared his throat. 'Well yeah, but if you say a word to any of my mates you're dead.'

The smile on Brian's face was extraordinary. It stretched from ear to ear and his eyes sparkled.

'Sorry,' he said. 'I didn't quite hear that. Could you say it again?'

Troy scratched his head. 'You deaf, man? I said yeah, I'm a train enfusiast. I'm not gonna say it again.'

Brian reached out and wrapped his arms around Troy.

'Thank you!' he cried. 'Thank you, thank you, thank you!'

'Get off me, man,' Troy said, looking startled and swiping at Brian's arms. 'Don't be gay.'

When Brian finally let go of him he straightened his sweatshirt, pulled his hood back up and looked down at his mobile.

'I've got to go now,' Troy said. 'I'm meeting my girl. Thanks for the number of that train club, Brian. I'll give 'em a ring.'

'You do that,' Brian said, still beaming from ear to ear. 'You'll love it. I promise.'

'You gonna be at their meeting?' Troy asked.

'No.' Brian shook his head. 'I'm going away, for a long time.'

'Anywhere nice?'

Brian grinned. 'Very nice.'

'All right then. Have a good one. See you.'

He gave Brian a half salute and sloped off across the bridge, his head down, mobile tucked between his hood and his ear. I waited until he'd disappeared round the corner and then enveloped Brian in a bear hug.

'You did it!' I squealed. 'You only bloody did it, Brian!'

'I did! I did do it!' He lifted me off my feet and spun me around and around. 'And I couldn't have done it without you, Lucy Brown.'

'So what happens now?' I asked, wobbling slightly

as he set me back on my feet. 'How do you become a ghost?'

'You still haven't read your manual, have you, Lucy?' Brian shook his head despairingly.

Just as I was about to reply, two tall, slim men in grey suits and dark sunglasses stepped onto the bridge. They walked side-by-side, each step in sync until they reached us, then they stopped.

'Brian Worthing?' said the one nearest Brian.

I looked at Brian with alarm but he looked unfazed.

'Yes,' he said.

'Phone call for you from Saint Bob,' said the other man, handing him a mobile phone.

'Yes,' Brian said, holding it to his ear. 'Yes, yes, that's right. Yes, yes I would. Yes, thank you, Bob. Good luck to you too.'

The two men watched, completely expressionless, as Brian ended the call and snapped the mobile shut. The one nearest me held out a hand for the phone, put it in his pocket and nodded at his companion. They turned stiffly and walked back the way they'd come.

'Well?' I demanded, hopping from foot to foot as Brian beamed at me.

'That was Bob,' he said. 'I get to become a ghost.'

'When?'

'Very—' Brian looked down at his hand. His age spots and freckles had disappeared and his skin was as pale and waxy as a church candle. 'Soon.'

'Quick,' he said, grabbing my hand and pulling me

along the bridge. 'We have to go somewhere private. We don't have much time.'

We ran, hand in hand, down one of the platforms, only stopping when we reached the men's toilets. Brian pushed the door open an inch and peered round it.

'I can't go in there,' I squealed as he pulled me inside.

'It's OK,' he said, ducking down and squinting under the cubicles. 'There's no one else in here.'

I stood in the centre of the small room and tried not to touch anything. The tiles were yellow and grubby and the smell from the urinals was indescribably gross. I pinched my nose and grimaced at Brian. Under the harsh glare of the strip lighting he looked almost transparent.

'Brian!' I gasped. 'You're disappearing.'

'That's what happens when you become a ghost,' he said, his moustache splaying across his top lip as he grinned at me. 'Sorry to drag you in here, Lucy, but the manual specifically says you cannot become a ghost unless you're out of public view.'

I stared at him, my eyes wide. 'You're not kidding. Your entire forearm is almost see-through.'

'Give me a hug then,' he said, opening his one and a half arms wide, 'while I've still got time.'

I wrapped my arms tightly around him, but he was no longer the firm, warm Brian I'd got used to. It was like hugging a sponge or a chocolate mousse. He didn't even smell of BO any more. He didn't smell of anything at all. He really was going to leave us.

'I'll miss you, Brian,' I said. 'I'm not sure how I'd have got through this without you.'

My hair moved as though a light wind was blowing through it, and I realised Brian was trying to stroke my head.

'You're stronger than you think, Lucy,' he said, his voice a whisper. 'You're a lovely girl and Dan is a very, very lucky man to have someone like you love him. If I could live my life over again, if I could be young again, I'd wish for a woman like …'

The word 'you' at the end of his sentence faded to a warm 'ooohh' in my ear and I was hugging thin air. I took a step back. Brian's shape shimmered in the air like a faded photographic negative, his face just about visible, a peaceful look in his eyes, a small smile on his lips.

'Be happy, Brian,' I whispered. 'Be happy.'

He nodded and I blinked back my tears. 'Go, Brian. Go. I'll be OK, I promise. Thank you for everything.'

He stared at me for a few more seconds, then took a step towards the urinals, walked through the wall and disappeared. I was still staring at the tiles when the door flew open and a young man in a train conductor's outfit burst into the room.

'Wrong toilets, love,' he said, looking me up and down. 'The Ladies' is next door.'

I returned to the House of Wannabe Ghosts to find Claire sitting at the newly cleaned kitchen table, a cup of tea in front of her, her head in her hands.

'Are you OK?' I asked, gently patting her dreadlock pineapple. 'Don't be upset, Claire. Brian passed his task and became a ghost. I've never seen him look so happy.'

Claire looked up at me as I pulled out the chair opposite her and sat down.

'It's not Brian,' she said, fiddling with her nose ring, 'although I'll really miss him.'

'Then what is it?'

'It's your friend Anna,' she said, looking me in the eye and then looking away sharply.

I felt sick. 'What about Anna?'

'Do you want the good news or the bad news?'

'The good news,' I said, clasping my hands together and pressing them against my lips.

'Anna told Jess she hasn't slept with Dan yet,' Claire said. 'They haven't even kissed.'

The table squealed across the kitchen tiles as I launched myself at Claire and hugged her tightly. Yes! Yes! Yes! Anna had lied when she'd shouted at me in the tube station and told me Dan was a great shag. Oh thank God.

'And the bad news?' I asked nervously, sitting back in my seat.

'She said she wants to spend the rest of her life with Dan and she doesn't care if he doesn't want kids. She just wants to be with him.'

'What?' I said, all the hairs on my arms standing up. 'She's lying. She wants him as a sperm donor. She's desperate for kids, it's all she's wanted since she split up with Julian.'

'But, Lucy, she said she's never loved anyone like she loves him,' Claire said softly, 'and she sounded like she meant it. She told Jess she's invited him to her birthday party on Wednesday and she's going to make a move on him and then tell him how she feels.'

'No,' I said. 'No, that's not true. It's not true.'

I reached out for Claire's hand but my fingers were shaking so badly I knocked over her mug, splashing hot tea all over the table, all over me, and then everything went black.

Chapter Thirty-six

Tuesday 14th May
Day Eighteen

What the hell? Why was Claire in bed with me? I closed my eyes and opened them again. Nope, she was still there, her dreadlocked head on the pillow beside me, the duvet pulled up around her shoulders. Her eyes were open and she was staring at me.

'Are you OK, Lucy?' she whispered, brushing my hair off my face.

'I don't know,' I said, glancing around warily, half-expecting Brian, Archie and Sally to pop out from the bottom of the duvet. 'Why are you in my bed?'

'I was really worried about you last night,' she said, propping herself up on one elbow. 'After I told you about Anna you blacked out, fell off your chair and hit your head on the floor. You didn't come round for ages and when you did, you were talking gibberish.'

'What did I say?'

'Dan and Anna's names over and over again. You tried to leave the house so I rugby-tackled you and sat on you until you agreed to go to bed instead.'

I flipped onto my back and groaned. 'Is that why my ribs ache?'

'Sorry about that.' She grinned nervously. 'I just didn't want you to blow your chance of becoming a ghost by communicating with Dan again. That's why I'm in your bed. I didn't want to risk you running off.'

I sighed. 'Thanks, Claire, you did the right thing.'

'Are you sure? You're not angry with me?'

'I'm not. I promise.'

I stared up at the ceiling, my mind working overtime. I had three days left until my twenty-one days were over and I had two choices:

1) Give up and go to heaven
2) Fight until the end

'Lucy,' Claire said. 'Are you sure you're OK?'

'I'm fine,' I groaned as I sat up and peeled back the duvet. 'Honestly. And to show you there are no hard feelings, I'll even make you a coffee. I just have to make a phone call first.'

It was 8 p.m. when I opened the door to Kung Po's restaurant and confirmed to a hassled-looking waitress that I'd booked a table for three. She showed me my seat, took my order for drinks, then set a bottle of wine and three glasses in front of me. I sipped at it gratefully, my stomach churning with nerves. It was my last chance to complete my task.

'Hi, Lucy,' said a cheery voice beside me. 'You look a million miles away.'

Sally pulled back a chair and sat down. She was

wearing a Hello Kitty T-shirt and jeans and her hair was tied in two yellow plaits on either side of her head. She looked impossibly cute and I felt sure Archie would find her irresistible. At least, I hoped so.

'Glad you could make it,' I said, smiling at her across the table. 'Do you want some wine?'

As I reached for the bottle, she glanced at the door.

'Don't worry,' I said, filling her glass to the top. 'Archie will be here.'

'Am I that obvious?' she asked, looking back at me, her cheeks pink.

'We're just three friends having dinner together,' I said, sounding more confident than I felt. 'No pressure.'

'No pressure,' she repeated and took a large gulp of her wine.

Convincing Sally there was no pressure was one thing, convincing myself was another. Everything rested on the dinner going well. Sally was too nervous and old-fashioned to make a move on Archie and he had no idea who he wanted, so my plan was to get them together, get the conversation going, then make my excuses and go. After that, I'd just have to cross my fingers and leave fate to do its best.

'Lucy,' Sally said, holding up her wine glass. 'I propose a toast.'

'Isn't it a bit early for that?' I asked, glancing at the door. 'Shouldn't we wait for Archie to turn up first?'

'No,' she said, shaking her head, her plaits flying everywhere, 'this is a toast for the girls.'

'OK ...'

She waited for me to lift my glass into the air, then bumped her glass against mine. 'Cheers!' she said as they chinked together. 'Here's to women, and getting our hearts' desires.'

'To our hearts' desires,' I said, knocking back my wine.

Sally took a sip of her drink and peered at me over the top of the glass.

'What?' I said. 'Why are you looking at me like that?'

'You're a bit of a mystery, Lucy Brown,' she said. 'You never really talk about yourself. You talk about work and Archie and you spent the whole afternoon at the *Star Trek* convention cracking jokes, but I don't know anything about you.'

I shrugged. 'I'm just a bit private, I guess.'

'You're not that private,' she said, propping her chin on her hands and gazing at me. 'When I made the toast and said that bit about getting our hearts' desires, there was a strange look in your eyes.'

'What kind of look?'

'A desperate one.'

I reached for the wine bottle. Was it really that obvious how desperate I was to find my way back to Dan?

'It's nothing,' I said, filling up my glass. 'I was just thinking about something else.'

'Or *someone* else?'

'Actually, I—'

I was saved from having to finish because the bell

322

above the restaurant door chimed and we both craned round to see who'd just walked in.

'Who's that with Archie?' Sally mouthed, looking back at me.

'That,' I said, rising from my seat to greet the woman who was stalking towards us, 'is Archie's gran.'

'Isn't this lovely,' Archie said as he flipped open his menu. 'My three favourite girls, all in one place.'

Sally grinned and fiddled with her napkin. Mrs Humphreys-Smythe gave me a look of unveiled contempt.

'Wasn't it nice of my grandson,' she said, turning her attention to Sally, 'to invite his lonely old gran out for a spot of dinner?'

'You're not old,' Sally said, sitting up straight and dropping her napkin. 'I thought you were Archie's mum when you walked in.'

'But not on closer inspection, I imagine,' said Mrs Humphreys-Smythe, narrowing her eyes.

'Oh no, not at all,' said Sally, 'you look even younger up close.'

'Well, thank you.' She rewarded Sally with a genuinely warm smile. 'It's always nice to meet such a well-brought-up young lady.'

Sally giggled and hid her face in her menu, just as Archie closed his with a slap.

'So,' he said, glancing round the table, completely oblivious to the glacial atmosphere between me and his gran, 'are we all ready to order?'

I gave him a look.

'Is that a yes?' he said, completely misreading my expression. 'Everyone yes? Grandmother? Sally? Marvellous.'

Archie nodded to the waiter who hurried over to our table and hovered by his elbow.

'Grandmother?' Archie said. 'Are you ready to order?'

Mrs Humphreys-Smythe proceeded to harangue the waiter with questions about the menu. Was there monosodium glutamate in absolutely everything? Could she have the mixed rice but without the egg (she didn't react well to eggs)? Was the chicken all breast meat (she couldn't abide thigh)? Was the house special very spicy (a little spice was nice, but not too much)? When she'd finally run out of questions she ordered a starter, a main course, a dessert and a coffee.

Oh my God.

She was planning on staying for the whole bloody meal. Even if I left as planned, Archie and Sally wouldn't get a single second alone. I was screwed. Completely, utterly, totally screwed. And, more to the point, so was my task. There was only one thing for it. Get very, very drunk.

By the time the main course arrived, I was already quite tipsy. Sally had switched to soft drinks after her second glass of wine (a decision that earned her a nod of approval from Mrs Humphreys-Smythe) and Archie had insisted on buying 'the best bottle of red you have' to share with his grandmother. That left me to finish the white wine all on my own. And finish it off I did. As the others tucked into their meals I pushed my chicken chow mein round my plate with my fork and clutched my wine glass with my other hand.

'Not hungry?' Archie asked, looking up from his half-finished plate of sweet and sour prawns.

I narrowed my eyes at him. 'I'm fine. Thanks for the concern.'

He swallowed nervously and didn't say another word to me until the dessert, and my second bottle of wine, had arrived.

'Thirsty, are you?' commented Mrs Humphreys-Smythe, raising an eyebrow as the waiter filled my glass.

'Yes, thank you,' I said. I necked half the glass and set it back on the table. It wobbled but didn't fall over.

Mrs Humphreys-Smythe stabbed her lychees with her fork and muttered something under her breath.

'Sorry?' I demanded, spinning round to face her. 'Was that aimed at me?'

Sally and Archie both stared at me with alarm. Mrs Humphreys-Smythe pursed her lips and squeezed out the tightest, falsest smile I'd ever seen.

'I said' – she mouthed the words slowly, as though I was thick – 'that there are places where people like you can go to get help.'

'People like me? What's that supposed to mean?'

My words were coming out slurred and there were three Mrs Humphreys-Smythes where there should have been one. And they all looked evil.

'There's no shame in admitting that you have a problem, darling,' she said, fingering the pearls around her neck. 'It seems to be all the rage these days. Every time you open the paper there's another Z-list celebrity checking themselves into rehab.'

'So you're saying I should go to rehab?' I said, raising an eyebrow.

'It might not be a bad idea,' she said tightly. 'From what Archie's told me, you do rather have a fondness for the grape.'

'Well, from what Archie's told me, you should bugger off into an old people's home and let him live his life.'

Archie, Sally and his gran gasped simultaneously.

'Lucy,' Archie said. 'I won't let you speak to my grandmother like that.'

'Well, someone's got to.' I snapped round to face him. 'You're obviously too chicken shit to speak up for yourself.'

'Lucy. Stop it.'

There was a definite warning tone in Archie's voice but I was too drunk to care. I'd done everything I could to help him and he was still siding with his grandmother instead of me. Sod him. Sod him and sod her and even stupid Sally who was trying, and failing, to hide her giggles behind her hand. I'd failed my task. I'd failed it. After Friday I'd never get to see Dan again or apologise for the argument and Anna would get her claws into him and that would be it, game over. It would be like I never existed. Like I never mattered. Like I was never loved. I lurched forward and grabbed the wine bottle. Fuck Archie and his grandmother. Fuck them all. What did I have left to lose? Nothing.

'I won't stop it,' I slurred. 'It's time I was honest with you, Archie. It's time someone told you what a sad loser geek you really are. Do you want to know why no one was interested in you at the speed-dating event? Because you're dull. Your life is dull, everything you talk about is dull. You're just dull, dull, dull.'

I was being unfair and horribly, horribly cruel but, even though I didn't believe what I was saying, I couldn't help myself. In that moment I blamed Archie for everything that had happened to me, every failure I'd suffered, every mistake I'd made, every night I'd cried myself to sleep.

'Lucy, please,' Archie said, placing his hand on mine.

I flinched and slapped his arm away with all the drunken strength I had. He recoiled and rubbed his arm, a look of shock on his face.

'I think it's time you left, young lady,' said Archie's grandmother, putting down her fork. 'You've embarrassed yourself quite enough for one evening.'

'Oh yeah, you think so, do you?' I turned round to face her. 'Well, I've got news for you, Granny Posh Arse. I'm not done yet. Why don't we talk a bit more about you, not that we haven't talked about you enough already this evening. Oh, so you love classical music. How marvellous. And you think the version of *Swan Lake* with the male swans is atrocious. Oh, *quel dommage*. But let's keep talking about you. Let's talk about the fact that the only thing that makes you happy is making your grandson as miserable as you, shall we?'

Then I winced. Archie had stood up and was gripping the top of my arm. His entire face was red and he was shaking.

'That's enough, Lucy,' he said. Not only that, but the entire restaurant was looking at our table. 'I want you to leave.'

I tried to shake him off, but he was stronger than he looked.

'What if I don't want to leave?' I said.

'Just leave.' He looked me straight in the eye and didn't look away. 'Now.'

Two waiters suddenly appeared at our table.

'Is everything OK?' one asked.

'Everything is fine,' I said, glaring at Archie. 'I was just leaving.'

He released his grip on my arm and stepped back. The entire restaurant was silent. I reached down to pick up my bag.

'I'll be going now,' I slurred, throwing my bag over my shoulder and hitting myself in the side of the head. 'Thank you all for a delightful evening.'

As I swayed towards the exit, one of the waiters scuttled ahead of me and held open the door. I squinted towards my escape route and tried to focus on putting one foot in front of the other.

'What a nasty piece of work,' said Archie's grandmother, loudly. 'An alcoholic *and* a foul-mouthed tramp. I told you she was dirt, Archie, I did warn you.'

I lurched round and stumbled back towards the table. 'Say that again?'

Archie's grandmother smiled beatifically. 'I think you heard me the first time.'

I smiled back at her. 'I just wanted to double-check. Before I did this—'

I'm not sure when she started screaming – as I reached for her glass of red wine or when I raised it above her head – but she was definitely screaming as it splashed onto her horrible old face and dripped down her cheeks.

Chapter Thirty-seven

Wednesday 15th May
Day Nineteen

I called Archie fifteen times on Wednesday morning. Fifteen times, each trill boring into my hungover brain, and he still refused to talk to me.

Mrs Humphreys-Smythe answered the first time I rang, but I was too mortified to say anything, not even when she said, 'You can be silent all you like, but I know it's you, and I know why you're ringing. You can forget about seeing or talking to Archie ever again. He's disgusted by your behaviour last night. Absolutely disgusted. Vile, Miss Brown. That's what you are: vile, and as common as muck.'

What could I say to that? How could I even begin to stand up for myself? I couldn't, because she was right. I'd been really, really cruel to Archie. She, on the other hand, had deserved everything I'd said, but I'd gone too far when I threw red wine over her. I knew Archie would never be able to forgive me for that, but I still wanted to say sorry. There were only two more days until my time was up and Saint Bob would summon me back to limbo. I couldn't leave without apologising. I just couldn't.

Claire found me in the kitchen, my hands wrapped around a cold cup of tea.

'It's my last day,' she trilled as she jumped into the chair opposite me, 'and I can't decide how to spend it. There's no point trying to complete my task. I haven't seen my guitar pupil in weeks. I'm tempted to spend the whole day making Keith's life a misery, but then again I could just get absolutely slaughtered instead. I don't imagine they have snakebite and black up in heaven, do they? Lucy … Lucy … are you OK?'

I shook my head. My mouth was so dry my tongue was stuck to the roof of my mouth.

'How was your dinner last night?' Claire asked excitedly. 'Did Archie and Sally fall in love with each other? Have you passed your task?'

I took a sip of cold tea and unglued my tongue. 'I totally screwed up.'

'How?' She twirled an errant dreadlock around her finger and grinned at me. 'I'm sure it can't be as bad as you think.'

'It's worse.'

'Oh shut up. You're such a drama queen sometimes, Lucy. Screwed up in Lucy language probably means you spilt a bit of wine down your front while Sally laughed hysterically at something Archie said.'

'I didn't spill any wine,' I said, running my finger over a coffee stain on the table. 'I threw some at someone.'

Claire laughed. 'Fuck off! That's something I'd do, not you. So who did you *allegedly* throw wine over?'

I closed my eyes. 'Archie's gran.'

'Shit.' She sucked in her breath like a builder quoting for a big job. 'You're kidding? You're not kidding, are you? I can tell by the look on your face. What happened?'

'It's a long story,' I said, tipping a drop of tea onto the stain and rubbing it in, 'but the short version is that I massively fucked up and now Archie won't talk to me. My task is over, Claire. I screwed it up.'

'What are you going to do?' she asked.

I shook my head. 'I don't know. What can I do? I can't force Archie to talk to me, and I can't go round and see him because I've got no idea where he lives. All I can do now is to try and stop Anna from telling Dan how she feels about him tonight. If I can just save him from her, at least I'll have done something.'

'Then I'll help you,' Claire said, clutching my hand. 'Sod Keith Krank and getting pissed. Let's stop that bitch from getting her claws into your boyfriend.'

It was dark as we walked down Anna's street and approached her house. It was alive with thumping house music and multi-coloured light streamed from the windows. Beautiful, trendy people spilled out of the front door and milled around on the patio, chain-smoking and drinking. A thousand years ago I would have been at that party too. I'd have been knocking back Anna's homemade cocktails and jumping around to the tunes.

Dan would be there too, grinning at me from across the room as the party bore chewed his ear off. By the end of the night we'd both be drunk and exhausted and we'd throw our arms around each other and stumble into a taxi, talking nineteen to the dozen all the way home. Then we'd fall into bed, laughing and giggling and, if we still had the energy, we'd make lazy love before finally passing out.

'Looks like a shit party,' Claire said as we parked ourselves on the low wall outside Anna's next-door neighbour's house.

No one in Anna's garden gave us a second glance. They were either too pissed or too self-involved to notice the dumpy goth girl and her brunette friend.

'What if Dan and Anna don't come into the garden?' I whispered. 'As soon as I set foot inside the house she'll spot me and I'll be thrown out on my ear.'

'I could go in,' Claire suggested. 'I don't know what Dan looks like, but I'd recognise Anna. Conniving bitch.'

'Thanks for the offer,' I said, staring at the door. 'I've just realised, Dan will be out soon enough. Anna doesn't allow smoking in her house.'

Claire reached into her black patent record bag and pulled out a packet of fags.

'Talking of which,' she grinned. 'May as well smoke this little lot. Can't imagine there's a roaring trade in tobacco in heaven.'

She chain-smoked her way through four fags and was just about to light her fifth, when I gasped and pointed at the door. A tall, dark-haired man was fumbling in his jeans back pocket with one hand as he slugged whisky from a bottle with the other.

I nudged Claire. 'That's Dan.'

She peered through the smoky haze that surrounded us. 'He looks pissed,' she said.

Almost on cue, Dan tripped over his feet as he stepped down onto the patio and only managed to stop himself from falling flat on his face by grabbing the arm of a random bloke nearby.

'Sorry,' he shouted, righting himself. 'My sincere apologies. Sorry. Sorry.'

The bloke shook Dan off and said something I couldn't hear. I watched as Dan stumbled through the crowd, lurching against them and spilling their drinks as he puffed on a cigarette. When he finally reached the wall he collapsed onto it, lying sprawled out on his back.

'Dan,' a female voice called. 'Dan, are you out here?'

Anna, resplendent in a tight black bodice, skinny jeans and ridiculously high heels, appeared in the doorway.

'Dan!' she called again. 'Has anyone seen Dan?'

'He's over there,' someone called, pointing towards the wall. 'I think he might need rescuing.'

'Then I'm just the girl for the job.'

I looked at Claire. Her eyes were narrowed and she was sitting up straight, her entire body rigid as she watched Anna sashay through the crowd towards Dan.

'Shall I thump her?' she hissed. 'I would you know, if you wanted me to.'

I shook my head. 'I already tried that. Didn't stop her.'

'You did what?' Claire stared at me, her cigarette dangling from her fingers. 'You're kidding me.'

'I'll tell you about it later. Long story.'

She inched across the wall, away from me and grinned. 'Should I be scared of you?'

'Shhh,' I said, holding up a hand. 'Dan's saying something.'

Dan, still prostrate on top of the wall, was staring up at Anna. She was bent over him, stroking his hair from his face.

'Are you an angel?' he cried. 'Are you a blonde angel come to save me?'

Anna's hair fell over her eyes as she leaned forward and whispered something in his ear. Dan found whatever she said hugely funny and only stopped laughing long enough to take another messy slug at his bottle of whisky. I'd never seen him so drunk before. Merry, yes, but he was absolutely slaughtered. His face was flushed pink and his eyes were half-closed. The bottoms of his jeans were dark with mud or dirt and he looked like he hadn't showered or changed his clothes for days.

'Save me, Angel!' he shouted again. A crowd of people standing nearby jumped, and stared at him. 'Save me from this cruel, cruel world.'

Anna smiled, first at Dan, and then at their audience. She was clearly delighted by all the attention.

'Would this help?' she said, raising her voice so everyone could hear her.

My heart was in my mouth as she leant over Dan again and kissed him on the forehead.

Dan shook his head. 'No. Still damned.'

'Then how about this?'

Anna kissed him on his cheek, leaving a scarlet lip print behind. Dan shook his head so hard he nearly fell off the wall.

'Lucy,' Claire whispered, grinding her fag out under the heel of her boot. 'I don't like this. I'm going to stop them.'

'Claire, don't,' I said as she stood up. 'Don't. We've both had final warnings from Bob. Claire, stop!'

I grabbed at her hand but she shook me off.

'I've got nothing to lose,' she said, straightening her tutu. 'I'm going to fail my task anyway, so it doesn't matter what I do now.'

I watched, frozen to the wall, as she strode towards Anna and Dan, her hands clenched into fists. Anna, totally unaware of the approaching goth girl, flicked back her hair and looked from Dan to her enraptured audience and back again.

'How about this?' she said.

The expression on her face when she looked down at Dan made my stomach turn. It was tender and gentle. She looked like a woman in love.

'Don't,' Claire screamed as Anna leaned forward and kissed Dan hard on the mouth. 'Dan, don't! Lucy still loves you. She loves you. She's here.'

There was a second, a horribly, horribly long second when time seemed to stand still and everyone froze. Anna and Dan were locked at the lips, his fingers in her hair. Claire was a fury in black, her blood-red fingers poised just above Anna's head. The crowd, drinks halfway to their mouths and cigarettes dangling in their fingers, stared, open-mouthed. Then my heart thumped in my chest and Anna and Dan, still wrapped together, tumbled onto the patio. Claire was shouting and pounding the air with her fists but no words were coming out of her mouth. The crowd stared at her, still frozen in their tight, shocked groups.

Dan was the first to his feet.

'What did you say?' he shouted at Claire. 'What did you fucking say?'

Her lips moved. Nothing came out. She swallowed and her lips moved again. Silence. Dan lurched forwards and tried to grab at her, but she was too fast for him and stepped away as he crumpled against the wall.

'Why would you say that about Lucy?' he said, his voice breaking as he said my name. 'Why would you say something like that to me?'

Now Anna was up on her feet, hair ruffled and her lipstick smudged. She threw a protective arm around Dan and pointed a manicured finger in Claire's direction.

'You have five seconds to disappear or I'm calling the police.'

Claire put her hands on her hips and faced up to

Anna. Oh God. She looked like she was squaring up for a fight. I jumped off the wall and took a step towards Claire. Our eyes met and the rage on her face drained away.

'Sorry,' she mouthed. 'Lucy, I'm so sorry.' And then she ran towards me, grabbed my hand and pulled me down the street away from the party, and Dan.

Claire's voice croaked back into life about ten minutes later, as we hurried down the steps of the nearest tube station, but it was still decidedly husky. She'd also changed colour. Her face, arms and the tiny bit of calf that poked out between the tops of her army boots and the bottom of her leggings were mottled. The veins in her neck and arms were raised and dark. She looked so unwell I would have worried about her health if she wasn't already dead. Claire, however, seemed completely oblivious to her change in appearance.

'Did you see the look on Anna's face when I pushed her off the wall?' she croaked proudly as we walked along the platform. 'She was absolutely mortified.'

I nodded, too shocked and miserable to comment. My arms were covered in goosebumps, the hairs refusing to relax and flatten. I felt like I couldn't breathe, like my heart was thumping against my lungs, squashing them as I slowly suffocated. Dan had kissed Anna back. My Dan. Dan who'd promised he'd love me for ever had put his hands in my best friend's hair and kissed her. He could have laughed her off, made a joke, pushed her away … anything, anything, but kiss her back.

I took a step closer to the edge of the platform and gazed down at the dark tracks. I could hear a train rattling through the tunnel, drawing closer and closer. The only thing that stopped me from jumping was Dan's reaction to what Claire had said. He'd looked genuinely upset. Shaken. But why? Did he feel guilty about kissing Anna? Maybe he just wanted to forget all about me. Oh God, what if Anna really was in love with him and he was in love with her too. That would explain why he'd called her an angel and kissed her so desperately.

'She really loves him,' I said, turning back to Claire as the train thundered down the tracks and pulled into the station. 'And I think he loves her too.'

'Lucy,' she said, her hand on my arm. 'I wish I knew what to say to make this right.'

I wished she did too.

'Claire,' I said, stopping on the corner of our street.

'Yes,' she said, looking up at me, her face soft with concern.

'I just wanted to thank you for what you did for me tonight.'

She pulled her jumper over her hands and shrugged. 'No problem. You're my friend and I wanted to help you out. I just wish, I dunno, that it had turned out differently.'

We both looked down at Claire's fingers. They were now the colour of concrete. From the look on her face I knew she'd noticed she'd changed colour, but if she was scared or concerned, she didn't show it.

'But what if limbo punishes you?' I said. 'What if they tell you you can't go to heaven? It's all my fault.'

'No, Lucy,' she said, her face firm. 'Whatever happens now is my doing. When I was alive I blamed other people for how shit I felt about myself. I can't go back and change my life or rewind time and stop myself from committing suicide, but I can decide what happens next. And I don't want to be some kind of psycho-ghost out for revenge. It wasn't Keith Krank's fault that I was so unhappy. It was mine.' She smiled. 'If you're right and you can find love in heaven, I've got my second chance, haven't I? I can still be happy.'

I gazed down at her with new-found admiration. For someone so young, she'd become incredibly wise.

'You will,' I said softly. 'You will be happy, Claire.'

'Come on,' she said, taking my hand. 'Let's get back to the house and see what happens next.'

As it turned out, we didn't have to wait long to find out because there, standing side-by-side in front of the door, were two men in grey suits I'd met before.

'Claire Walters,' said the one on the left.

'I'm Claire,' she said, letting go of my hand and stepping forward.

'Claire Walters,' the man said sternly, 'you have broken rule 520.5 of the manual of wannabe ghosts – aiding and abetting a member of the living dead by making verbal contact with one of their life acquaintances.'

'I didn't abet,' Claire interrupted. 'Lucy asked me not to do it, but I did it anyway.'

'We are aware of that,' said the second grey man.

'Lucy Brown's attempt to stop you has been noted and, as a result, she was not found guilty of rule-breaking on this occasion.'

'However, Claire,' continued the first grey man, 'you also broke rule 501 on 28th April and rule 501.5 on 9th May. You were warned after your second violation that there would be consequences if there was a further incident of rule-breaking.'

'Yeah, yeah,' said Claire, who was shaking, despite her defiant tone. 'Just tell me what the consequences are.'

Both men took a step towards her.

'You will return immediately to limbo,' said the second grey man. 'Once there, you will be escorted to the heavenly escalator. You will remain in heaven for eternity, with no opportunity to return to earth, limbo or any other celestial place, and you will not qualify for angel status.'

'Sod angels,' Claire said, grinning at me. 'I look shit in white. I'm going to heaven, Lucy. See, I told you it would all turn out OK.'

I reached out and pulled her towards me, wrapping her in a tight hug.

'I'm going to miss you,' I whispered, inhaling the warm patchouli scent of her hair. 'I'm going to miss you so much.'

'Don't say that,' she whispered back. 'You'll make me cry and I've done enough of that for one lifetime.'

'Claire,' barked one of the grey men. 'It's time to go.'

We slowly peeled ourselves apart. Claire looked up at my face and shook her head.

'Whatever happens, Lucy,' she said, 'whether you pass your task or not, just make sure you do the right thing. Just promise me that.'

'I promise,' I said as she put her keys in the lock and walked into the House of Wannabe Ghosts and up the stairs, followed by the two grey men. She paused at the top and waved at me, then disappeared down the corridor, towards my room.

'I promise I'll do the right thing,' I shouted again, but I had no idea what that was.

Chapter Thirty-eight

Thursday 16th May
Day Twenty

Do the right thing, Claire had said. Do the right thing. I crawled out of bed, wrapped my dressing gown around me and sat down in the chair opposite the wardrobe. The house was strangely quiet, and every creaking floorboard and rattling pipe made me jump. For the first time since I'd fallen through Brian's wardrobe twenty days ago, I was completely alone. I pulled my knees up to my chest and hugged them. What had Claire meant by 'do the right thing'? Had she been telling me to fight for Dan, or give up and follow her to heaven?

Damn the men in grey for marching her up the stairs. If we'd had just a few more minutes to talk, I could have asked her what she meant. How was I supposed to fight for Dan when I'd obviously failed my task? Maybe she was suggesting I ignore Saint Bob's warning and try and talk to him? But I'd just lose my voice again. Or was she telling me to move on? She'd told me Anna was in love with Dan and I hadn't believed her. But I'd seen it for myself now. The way Anna felt about Dan was written all over her face. I'd only seen that expression once before.

I eased myself out of the chair, kneeled on the floor beside the bed and peered underneath. My photo album was still there, lying dustily amongst the vacu-packed clothes and the piles of shoes. I pulled it out and flicked through a few pages until I found what I was looking for, a photo of Anna and her ex-boyfriend Julian. It was taken at Dan's birthday party, three years ago. Dan and Julian were sitting on our sofa, their arms around each other, cans of beer in their free hands. They were beaming at the camera but it wasn't them I was looking at, it was Anna, perching on the armrest. She was gazing at Julian with a look of unadulterated adoration.

Anna had met Julian when he'd started as an account manager at her work. He was her junior and a couple of years younger, but she fell for him immediately. She even rang me after his first day at work and told me she'd just met the man she was going to marry, and Anna wasn't the kind of woman to make a sweeping statement like that without being very, very sure. She'd even sworn there wasn't a romantic bone in her body and that she'd rather die than dress up in a white frock and sashay down the aisle, so I was even more excited about her news. By the next weekend they were an item and Anna declared she was madly in love with Julian. He had a few issues, she told me, but they weren't a big deal. He just liked a bit of a drink now and then, but didn't we all?

Several months later, when Julian started ringing in sick after drinking binges, Anna covered for him. 'It's fine,' she'd said at the time, 'we all pull sickies after a big night out every now and again.'

A year later, when Julian finally acknowledged that he had a problem and went off to rehab, Anna called him every day and cleared her flat of bottles. When he returned to her, pale and exhausted, she held him, talked to him, and arranged for them to go out and do stuff that didn't involve drink. She would do anything for him, she told me once, because she knew he was the right man for her. She really believed that too, right until she returned home from work one evening to find Julian in her bed with one of his fellow rehab attendees.

Jess and I nursed her through her heartbreak. We drank with her, talked with her, we slept beside her on her bed, and we held her as she cried herself to sleep night after night. Slowly, over the next few months, Anna became hard, bitter and cynical. She slept with so many men we lost count. She fed them false numbers and false names, then kicked them out of her apartment in the middle of the night. No one, she told us, would ever screw her over again, and we believed her.

Last year she decided she wanted to get pregnant more than anything in the world and came up with her sperm donor plan. Jess and I were both worried about her, but what could we do? She was so headstrong that there was little we could do to stop her. And after hating men for so long, it almost made sense.

I slapped the photo album closed. Anna had hated all men ... until Dan. No matter how hard I tried, I couldn't forget the tender look on her face right before she kissed him. Somehow Dan had melted her hard heart and she'd changed back into 'soft' Anna again, the Anna that secretly believed in soulmates and love. 'Soft' Anna would stop Dan from feeling lonely and drinking himself into an unconscious mess. She would hold him, comfort him, protect him and look after him. She would do all the things I couldn't. Even if I hadn't screwed up my task, I'd never be able to physically comfort Dan or talk to him. What could a ghost actually do? Hover around at the end of the bed? Who'd be comforted by that?

I pulled myself up from the floor and padded over to the wardrobe. My wedding dress was still encased in its plastic tomb, but it had been pushed over to one side, revealing the door to the limbo escalator. The escalator Claire had taken the previous night. I pulled down the zip of the plastic bag and my fingers wandered over the silk. When I was alive my wedding dress represented my future. Now it symbolised everything I had lost. I'd been so convinced I was returning to earth to help Dan, but I was fooling myself. I'd been fooling myself for nearly three weeks. I wasn't trying to complete the task for Dan; he didn't need me, not in ghost form anyway, but I needed him. I needed to pretend that I wasn't really dead and that we could still be together for the rest of our lives. But there was no rest of our lives. Mine was over, but Dan's could still carry on.

How selfish was I to think he should mourn me for the rest of his life?

I zipped the wedding dress back into its bag and stared at the door to the escalator, Brian's words echoing in my head. 'Sometimes, Lucy,' he'd said, 'people pass their tasks and choose not become ghosts.'

I hadn't understood that at the time. I'd just felt hurt that Mum had returned to earth to be with me and then chosen to go up to heaven instead. Now it made sense. She would have seen Dan taking care of me and holding me together. There was no need for her to appear as a ghost to reassure me she was with me, if Dan was looking after me. And now Anna was doing the same for Dan, and he'd called her his angel and kissed her. He still loved me. I was sure he still loved me, but he was doing what everyone does when they lose someone they love; they grieve and they cry, and then they move on and rebuild their lives.

I reached out and laid my hand on the doorknob to the escalator. If I really loved Dan, there was only one thing to do ...

A piercing squeal made me jump back from the door. What was it? Some kind of alarm? The squeal continued, ringing out through the house. It was the phone, I realised slowly. Was Saint Bob calling to tell me not to open the door? I sprinted out of the bedroom and ran down the stairs, two at a time.

'Bob?' I panted into the phone. 'This is Lucy.'

'Who's Bob?' said a familiar voice.

'Archie?'

'Yes. Who's Bob?'

I said the first thing that came into my head. 'He's my uncle.'

'Bob's your uncle?' Archie started to laugh and promptly stopped himself. 'Listen, Lucy, I can't talk right now because Grandmother's about to come home, but I do need to talk to you about the other night.'

I felt sick. 'I'm so sorry, Archie,' I gabbled. 'You've got no idea how bad I feel about what—'

'Save it for tomorrow,' he said sternly. 'Meet me in Café Rio on Wardour Street at 2 p.m.'

The line went dead before I had chance to reply and I stared at the phone in my hand. Archie wanted to talk to me. He actually wanted to talk to me. I'd be able to apologise and everything. I couldn't stop grinning. It was the best news I'd heard in days. Heaven would have to wait.

Chapter Thirty-nine

Friday 17th May
Day Twenty-one

I was in my seat, with a hot cup of coffee in my hands, a good fifteen minutes before Archie and I were due to meet up. I needed the time to go through everything I wanted to say to him. There was nothing else I could do for Dan before I left for limbo, but I could try and put things right with Archie. I could say sorry, at least.

I sipped my coffee slowly, savouring the hot, slightly bitter sensation as it warmed my mouth and throat. It was great that I'd get to see my parents again in heaven, but there was so much I was going to miss about being alive: the sunshine on my face, the wind against my skin, the roar and rush of London traffic in my ears, the sound of an entire room exploding into laughter, the taste of chocolate and ice cream, the softness of Dan's skin after a shave, the scent of the hollow between his neck and his collarbone …

'Lucy.'

Archie was standing beside me, his expression grim.

'Hi, Archie,' I said, smiling nervously. 'I'm really glad you came. Do you want to sit down?'

We stared at each other across the table for several seconds until I lowered my gaze and looked away, upset by the anger I'd seen in Archie's eyes.

'Can I get you a coffee?' I asked as he sat down.

He shook his head. 'No thank you, Lucy. I won't be staying long.'

'Archie …' I reached for his hand, but he snatched it away, leaving my fingers trailing the plastic table top. 'I'm sorry,' I said. 'Archie, I'm so, so sorry for what happened the other night—'

'Did you know,' he said, interrupting my apology, 'that my grandmother was married to my grandfather for forty-five years. Did you know that, Lucy?'

I shook my head, too ashamed to say anything.

'And when he died' – Archie rested his elbows on the table, leaned forward, and looked me straight in the eye – 'she didn't just lose her husband, she lost her soulmate. Her soulmate, Lucy, the man she'd loved since she was twenty years old. And I'm all she's got left. Is it any wonder she doesn't want to lose me too?'

'I didn't think …' I said, feeling wretched. Worse than wretched. Like something you'd scrape off your shoe. And I hadn't thought, not about the fact that Mrs Humphreys-Smythe was a widow, anyway. All I'd focused on was the fact that she hated me and was hell-bent on screwing up my task. It never occurred to me that she might be grieving for her own soulmate. That she was scared of being alone, too.

'I'm sorry, Archie,' I said. 'I'm so, so sorry. What I did was completely out of order and I can't even begin to explain why I did it.'

He leaned back in his chair and folded his arms. 'You'll have to do better than that, Lucy. *I can't explain* just doesn't cut it, I'm afraid.'

What could I say? I couldn't tell him the truth. I couldn't say, 'The truth is, Archie, I'm dead and I came down from limbo to complete a task so I can be with my fiancé again. Oh yeah, and you're the task.' The minute the words left my mouth I'd be struck dumb by Saint Bob and Archie would think I was messing around.

'The thing is, Archie,' I said, gazing down at my mug, 'it was really important to me that you and Sally got to know each other. I can't tell you why, but it was more important to me than anything else in the world, and when your grandmother showed up to dinner I was incredibly frustrated.'

'Frustrated? Why? It was just one dinner. You could have arranged other meals out for just the three of us.'

'I couldn't, there wasn't time.' I looked up. 'You and Sally had to get together that night because ...'

'Yes?' Archie leaned forward and nodded. 'Yes?'

'Because I'm going away tonight.'

'Where?' he said, his angry expression fading.

Limbo? Heaven? What could I say? It needed to be somewhere very far away.

'Australia,' I finally said.

'Are you coming back?' he asked, frowning.

'No.'

He sighed, ran his fingers through his hair and stared up at the ceiling. When he finally looked back at me there was a pained expression on his face.

'Let me get this right. You're telling me your highest priority before emigrating to Australia was getting me and Sally together?'

'Yes.'

'So important, in fact, that when my grandmother joined us for dinner, you chose to insult us both and pour wine over her head.'

'I know it sound ridiculous—'

'Ridiculous?' Archie snorted. 'It sounds positively insane.'

What could I say to that? Of course it sounded insane. I'd acted like some kind of psycho.

'What hurts me most,' Archie continued, 'is that I truly believed we were friends. I really thought you liked me, Lucy.'

'I do like you,' I said.

'Then why did you call me a loser and humiliate me?'

'I didn't mean it. I only said that because I was so frus—'

Archie's chair squealed against the floor as he pushed himself back from the table. 'If you say frustrated one more time, Lucy, I'm walking out and you'll never see me again.'

'Please,' I whispered as everyone in the café stopped talking and stared at us. 'Please just listen to me. I'll explain everything. Don't go.'

He pulled his chair closer and put his elbows on the table. 'I'm listening.'

'Archie,' I said, 'the reason I was so frus … horrible that night was because I suspected my boyfriend was in love with someone else.'

Archie's mouth fell open. 'You've got a boyfriend?'

'Yes.'

'So you lied to me when you said you were single?'

'Yes.'

For one terrible second I thought he was going to keep his word and walk out. Instead, he sat up straight and folded his arms.

'So how long have you been together?'

'Seven years.'

'Seven years.' He raised his eyebrows. 'So there was no reason for you to go to speed-dating events?'

'No, apart from trying to find someone for you.'

'Why me?' he said, holding out his hands. 'Why me? I'm not a bloody charity case, Lucy. You can't dabble with my life just because your own love life is screwed up.'

'I know that now.'

Archie sighed and shook his head. 'So, and correct me if I'm wrong, because this is the only logical explanation I can come up with to explain this whole mess, you thought your boyfriend was cheating on you so you decided to emigrate to Australia but, before you left, you wanted to prove to yourself that there was such a thing as true love, so you set about trying to find a soulmate for me. It was your little mission, so to speak. Is that what happened?'

'Something like that.'

'Oh, Lucy,' Archie said, his eyes soft. 'I had no clue you were feeling so bitter and miserable.'

I looked down at my hands. They were shaking. 'I just had so many dreams,' I said, 'and I couldn't accept it when they were destroyed. I was looking for a way to make everything right again, but I didn't realise how selfish I was being until very recently.'

Archie's hand drifted towards mine, but stopped short. 'You upset a lot of people the other night, Lucy.'

I looked up at him. 'Yes, I did, and I'm very sorry.'

'Grandmother's still angry, and won't have your name spoken aloud.'

'I don't blame her.'

'But you did do something right, Lucy.'

I felt sure I hadn't done a single thing right, but a smile was playing on Archie's lips so I asked the question anyway. 'What was that?'

'You brought Sally and I closer.'

I looked at him with surprise. 'I did?'

'Yes, you did.' He smiled. 'Grandmother decided to go home shortly after the wine incident and left Sally and I alone. The conversation was stilted at first, surprised as we were by your actions, but we started to talk and relax, and we ended up having a very enjoyable evening together.'

'You did?' I said.

'Yes. And it turns out Sally and I have a lot more in common than I realised. She must be the only other person I've ever met who likes rap, Warcraft, Italian food, Miro and Dostoyevsky in equal measures.'

'You like Dostoyevsky?' I asked incredulously. I'd always thought he was more of a *Lord of the Rings* kind of man.

He nodded. 'And so does Sally. In fact, we have very similar tastes in art and literature, and we share an interest in philosophy.'

I couldn't speak. Bratz fan Sally was into art and literature? I never would have guessed. I also wouldn't have guessed that Archie was into rap, Claire was an insecure romantic, and Brian was a thoughtful, caring man. To me, when I first met them, they were the geek, the goth and the trainspotter, and not a lot more. So much had changed in twenty-one days.

'And I was dreading telling you this,' Archie continued, his eyes on my empty coffee cup, 'before your boyfriend revelation, anyway. But the way you acted the other night, and the things you said, made me see you in your true colours.'

I opened my mouth to speak, but Archie held up a hand.

'You're not a bad person, Lucy, far from it, but you're not the girl I fell in love with. Do you know why?'

I shook my head.

'Because I wasn't really in love with you. I was in love with the idea of being in love. On the surface, and because you showed an interest in me, it seemed like you were the woman for me, but I was wrong. My match was far closer to home.'

I bit my lip. Was he about to say what I thought he was going to say?

'It's very early days,' he continued, 'and it would be wrong of me to use a word like love so readily again, but … ' He swallowed, '…I have very strong feelings for Sally and it appears she has similar feelings for me. And we'd like to see where they lead. Grandmother seems to be very fond of her too.'

Archie's gaze flickered up and met mine. I smiled at him, a huge smile, a genuine smile, my first real smile in days.

'I'm so happy for you,' I said, reaching across the table and squeezing his hands. 'So, so, so happy for you. You have no idea how pleased I am.'

'Really?'

'Absolutely.'

'So mission accomplished then?'

'Sorry?'

'Your little mission to get Sally and I together – it worked. Happy endings all round.'

Archie looked so delighted I didn't have the heart to tell him it really didn't matter whether I'd got them together or not. Saying he had feelings for Sally wasn't the same as saying she was his soulmate. Telling me he 'wanted to see where things lead', wasn't the same as telling me he'd met the love of his life. Sooner or later, the men in grey would show up and, no matter what they told me, there was no happy ending for me. Even if, by some miracle, I *had* passed my task, I'd already made my decision. And it involved leaving Dan behind. I was just about to say something when Archie's phone bleeped.

'It's Sally,' he said. 'We're going for a picnic in the park this afternoon and I'm responsible for the food so I'd better get moving.'

'That sounds lovely,' I said.

'Oh, how rude of me,' Archie said, shifting in his seat. 'I don't suppose you'd like to join us, Lucy?'

I shook my head. 'I've got a few things to do.'

'Of course you do,' Archie said, standing up and grinning down at me. 'You're emigrating to Australia. How exciting. A new start and all that. That's not to say I won't miss you. We both will. Maybe we could visit you next year, when you're settled.'

'Don't take this the wrong way,' I said, thinking about where I was actually going. 'But I hope I don't see you and Sally for a long, long time.'

Archie looked puzzled, but he reached out his arms anyway. 'Hug? No hard feelings, Lucy.'

'No hard feelings, Archie,' I said, gripping the sides of my seat, 'but do you mind if we don't hug? I've said a lot of goodbyes recently, and I'll only start crying again.'

'If you think I'd accept a poor excuse like that, you've got another think coming,' he said, rounding the table and wrapping himself round my shoulders. 'You'll be happy again, Lucy. I know you will.'

'I do hope so, Archie,' I said, hugging him back.

'Right,' he said, letting go of me and hoisting his bag onto his shoulder. 'I'm off to the picnic. And you're packing, I presume?'

'Soon,' I said. 'There's someone else I have to say goodbye to first.'

I'd just crept out of the coffee shop when I spotted two very familiar men in grey suits walking towards me. I paused on the corner of Wardour Street and waited for them to catch up.

'Lucy Brown?' said the one on the left.

I nodded. 'I'm Lucy.'

'Let's go somewhere more private,' said the one on the right, as shoppers and tourists weaved around us and crowded the pavement.

The two men set off at such a pace I had to jog to keep up with them. They finally stopped walking when we reached the Southbank. Neither of them had broken a sweat but I was panting. I slumped over the high wall above the Thames and stared down at the dark water beneath me until my breathing returned to normal.

'Can we sit down?' I asked, standing back up and pressing my fingers into the stitch in my side. 'There's a bench over there.'

The men glanced in different directions like a pair of identical mantlepiece dogs, then looked back at me.

'OK,' said one. 'But if anyone joins us we'll have to move.'

'Fine,' I said, slumping onto the bench. 'But you might have to drag me off.'

Both men raised their left eyebrow in my direction and shifted along the bench towards me so I was pinned between their shoulders.

'I didn't mean I would refuse to go with you,' I said, wriggling madly. 'I'm just too tired to walk anywhere else.'

As they relaxed and inched away from me, a phone trilled loudly. The man on my left reached into his inside pocket.

'Yes, Bob,' he said into the mobile. 'Yes, we have her here. OK. Here she is.'

He handed me the phone and I pressed it against my ear.

'Congratulations on completing your task, Miss Brown,' said Bob, his voice as warm and jovial as ever.

My heart double-thumped. 'What?'

'You've passed your task.'

'But Archie didn't say Sally was the love of his life.'

'I know.'

'But … but …' I stuttered, 'for Brian's task, he had to get Troy to admit he was a railway enthusiast. I didn't get Archie to admit he'd found his soulmate.'

'You didn't have to,' Bob said, his voice as clear as if I was standing right next to him. 'Your task clearly stated that you should find Archibald Humphreys-Smythe the love of his life, and you did. Sally was always destined to be Archibald's soulmate. They just needed bringing together, and that's what you did. You passed your task, Lucy.'

I gasped with delight. I did it. I actually did it! Sally

359

and Archie were destined to be together. They'd live happily ever after and I'd made it happen.

'So,' Bob continued, 'on to the big question. As you have now qualified for ghost status, you may now decide whether you'd like to become a ghost or if you'd rather return to limbo and go on from here to heaven.'

My elation at passing my task deflated like a leaky balloon.

'If I choose limbo,' I said quietly, aware the men in grey on either side of me were listening intently, 'do I have to leave immediately or can I have a bit of time?'

'Time?'

'To say goodbye to someone.'

'Lucy,' Bob said, immediately adopting his officious tone. 'You are still expressly forbidden from contacting or communicating with anyone you knew when you were alive, as stated in the manual, rule—'

'I know,' I interrupted. 'I know that, Bob. And I'm not going to communicate with anyone. I just want to see someone for the last time and say goodbye to them. Silently,' I added before he could object.

'You will be stopped if you try and communicate with anyone,' Bob said.

'I won't. I promise. Please, Bob. Please just give me a bit of time to say goodbye. This hasn't been an easy decision to make.'

'And your decision is?'

'Limbo, then heaven.'

'You have until midnight tonight to say your good-byes. If you break the rules of the manual or fail to return to the House of Wannabe Ghosts before midnight, you will be apprehended and escorted back.'

'I understand that.'

'Lucy,' he said gravely. 'This is your last chance to change your mind. If you want to become a ghost you must tell me now. What you say to me next will be set in stone and cannot be changed. So, what is it to be? Ghost or heaven?'

Ghost, my heart called. Choose ghost. If you don't, you'll never see Dan again after today. You'll have to wait years and years to see him again and when he does make it to heaven, his heart will belong to Anna and not you.

Heaven, my brain said. Lucy, you have to go to heaven. You have to do what is right for Dan. If you love him you'll let him go so he can find happiness again. You have to do what's best for Dan, not what's best for you. That's what true love is all about – putting someone else's happiness ahead of your own.

I took a deep breath. 'I choose heaven, Bob,' I said.

I sat on the bench for a long time after the men in grey had pocketed the phone and disappeared over the bridge. The sun set slowly over London and thousands of lights flickered and glowed through the gloom. All over the city people were leaving their offices and pouring into bars, clubs and restaurants. I'd always loved London at night. You never knew what adventure you were going to have or who you were going to meet. As I gazed at the city that had been my home for so long, I said goodbye to the life that I'd had. No more cold mornings snuggled up under the duvet, no more hot summer afternoons, no more dipping my toes in the sea on the first day of a holiday, dancing naked in the kitchen, singing at the top of my voice or melting chocolate on my tongue. No more shopping, reading, cinema or birthdays. I'd never again arrange the twinkling lights on a Christmas tree and watch pine needles fall as I stuffed my presents underneath. I wrapped my arms around me and thought about all the people I'd loved in my life. I remembered kisses, laughter, arguments, tears, giggles and jokes. I drank in the view before me, knowing I'd never see it again, never experience those things again, and I said a silent goodbye.

I felt strangely peaceful as I stood up from the bench and walked along the Southbank as the Thames flowed silently beside me. I had one more person to say good-bye to and then I'd leave. For ever.

The lights were on in 33, White Street. I sat down on a low wall on the opposite side of the street and gazed through the window. The curtains were open and I could see Dan's long shape on the sofa, his head on my favourite cushion, a can of lager in his hand. I couldn't tell if he was asleep or not, but he was very still. I was relieved he was at home on a Friday night instead of out at a bar or, worse still, at Anna's house. It was right that it was just the two of us, separated but to-gether, on my last night on earth. Maybe, deep inside,

Dan knew tonight was the night I'd say my final good-bye.

'I love you, Dan,' I whispered across the street. 'I love you more than anyone else in the world. You were the man I wanted to spend the rest of my life with, the man I was going to marry. I thought you'd cry at the altar as I walked up the aisle in my wedding dress and spin me round the dance floor at the reception and nestle your face in my hair. I wanted you to be the father of my children, Dan. I wanted you to lift me up and spin me round when I said I was pregnant and hold my hand as I went into labour. Your beaming smile would light up the room as our son or daughter was brought into the world. I wanted to share all my joys and disappointments with you, to grow old with you. You were the only man I ever loved, ever wanted, ever needed. I love you, Dan, and I'll never stop loving you. You are, you were, and you will always be, my soulmate. I love you, Daniel Harding. I love you. I love you. I love you.'

Tears were streaming down my face as I stood up and dragged myself away from my house, away from Dan, away from everything that could have, should have, been. I stopped. I couldn't do it. I had to take one last look at him. I had to see his face one more time. I turned, slowly, and caught my breath. Anna was standing at the front door, her finger on the bell.

No, I thought, no, no, no. Please, Anna. Please go away. Don't spoil this for me. You can have Dan for the rest of your life, but this is my moment. This is my goodbye. Don't answer the door, Dan, I willed. Please be asleep. Please don't hear the bell.

But Dan didn't hear me.

He pulled himself up off the sofa and disappeared into the hallway. Every bone in my body told me to turn around and walk away, but I couldn't. I couldn't stop myself from crossing the road and approaching the house. Anna, her attention totally focused on the door in front of her, didn't notice me crouch down behind the next door neighbour's car. She straightened her mini-skirt and smoothed down her hair.

'Hi, Dan,' she said as he opened the door and slumped against the doorframe. 'Are you going to invite me in then, or do I have to stay out here all night?'

Dan shook his head and said something I couldn't hear.

'What's up, Danny?' Anna said, reaching out to stroke his cheek. 'Are you embarrassed about what happened the other night?'

'I wasn't expecting you,' Dan said sharply, moving his head so Anna's hand fell from his cheek to his shoulder.

She took a step back. 'Sorry. I should have rung, but I fancied a drink at the White Horse and thought I'd see if you fancied joining me.'

Dan shook his head. 'I'm not in the mood.'

'Oh come on,' said Anna, pulling at his hand. 'You'll love it when you get there. Look, you've already got your shoes on.'

Dan looked down at his feet. He was scuffing the

toe of his shoe against the doorstep. I'd seen him do the same thing a thousand times before, when he was forced to do something against his will.

'I haven't got my wallet,' he said.

'No problem,' Anna said cheerily, 'I've got cash. Come on, please. I'm lonely. Come and have a drink with me, Danny.'

She yanked at Dan's hand again and pulled him onto the path. To my dismay, he reached round and pulled the door shut after him as he let her lead him to the street. I ducked down behind the car again as they approached me.

'We can go clubbing afterwards,' Anna said. 'I'll even let you take me to an indie club. I know how much you like a bit of indie.'

'I don't want to go clubbing,' Dan replied, pulling his hand from Anna's. 'Actually, let's just forget this whole thing. I just want to be at home tonight.'

Anna laughed, but there was something desperate in the tone. 'I can come with you,' she said. 'We can get a bottle in and watch a film or something.'

Dan took a step back and folded his arms. His jaw was tense, but his eyes looked exhausted. 'I just want to be on my own, OK?'

Anna stood up straighter, straining to make eye contact with him.

'This is about the other night,' she said, her voice tight, 'isn't it?'

'Just leave it, Anna,' Dan sighed. 'Please.'

'No!' she shouted, stalking back and forth on the

pavement. 'I don't want to leave it. I want to talk about the other night. You've ignored all my phone calls, which was a surprise considering how much you seemed to enjoy kissing me.'

'I'm sorry,' Dan said, passing a hand over his forehead and shielding his eyes with his fingers. 'I was drunk.'

Anna stopped pacing and froze. For a split second she looked devastated, then almost as she blinked, defensive Anna was back.

'Oh yeah?' she spat out. 'Well, you seemed to know exactly what you were doing. You called me your angel, remember? You told me to save you? You wanted me as much as I wanted you, Dan.'

'I was confused, Anna,' Dan said, stepping away from her. 'I didn't know what I was doing. It shouldn't have happened.'

I hung onto the back bumper of the car, my heart thumping like mad. I'd made a terrible, terrible mistake. Dan didn't love Anna. He didn't want to be looked after or cared for by her. I'd got it totally wrong. And I'd told Bob I'd go up to heaven. What had I done? What the hell had I done?

'Confused!' Anna said, thumping him on the chest. '*You* were confused? You told me I was important to you. You told me I was helping you deal with Lucy's death. You told me how much you liked being with me.'

Dan shrugged. 'I do ... did. You were one of Lucy's best friends.'

'You don't get it do you, Dan?' Anna screamed at

the top of her lungs. 'I'm in love with you. I have been for weeks. I thought you felt the same way. Kiss me again, Dan. Kiss me and tell me I'm wrong!'

I stood up just in time to see Anna launch herself at Dan, her arms round his neck, scarlet lips on his. Dan's hands floundered on her back until they found her waist, then he pushed her away. He took a step away from her, towards the road.

'You've got the wrong idea, Anna,' he said. 'The kiss meant nothing. I'm sorry, but it didn't. I was drunk and miserable. It was a mistake.'

'You love me,' Anna said, grabbing hold of his wrist and pulling him towards her. 'You love me but you won't admit it.'

'I don't,' Dan shouted, pulling away from her. 'I'm still in love with Lucy, Anna. I'm still in love with her.'

He yanked his arm out of Anna's grip and stumbled backwards. His ankle twisted and, almost in slow motion, he slipped off the kerb and flew backwards into the road. There was a squeal of brakes and two women screamed. One of them was me.

The short, stocky bus driver was shaking as he stepped from his bus and stared, open-mouthed, at the crumpled man laying metres from his front bumper.

'Call an ambulance,' he shouted at Anna. 'Call an ambulance now.'

Anna, pale and trembling, fumbled in her bag and

pulled out her mobile phone. She stabbed at the keypad.

'Hello,' she said, her voice shaky. 'Come quickly! A man's been hit by a bus and he's bleeding heavily. Yes. Yes. White Street. No, I don't know if he's breathing or not. Please come quickly. Please, I don't want him to die!'

'Did you see it?' the bus driver said to me. 'Did you see what happened? He just fell in front of my bus. I tried to stop, but I couldn't stop in time. Did you see what happened?'

I walked, as though in a trance, past the bus driver and the passengers that had spilled from the bus and were surrounding Dan. I walked past Anna and crouched on the cold concrete beside Dan's body and stroked the bloodied hair from his face.

'Lucy,' he said, opening an eye. 'Lucy, is that you?'

'It's me,' I whispered, brushing his lips with mine. 'It's me, Dan.'

'I knew you'd come back,' he sighed. 'I always knew you would.'

I pulled away from him so I could look into his eyes again, but they were closed. His lips were slightly parted and his chest was still.

'CPR!' Anna screamed, pushing me out of the way. 'Can someone do CPR? Please, please don't let him die. Please do something. Someone do something!'

Chapter Forty

I burst through the front door of the House of Wannabe Ghosts and took the stairs, two at a time, to my room. I'd stayed at the scene of Dan's accident until the ambulance had arrived. They immediately took over CPR from one of the bus passengers and, when that didn't work, applied two paddles to Dan's chest.

'I'm sorry,' they'd said to Anna who was crouching next to Dan's body. 'There wasn't anything we could do. He's gone.'

When Anna screamed, two of the male passengers immediately rushed to her side. No one noticed me slip away from the scene and sprint, as fast as I could, down the road.

'Shit,' I shouted, wrenching open the wardrobe and pulling at the handle to the limbo escalator. 'Open up! Let me in, Bob. Let me in!'

I was just about to turn the handle again when I remembered ... my ring. It was still on the bedside table. I snatched it up and pushed it onto the third finger of my left hand and ran back to the door. When I twisted the handle again the door opened.

*

I ran up as many steps as I could before I ran out of breath and sat down.

'Come on,' I begged as the escalator rolled upwards and the atmosphere gradually turned from murky green to dull grey. 'Come on.'

My emotions were so all over the place I couldn't pick them apart. Watching Dan die had been horrific and I couldn't wipe the image of the bus hitting his body and tossing him into the air from my mind. But he'd recognised me. He knew I'd come back for him. He knew.

'Please,' I said aloud. 'Please let him be in limbo. Please.'

Saint Bob was waiting for me at the top of the escalator, looking even more golden and sparkly than the last time I'd seen him.

'Lucy,' he said, opening his arms wide. 'I'm so glad you could make it. You cut it a bit fine, mind you, but you're here now.'

I hugged him. 'Good to see you again, Bob.'

He looked at me with surprise. 'Really? I thought you were dead-set on becoming a ghost. At least, that's what you said before you left here.'

'Things change,' I said. 'People change their minds.'

'Good, good,' grinned Bob, steering me towards the up escalator. 'I hoped that might happen.'

'No, Bob,' I said, pulling away from him. 'I can't go up there now.'

'I'm sorry?' he said, raising his bushy eyebrows. 'What did you say?'

'I will go up there,' I said, taking a few steps back. 'I promised I would and I will, but there's someone I have to find first.'

'Lucy,' Bob shouted as I sprinted away and threw myself into the crowd of grey people. 'Lucy, come back here now!'

I ignored him and ploughed through the crowd, pushing grey people out of my way as I squeezed past them.

'Dan,' I shouted. 'Dan, it's Lucy. Where are you? Dan! Dan!'

No one replied and no one reacted to me. I pushed on, cold bodies brushing against me as I weaved through them.

'Dan,' I screamed. 'Dan, where are you?'

I burrowed my way through the crowd until I reached a wall.

'Where are you?' I shouted as I followed the wall round. 'Dan, where are you?'

'Could Lucy Brown please report to the up escalator, immediately,' an overhead Tannoy boomed.

'Give me a minute,' I shouted. 'Please, just one more minute.'

I was just about to round a corner when I spotted two men in grey suits charging towards me. I darted back into the mass of moaning grey people.

'Dan,' I called. 'Where are you? It's Lucy. I love you.'

'Lucy,' a male voice croaked above the hum. 'Lucy?'

'Keep shouting. I'm coming to get you. Keep shouting.'

I followed the sound of his voice, shoving a Victorian gent, a medieval knight and a cavewoman out of my way. The crowd seemed to thin and part until finally, there he was, balled up on the floor, his knees hugged to his chest, his eyes closed. He was wearing the same dirty jeans, black T-shirt and grubby trainers he'd been wearing when his accident had happened, but the back of his head was free from blood and his limbs were straight and unbroken.

'Dan,' I said softly as I crouched beside him. 'It's Lucy.'

His eyelashes flickered and he opened his eyes. 'Lucy?'

I stroked his cheek. It was grey but still warm, his stubble pricking my fingertips. 'I'm here,' I said.

'I'm dreaming,' he mumbled. 'You're dead. I'm dreaming about you again.'

'You're not dreaming. I'm really here.'

He smiled up at me and stroked my hair. 'Your hair feels real.'

'That's because I'm really here with you, Dan.'

'I love you, Lucy,' he whispered. 'I never stopped loving you.'

I pressed my face into the hollow between his neck and his collarbone. He still smelled exactly the same.

'I love you too,' I said. 'I love you so, so, much. And I'm so sorry about the argument we had before I died. I didn't mean what I said. I was a stupid, stressed, selfish idiot.'

Dan pushed himself up onto one elbow and squinted

at the grey legs that milled round us. 'Argument? I wasn't arguing with you. I was having an argument with Anna on the street outside our house and then ... then I pulled away from her ...' He frowned. '... and I'm not sure what happened next. Where am I, Lucy?'

I opened my mouth to reply but a hand on my shoulder made me pause. Saint Bob was standing beside us shaking his head.

'Let me deal with this, Lucy,' he said firmly. 'You can see him again in a minute.'

'Who is this guy?' Dan said, looking from me to Bob and back again. 'And why is he glowing?'

I smiled. 'Go with him,' I said. 'I'll be waiting for you outside the office door.'

I crouched outside the door to Bob's office, my ear pressed against the keyhole, but I couldn't hear a thing. Dan and Bob had been in there for ages and I wasn't sure if that was a good thing or a bad thing. I'd been really excited to see Dan in limbo but he was so confused I really wasn't sure how he'd react when he found out he was dead too.

When the door finally swung open I stepped back and gasped.

'Lucy,' Dan said, his expression blank.

'Yes?' I said, my undead heart thumping wildly.

'It really is you, isn't it?' he said, staring at me. 'It really is you?'

I nodded. 'It's me.'

'And we're both dead?'

'Yes.' Tears rolled down my cheeks. 'We're both dead, Dan.'

He laughed, charged towards me, wrapped his arms around me and lifted me off my feet.

'Lucy,' he breathed as he spun me round and round. 'My Lucy, my beautiful Lucy. I've missed you so much.'

'I've missed you too, Dan. More than you know.'

'Do you have any idea how much I love you?' he said, lowering me to the ground, his arms still tightly wrapped around me

I shook my head.

'I loved you the minute I first set eyes on you,' he said, gazing into my eyes, 'and I've loved you every minute since. Every single minute.'

'So you don't hate me for not saying' I love you, too' before I died?'

'Hate you? Of course I don't hate you. I love you, Lucy. I blamed myself for leaving you that night and for putting that damned box in the attic ...' His eyes filled with tears. 'I blamed myself for your death.'

'It wasn't your fault, Dan,' I said, stroking the tears from his cheeks. 'It wasn't your fault.'

He lowered his head and kissed me gently on the lips. 'I love you, Lucy,' he said between kisses. 'I love you so much.'

Bob cleared his throat. 'Sorry to break up the reunion, folks, but there's one more piece of business to attend to before you two die happily ever after.'

Dan and I turned to look at him.

'What's that, then?' I asked, terrified there'd been some terrible mistake and we were going to be parted again.

'Over there,' Bob said, pointing into the distance, 'is an escalator marked up. I suggest you both board it forthwith.'

I looked at Dan and grinned. 'What do you think?'

He squeezed my hand. 'Wherever you go, I'm going too. I'm never going to lose you again, Lucy Brown.'

Acknowledgements

Thank you to everyone at Orion for being so supportive and enthusiastic, particularly Kate, Gail, Sophie and Julie. Huge thanks to Darley for dragging my novel out of the slushpile and seeing its potential and a massive hug to Maddie, my superstar agent. You're the best! Thanks also to Kasia for all her hard work.

The wonderful ladies and gents in the Novel Racers - you're all brilliant. Thank you for encouraging me and cheering me along every step of the way. Your support means a lot to me and I know it's only a matter of time until I'm cheering one of you. SAF ladies - you're ace. I couldn't ask to work with a group of more talented and dedicated writers.

I'd also like to thank my wonderful family - Jenny, Reg, David, Bec, Suz, Leah and Sophie - and all my friends for their love, support and encouragement. Kellie, Laura, Becky, Lisa and Heidi - you're the best friends a girl could ask for and I'm so lucky to have you in my life.

And to Sheps, who inspired me to write this book, you are, and always will be, hugely missed.